VIGIL

Z.A. MAXFIELD

mlrpress
www.mlrpress.com

MLR Press Authors

Featuring a roll call of some of the best writers of gay erotica and mysteries today!

M. Jules Aedin	Maura Anderson	Victor J. Banis
Jeanne Barrack	Laura Baumbach	Alex Beecroft
Sarah Black	Ally Blue	J.P. Bowie
Michael Breyette	P.A. Brown	Brenda Bryce
Jade Buchanan	James Buchanan	Charlie Cochrane
Jamie Craig	Kirby Crow	Dick D.
Ethan Day	Jason Edding	Angela Fiddler
Dakota Flint	S.J. Frost	Kimberly Gardner
Roland Graeme	Storm Grant	Amber Green
LB Gregg	Drewey Wayne Gunn	David Juhren
Samantha Kane	Kiernan Kelly	J.L. Langley
Josh Lanyon	Clare London	William Maltese
Gary Martine	Z.A. Maxfield	Patric Michael
AKM Miles	Jet Mykles	William Neale
Willa Okati	L. Picaro	Neil S. Plakcy
Jordan Castillo Price	Luisa Prieto	Rick R. Reed
A.M. Riley	George Seaton	Jardonn Smith
Caro Soles	JoAnne Soper-Cook	Richard Stevenson
Clare Thompson	Marshall Thornton	Lex Valentine
Haley Walsh	Stevie Woods	

Check out titles, both available and forthcoming, at
www.mlrpress.com

VIGIL

Z.A. MAXFIELD

mlrpress

www.mlrpress.com

Copyright 2010 by Z.A. Maxfield

Published by
MLR Press, LLC
3052 Gaines Waterport Rd.
Albion, NY 14411

Visit ManLoveRomance Press, LLC on the Internet:
www.mlrpress.com

Cover Art by Deana Jamroz
Editing by Kris Jacen

ISBN# 978-1-60820-171-6

Issued 2010

To Carol P., Donte's superfan, with love and gratitude, and to Elisa Rolle and Antonella Piazza, for language help when I needed it, thank you very, very much.

CHAPTER ONE

Clearly, it was time to kill Ned Harwiche III. Adin checked his watches yet again and decided he'd waited long enough. Everyone had their rituals, but Ned's had to be the stupidest of all, and the most macabre. As it would be getting dark before long, Adin began the lengthy walk back to the street.

Adin had always loved Père-Lachaise cemetery. He'd spent many a fond hour there getting drunk and emotional with his friend Edward, who had always been prone to such things, when they'd been silly and young and given to excess and guyliner. But even though they bore the same first name, Ned Harwiche and Edward Sheffield were two entirely different people.

Only Ned—in a bid to make what was probably a pretty lackluster day in his boring life seem more exciting—would have mysteriously requested that Adin meet him at *The Wall* at Père-Lachaise to discuss a business proposition. Adin had come willingly enough, even if the location was a little bizarre. He doubted Harwiche chose it for either its personal or its historical significance.

Adin had decided to twit Harwiche and his fastidious, button-down, nelly ass that day by dressing, in what he liked to think of as full vampire boyfriend mode, complete with leather pants, a black silk T-shirt, enough jewelry, chains, and studs to open a hardware store, and eye makeup. A dramatic long silk coat swept the gravestones when the wind whipped it around his calves. A paisley scarf lent the entire ensemble a touch of class. A sure sign that Adin's vampire lover Donte's sartorial splendor was rubbing off on him.

All in all, Ned Harwiche didn't deserve the care he'd taken, but Adin missed Donte—badly—and felt like making trouble. Adin could swear one of the guards still remembered him from when he was a kid. But maybe he'd looked at Adin with vague distrust when he'd passed through the gates earlier that afternoon because of his clothes. The guards probably had their hands full with kids who looked just like he did right then.

Ned Harwiche, however, would find it appalling and appealing at the same time, and he'd spend their entire meeting at war with himself. Since Adin and Ned were minor adversaries at book auctions, Adin was ready for a little passive revenge. He still wondered why Ned had asked to meet him. It looked like his curiosity would go unsatisfied for the moment, because Harwiche, even after all the annoying phone calls and rescheduling he'd done, had failed to show up.

As Adin turned from saying a final good-bye to the wall, two dour-looking men in business suits approached him.

"Will you please come with us Monsieur Harwiche?" one of them asked politely in French.

Adin gave the man a disinterested smile in return and prepared himself to say they had the wrong man. But before he could open his mouth the man who had not spoken lifted his jacket, showing off a gun in a shoulder holster, neatly clearing Adin's mind of all coherent thought.

"Let's just say it's not a request M. Harwiche." You had to hand it to the French *H aspiré*. Often one got *une grande* whiff of whatever had been consumed for lunch. The man grabbed him with a hand attached to an arm so rock solid that it could probably lift him off the ground.

Adin frowned and refused to move. "I believe you're making a mistake."

The man who spoke first, whose glasses covered a nervous expression completely at odds with how well he wore his suit, caught Adin's arm in an unrelenting grip.

"Don't make us shut you up in a painful way," he murmured in English. "Just come quietly."

"But—" Adin tried again, getting only the one word out before the first man shoved him forward and the second head-butted his forehead brutally.

Together, the two suits dragged him to the car and pushed him in, but not before he caught a glimpse of Ned Harwiche crouched behind a tall memorial.

That prick.

On the car ride Adin kept his mouth shut and his ears open. He was vaguely aware of heading toward the river and the area known as the Marais. If he chanced a glance at the man who'd gotten into the back with him, the armed man, he got nothing for his trouble. The man stared passively ahead, virtually immobile, and said nothing at all for the entire ride. The car came to a halt on the narrow street in front of what had—by its sign—at one time been a bakery in the historically protected neighborhood, but now housed what seemed to be a curio shop. The driver got out, and then opened the door on Adin's side to pull him from the car. The other man emerged behind Adin, unfolding his long legs and taking his time.

"Wouldn't it be better—?" Adin began but the man with the gun shoved him roughly forward.

"What would be best is if we could all just go inside and do what we came here to do."

Adin complied. There didn't seem to be anything for it but to imagine just exactly what he was going to do to Ned Harwiche when he caught up with the little weasel. They opened the door into the shop, causing the jangling of wall-mounted brass bells. An odd-looking man ushered the three of them inside. He closed and locked the door behind them, pulling the blinds to the street shut.

Since meeting Donte, Adin often found himself in surreal situations, but this one was shaping up to be at the top of the list. Everywhere he looked, shelves jammed with books and trinkets lined the walls from the floor to the ceiling. The place was an obstacle course of tables on which rocks and crystals sat in haphazard jumbles. Behind the counter with its ancient cash register, there were apothecary jars filled with various organic things, twigs and leaves and balls of fluff he thought might be the exploded remains of thistle or clumps of down feathers.

There were things suspended in acrid-looking fluids he didn't care to speculate about.

The place looked to be the perfect hokey *magick* shop; one he thought better suited to Los Angeles and its Buffy wannabes than Paris. But if it had to be here it made sense for it to be in the Marais. It stood only blocks from the Auberge Nicolas Flamel, where the famed fourteenth century alchemist once lived and supposedly turned lead into gold.

The odd man spoke. "I'm Thierry." His accent was thick and elegant. "You are a not an easy man to pin down, M. Harwiche. I beg you not to insult our intelligence again. The item you asked us to procure will be difficult to conceal for long, and I assume you intend no further delays."

Adin's ears burned at the mention of something Harwiche wanted to buy. Ned had given him fits by routinely bidding against him for manuscripts Adin knew for a fact he had no interest in. Harwiche collected erotica, certainly, and that had led them to square off more than once over a particularly good piece. Between Adin's friends in the business, and the university's faith in him he'd more than once come out the victor. But this had the effect of turning Harwiche into an even more determined and implacable foe, and he rarely passed up the chance to drive up the price of something Adin wanted—to spite him—whether it was something he collected for his own pleasure or not.

Adin couldn't begin to imagine how they could be confused for each other. There were photos of both him and Harwiche on the Web. A quick glance into the reflecting surface of a thick glass bottle reminded him he was dressed outlandishly and wearing makeup. Perhaps these men simply thought he must be Harwiche, who was known as widely for his bizarre affectations as he was for his money and the way he spent it. But Harwiche was a fucking troll, and Adin felt more than vaguely insulted by the mistake.

The situation seemed to present the possibility of payback, though, and Adin liked the sound of that very much.

"The item in question. Yes. I'd have to see it first." He hoped to buy himself time before he had to make up his mind one way or the other about telling them the truth. They didn't look like they'd take it well.

"I don't expect you to be disappointed. We went to rather a lot of trouble. This has required a level of logistics and planning that taxed even our considerable resources. I hope to hell you have no plan of backing out."

"No," Adin demurred. *Shit.* "Of course not."

"Then follow me, please," the odd man said and led the way to the back of the counter where he drew aside a curtain and then passed through. Once in the back room he opened a door on an interior wall that led to a set of stairs.

The minute Adin set foot on the first stair the hair on the back of his neck prickled, and Adin very clearly heard Donte's baritone voice say, "*Adin! No,*" inside his head. He ignored it as usual. Which was all part and parcel of how he'd come to be here in the most romantic city in the world without Donte in the first place, damn the man's stubborn vampire fustiness.

The stairs were narrow and the carved stone treads were short, his own foot barely fit, and it was a smallish foot by modern standards. These stairs had probably been built in the sixteenth century, when the average man's foot would have been considerably smaller.

"Once you've seen the merchandise, I'm going to ask you to wire the money into our account. I'll give you the numbers. As soon as the money is transferred, the merchandise is yours, and I'm sure you'll understand if we return you to your hotel with it. I, for one, will be glad to be rid of it."

"I see." Adin kept a hand on the railing on the dark stairs, afraid not only of slipping, but also of being shoved from behind. Which probably wouldn't happen.

Probably.

"No, you don't see, but you will. I assure you." At this Adin heard a *snick* sort of sound he identified a moment later as a lighter.

Aw, *fuck Ned Harwiche*. He wasn't exactly the kind of man Adin had pegged for a clandestine meeting in a cloak and dagger, basement-of-a-hoodoo-shop in the middle-of-nowhere. Now that the odd-looking man was lighting antique oil lanterns with a stick lighter, Adin's urge to go along with the charade was fast dissipating.

When his eyes adjusted, Adin glanced around. The smell was musty with decay and slightly foul, as if there was old food sitting around. There was also the distinct odor of urine, possibly, a kind of chamber-pot smell Adin associated with hospitals and bedpans.

Adin jumped when iron clanked against stone right in front of him. He took an apprehensive step back and that's when the circle of light from Thierry's lantern fell onto the face of a young boy. And *fuck*, he was chained to the wall, manacled and leg-shackled in a space even Adin could barely stand up in, with only a rusted iron cot and tattered sheets to sleep on, unable to go more than a couple feet from the bed in any direction, kept in the darkness and terrorized, given the way the boy cringed from the light. What. The. Hell? Adin thought his heart must be clattering so loudly Thierry could hear it.

"It's all right. He can't hurt you." Thierry's tone was reassuring. Adin gaped at him. "The iron makes him weak. He has less strength than a child half his age."

Adin ground his teeth. He'd never encountered anything as appalling as this. *How long has Harwiche been trafficking in underage boys?* The boy looked up at him as though he'd heard.

"What is your name?" Adin asked stupidly.

"He doesn't speak, Harwiche. He probably can't. Not with the iron around his throat. I thought you had some idea of what you were getting into here?"

"I'll set up the transfer; prepare him to be moved." Adin wondered how he'd bluff his way through this. He had no idea who he needed to pay, and he didn't know how much. But whatever it was, he'd do it. This was intolerable on so many levels it was difficult for him to breathe. "Let's go through the particulars again, though. I find I drank rather too much last night and I'm just a little—"

"Fine." Thierry led the way back to the stairs. "I have the computers we'll need in the storeroom."

"After you," Adin indicated Thierry should go ahead. "Give me a minute."

Thierry frowned down at him from the stairs. "I don't have to tell you I've spent a tremendous amount in terms of manpower and money to make this happen. If for some reason you're thinking of trying to cheat me or the men I work for, I'd advise against it."

"How could I cheat you? You'll be at the top of the stairs the entire time." Adin looked from Thierry to the boy again. Thierry's face was impassive, but the boy's spoke volumes. Adin wondered if Thierry saw the hunger for revenge that seemed written there. After shooting Adin a reluctant glance, Thierry left them alone.

Adin took a step toward the prisoner. Adin guessed his age to be around thirteen. His hair was matted and his eyes were clotted-looking shadows in his pale face. The chains reached barely beyond the bed and they clanked as he moved. There was food, Adin discovered; plates stacked on trays on the floor, as though they'd been left there for a dog.

"I'll be back as soon as I can and then I'll get you out of here," Adin told him quietly. His heart started to pound again and his gag reflex threatened. He knew even if it cost him everything he had, he'd find a way to liberate this kid and help him make his way home. That's when Adin realized the boy was gazing at *him*, giving him a look that could only be considered contemptuous.

Adin shook his head, and walked two more steps toward him, squinting his eyes in the dim light to get a better look. Without moving a muscle, the boy hissed at him.

"It's going to be all right." Adin spoke softly "I'm going to find a way to help you."

It was a shock when Adin very distinctly heard the boy say,

"You can't even help yourself, vampire pet. You should leave before the blokes out there find out you're not who you say you are."

CHAPTER TWO

Adin moved the curtain back a little to look down at the street again. Once he'd made a number of impromptu financial arrangements, the boy—the little monster—as Adin privately thought of him, was his. That was only when he could think around the constant stream of annoying patter—English with a decidedly northern British accent—the boy hurled at him from where he sat on the bed. He'd been like that ever since Adin c losed the hotel-room door, which surprised Adin because the boy seemed to accept him at first, following him meekly back to his hotel. Together, they'd walked sedately across the elegant lobby and stepped into the old-fashioned elevator.

Of course, the boy had still been *in chains*.

Even in France someone was bound to ask about that.

"Come on, Edward. Come on… *Come on…*" He held his cell phone and waited for Edward's voice in his Bluetooth earpiece. After the third ring, the call went through to voicemail and Adin cursed. He tried another number with the same result.

"What's the matter?" the adolescent voice grated on him. "Had a spat with your blood drinking boyfriend?"

The little monster had that right, because Adin had left Spain and his vampire lover Donte under a cloud of disappointment and mistrust. Donte didn't like him traveling alone and treated him as though he required constant supervision. Adin was hoping Donte might lighten his grip when he realized he didn't need to hold so tightly, but it hadn't happened. After five months of kendo classes and hyper-vigilance and constant lecturing, he'd left a note saying he was heading for France, and he'd be back, but Donte was going to have to get used to letting him come and go.

This new situation with Harwiche wasn't going to endear him to Donte at all.

"Vampires can be all fickle like that. One minute it's all nom-nom-nom, and the next minute they're up for something foreign. Get a yen for something more exotic, did he?"

"Shut up."

"Maybe your bloke doesn't trust you. Maybe he thinks you're on holiday, filling out the menu on someone else's buffet table."

Adin turned on the boy. "Look *you*. Get out of my head. You need to *shut up* and let me think. Did you natter on like this to your captors all the time? They should have paid me to take you. Talk about *The Ransom of Red Chief*."

"Let me go. You have the key, just let me go."

"I can't." Adin stepped toward him but still carefully kept out of range of the boy's hands and feet. "I paid a hundred thousand dollars of my own money to someone I don't know, merely to take you out of that basement. I can't let you go until I know you're safe."

"Safe?"

"Yes. You don't have to be afraid of me, you know. *I'm trying to help you*."

"I'm not scared of you." The boy frowned, but Adin thought it was mostly bravado.

"I—" Adin sputtered. "I take it that although you can—apparently—rummage around in my head, you're not entirely privileged to its contents, because right now I'm picturing things that *would* scare you, starting with giving you back so they can do whatever it was they had planned before they picked *me* up by mistake."

The boy's gaze was assessing, as if he were trying to judge the truth of what Adin told him. "Mistake? You really don't—"

"I have no fucking clue who or *what* you are. I don't even care, except that it seems wrong to keep a boy chained in a basement."

"Why did you—"

"Stop *AT ONCE*." Adin whirled back toward the window

when he heard the familiar *wee-oo* sound of French sirens and tires screeching in the street below. "And by that I mean stop fumbling inside my head and blabbering outside of it. Sit on the far side of the bed," Adin commanded, knowing it couldn't be seen from the door. "And shut the fuck up." He dialed Tuan's number from memory and waited as that also rang through to voice mail. It was mid-morning in California.

Where are they?

A sharp rap sounded on the door. "Whatever you are, I can give you to the police. They'll treat you like a boy who has been abused. You could be safe with them."

Fear drew the boy's face taut. They gazed at each other for a long time. Adin said nothing and the boy gave nothing away.

"I don't know what I can do. I'd like to figure out how to get my money back." Adin sighed and turned to the door. "In the meantime I'll try to protect you, but you have to know I have very little hope of succeeding. And I'll probably be arrested for trying to help you. My name is Adin, by the way."

"Adin," the boy repeated. "I'm Bran."

"Bran." Adin scrubbed a hand through his hair before reaching for the doorknob. He left the chain in place. "*Perfect.* You're already a pain in the ass."

Adin barely had time to twist the knob when the door frame shattered and the chain gave way, sending the old wooden door flying at his face with stunning velocity. He was knocked back by the blow and staggered for a few feet until he felt cool hands catch his arm.

"*Adin.*"

Adin put a hand to his forehead and it came away bloody. "*Ow...*" He blinked until his eyes could focus. When they did he saw a familiar diminutive face gazing at him with worried brown eyes.

"*Boaz?*" Adin asked stupidly. It hadn't yet occurred to him why his lover's erstwhile right hand man might be standing in his room.

Boaz spoke sharply. "You didn't have to do that, Santos." He helped Adin to a chair. "You're such a shit sometimes. Come on in."

"Sorry." Santos murmured politely as he stepped into the room, welcomed by Boaz. Adin had trouble reconciling the fact that Donte's right hand man seemed to work for Donte's mortal enemy, Cristobel Santos. He wasn't adept at the vagaries of vampire politics, but it seemed to him that the entire world was one big episode of *Survivor, the Undead Edition*.

For good or ill Boaz was here, and even though he'd brought Santos with him, it was a safe bet Donte had instructed him to clean up whatever messes Adin got into. Again.

Adin sighed.

Santos approached the boy on the bed. Adin noticed that he kept his distance. "Well, well."

"Vampire." The boy's voice—while it seemed to hold contempt—was laced with fear.

"You. You, on the other hand—"

Bran hissed something and Adin didn't hear the rest of what Santos said. Boaz entered the ensuite bathroom then returned with a damp towel, which he pressed against Adin's forehead.

"Hello, Santos." Adin took hold of the compress. "To what do I owe the pleasure of your company?"

"Ask Boaz. I'm here because he insisted we come." Santos went to the door and closed it. He pulled the wood bits off, threw them away, and let the chain dangle. "I suspect he was ordered here."

"Boaz?" Adin addressed his friend. Boaz had entered Adin's life in the guise of a hotel limo driver, but Adin later found out he worked for Donte Fedeltà. Boaz was only the first of the many safety measures Donte put in place when he'd become interested in Adin, whom he'd considered his oh-so-fragile human lover.

"Donte telephoned." Before Adin could vent his frustration, Boaz held up his hand. "He's right. If you didn't get yourself into these things in the first place…"

Adin ground his teeth again. He worried this new habit would wreak havoc on his bite.

"That's not important right now." Santos turned and barked at Bran to freeze, and Bran backed into the corner of the room behind the bed. "Boaz, lie down on the bed and be…*impish*. I'll deal with this."

Adin felt the need to speak. "Santos, I hardly think—"

"I'm beginning to believe that, Adin. At first I thought Donte was exaggerating the problem." A knock sounded on the door, which Boaz held shut in its broken door frame. "Now, do you believe you can be quiet, or shall I have to tear your head off and put you in the bathtub to bleed uselessly down the drain."

Adin pressed his lips together.

"Very good." Santos had Boaz open the door to the hotel manager and four uniformed police officers. The look he gave them was one of surprise as he spoke to them in heavily American-accented English.

"What can I do for you gentlemen this evening?"

"Dr. Tredeger?" The manager looked beyond Santos to where Adin stood.

"That would be me," Adin acknowledged with a nod. He continued to press the towel to the wound on his forehead and wondered what *les flics* would make of that.

"My name is Villiers, I'm the hotel manager. May we come in?" he asked politely. Adin's heart slammed against his ribcage as he turned to find Bran's terrified eyes on him.

Santos spoke. "Certainly you may, M. Villiers. I confess Dr. Tredeger and I were expecting you, under the circumstances."

"*Santos*," Adin hissed.

"Now, Adin, you've been a very, very naughty boy. Admit it. I had to break the door down to our own room. And you got hurt in the process."

Adin gazed at Santos, uncomprehending, as the vampire came to him and pulled the compress from his face. "Poor baby. Our Boaz has been naughty too. What did I tell you about taking play too far? Someone always ends up needing stitches. Say you're sorry, Adin."

Adin's eyes narrowed. "I'm not sorry."

"No you're not, you stubborn man." Santos chided, even as he tapped the tip of Adin's nose affectionately with his index finger. "Well, M.Villiers my partner and I normally have rules, but I admit that he broke some of them this evening. And a few commandments. And the door, I'm afraid, for which Adin and I will gladly pay. But no actual French laws, I think."

As M. Villiers and the police officers advanced into the room, Adin held his breath. He didn't dare look anywhere but at Santos. He was trying to figure what Santos's game was, when one of the police officers, a woman, uttered a startled exclamation and backed from the room.

Adin's gaze went to the bed and even he was shocked by what he saw there. Boaz lay on the bed, nude, stroking a monstrous erection with manacled hands. He was the very picture of erotic abandon, all dark eyes and wavy hair, like one of the boys in a Caravaggio painting. His lips glistened and his cheeks and chest bore the flush of his arousal. He was chained at his neck, wrists and ankles just like Bran, who still cowered in his chains against the wall of the small room. Adin's gaze flew to Santos, who simply stared straight ahead. He didn't have time to wonder whether it was an illusion, and if so, who was creating it, because M. Villiers cleared his throat by coughing and politely placing his closed fist tightly over his mouth as though to hold in a shout of alarm.

Adin glanced at the police officers. They had furious color high on their cheeks, but none of them spoke.

"Boaz, my dear, please tell the nice M. Villiers that you are a guest and not a hostage."

Boaz pouted, and Adin could see he was having fun in his new role. "What's in it for me?"

"What is always in it for you, my dear? Whatever you choose. So, M. Villiers," Santos asked. "What may I do for you?"

"I'm very sorry. Dr. Tredeger, I received a report of an underage boy…"

The police officers rolled their eyes when Santos said, "Did you hear that, Boaz? A pretty compliment. Thank the man."

Boaz licked his lips deliciously and stroked himself again. The head of his cock was darkly engorged, glistening from within a hood of foreskin, and Adin found it difficult to take his eyes off it. Through half-closed eyelids, Boaz gazed at M. Villiers whose own eyes nearly bugged out.

Boaz uttered a breathy "Thank you." And his lips curled into a satisfied smile.

"Adin, is there anything you'd like to add?" Santos gave the back of Adin's neck a gentle pinch.

Adin tore his gaze away from the figure on the bed—not an easy thing by any means, as Boaz appeared to be an erotic fantasy come to life—and finally found his wits. "I stay in this hotel whenever I'm in Paris, M. Villiers. Has the management suddenly become interested in my personal life and my…hobbies?"

Bran still stood frozen in the corner of the room behind the bed, but for whatever reason, M. Villiers and the police officers said nothing about him.

"I apologize for the intrusion. It is, as always, your business how you spend your time."

"Well, I thought so. Provided that I'm careful with the furnishings, and kind to the staff."

"And you've always been that, Dr. Tredeger. Please forgive the intrusion."

"Of course."

"Thank you." Villiers motioned for the police officers to go ahead of him and saw himself out.

When they'd all left, Adin let out the breath he'd been holding.

"How the fuck did you do that?" He turned to find Boaz sitting demurely on the edge of the bed, fully clothed, while Bran looked on from where he remained with his back to the wall.

"Does Donte never tell you anything?" Santos murmured. "I daresay he'll be fit to be tied over this." Santos used a finger to pull the compress away from Adin's face and then, to Adin's horror, he licked the skin there, teasing at the wound with his tongue to close it.

As if someone had reached out and snapped Adin's spine at the place where his head met his shoulders, Adin felt the tremendous zing of an electric shock all over his body, and his knees buckled.

"*Ow.*" Adin lost his footing.

"That will be your master—" Santos chuckled, helping Adin sit next to Boaz on the side of the bed, "—expressing his displeasure."

"I have no master, Santos," Adin ground out, holding a hand out to Bran to indicate that it was safe for him to sit. "I have a lover. And he can see how much it pleases you to mess with him."

Bran sat down warily. Adin wondered if he was subdued by a visit from the local police or by the presence of what was obviously a very powerful vampire.

"You have a master, Adin. To him, you are no more than an exotic pet. I suggest you keep in mind that vampires are easily bored. I'm already bored, but I thought we might take a walk. Have a late supper. Boaz will watch the child."

"Are you kidding?" Adin asked. "The last time we were together for a meal, I was very nearly the main course."

"But you can't accuse *me* of ever trying to eat you," Santos said playfully. "Except once, at the airport in San Francisco, and then only a little to soften you up. You are perfectly safe with me, for now. Tell him Boaz."

Boaz nodded and Adin shrugged. "All right. What the hell?"

Boaz reached for Bran's hands where the manacles had chafed

his wrists. "Poor baby. I'll see what we can do about these while you're gone, Adin."

"You'll see if you can get them off?" Adin asked.

"*No*." Santos said abruptly. A look passed between Boaz and Santos that Adin didn't understand. "We can't take the iron off. But Boaz can make him more comfortable."

"What do you think, Bran?" Adin reasoned that if the boy could see inside of him, perhaps he could see inside Boaz as well.

"He means me no harm," Bran answered, indicating Boaz.

"What about this one?" Adin gestured toward Santos.

"He is un-living. His mind is closed to me."

At this, Santos laughed. "Un-living. That's certainly the glass half-full, boy. Adin is an optimist as well." Santos took Adin by the hand and began to lead him from the room. "Do you know what an optimist is to a vampire, Bran?" Santos opened the door and motioned for Adin to pass through before him.

Bran showed no outward trace of what he was feeling, but Adin could sense he was frightened. "No, what?"

Santos grinned. "A happy meal."

Adin looked back past Santos as he started to leave, giving Bran a last opportunity to speak. "Say the word and I won't leave you here by yourself, Bran."

"Well, *thanks a lot*," Boaz grumbled.

"It's all right," Bran answered. "But...you should never trust a vampire."

Santos shot Bran a glare but Bran stood his ground, his face impassive.

Adin winked at Bran, and he colored furiously. "Got it."

CHAPTER THREE

"*Zut*," Santos exclaimed, extending his arms in an encompassing, embracing gesture. "I love Paris. I never get tired of it. Walk with me?"

Adin hoped for the best as he walked beside the vampire for a while, enjoying the way the chilly night air clung to his skin and clothing. He imagined what it might feel like to walk on the quays by the Seine with Donte, and it caused such a wave of longing to come over him that he clasped his hands behind his back to keep from reaching out.

"Doesn't it just fill you with an indescribable contentment to walk the streets of Paris at night? It's such a mixture of the old and new, of history and hope and passion and humanity, all brazen and tarted up."

Adin grinned. "I feel the same way, but you put a far more poetic spin on it. I wish Donte were here."

Santos growled, "Why ruin a lovely night?"

Adin followed Santos in almost complete silence as he led the way to the Pont Neuf, and across the river to the Île de la Cité, stopping—finally—when they were standing in the park-like square in front of Notre Dame's cathedral doors. The cathedral was lit, like all the monuments, and glowed beautifully in the velvety blue darkness.

"This is arguably my favorite place on earth."

Adin gazed up. The cathedral was at once monstrous and brilliant, beautiful and grotesque. He'd certainly never tire of looking at it, and he didn't think if he had the advantage of Santos's years it would diminish his love for the place. "Mine too, maybe."

Santos sighed. "You may have guessed I don't like to have my plans disrupted."

"The thought occurred to me, yes," Adin said drily. He'd

more than upset a few of Santos's plans, and he knew Santos had definitely been unhappy with him at the time.

"You derailed any hope I had of destroying Fedeltà's diary. Even though he's your lover, you preserved a journal chronicling his passion for my father—another man. I understand him better and acknowledge that he cared for my father in a way I didn't—and still don't—understand. Now he seems to care for you in a similar way."

"He loved your father very much," Adin admitted. "He still carries it in his heart like a flame. What he feels for me is different, but I don't think it's less… Maybe I'm kidding myself."

Santos kicked at a pebble on the ground. "I don't understand this passion between men at all."

"Because you don't share it. Believe me, if the situation were reversed I couldn't…well. That's not entirely true, is it…? Whether I can feel sexual attraction with a woman or not, I enjoy any truly great literary love story. I have a particular fondness for *Tristan and Isolde*."

"I've had comrades in arms I have mourned. Men I trusted like brothers." Santos frowned.

"I have a sister that I love very much, but I would be incapable of romantic love for a woman. I just think that's how I was made."

Santos gazed at the cathedral again. "It flies in the face of religious tradition."

"I can see where you might have a problem with homosexuality, biblically speaking—" Adin tried not to laugh, but it wasn't easy. "—after its injunction in the Pauline Epistles. Unlike becoming a blood-sucking monster, homosexuality seems to be forbidden to Christians. Why, just the other day I was reading that glowing welcome to the Christian vampire brotherhood in the apocryphal *St. Paul's letter to the Undead*."

"You simply can't help yourself, can you? You always make a joke when you should be pissing yourself with fear." Santos reached out and cuffed Adin on the shoulder. "A better question is why you're still human?"

Adin paused. "Why wouldn't I be?"

"Look around you. Man reaches for immortality like a frantic junkie looking for drugs. He will claw and devour and kill for it if he sees it within his grasp. You remain human, and *I* want to know why." Santos turned so they were facing one another. "Have you already displeased your vampire protector? Is my father's eternal flame proving hotter than your human love?"

Adin swallowed hard. *Why does that feel like tearing off a scab?*

"For your information, I don't choose immortality. I don't want it. I've told Donte that, and we don't see eye to eye at all. He worries that I'll be hurt, and so he wants to turn me. For the last three months there have been alternating bouts of heated debate and brooding silence, interminable kendo and self-defense lessons, and what Donte tells me are bodyguards, but can only be described as sloe-eyed, brooding undead nannies."

"What an inconvenient pet you've turned out to be." Santos laughed. "Color me delighted."

"I'm thrilled you approve."

"Since your lover is my oldest enemy, don't you worry that we're meandering around Paris together in the middle of the night? Tell me you fear me still or I will weep."

"It's always the same with the undead. Do you ever ask why people skydive or swim with sharks or walk on hot coals?"

"I do not. In general, people are fairly stupid, and you may consider it a compliment that I don't think that's true of you, Adin."

"Actually, I see that it's a compliment. Thank you." Adin stopped midstride. "I didn't get the chance to thank you for your help this evening. You and Boaz saved me a great deal of trouble."

"You may thank Boaz; he insisted." Santos stopped in front of a café that was still open for business. "Are you hungry?"

"No." Adin stepped aside as Santos opened the door. "But after everything that's happened, I could very definitely use a glass of wine."

Adin entered the café first, and Santos helped him out of his coat. He found a rack and hung it up before they scouted a suitable table. After sitting, they ordered a bottle of Bordeaux. When the waiter uncorked and poured it, Santos showed the same disinterest Donte usually displayed. Adin wished it were Donte sharing the cool Parisian evening with him. He felt hollow and sad at the thought of Donte brooding alone somewhere.

"What?" Santos asked. "You're thinking of Donte again…?"

"It's nothing. What brings you to Paris? If it's not a deep and arcane secret…"

"It is!" Santos's eyes fairly sparkled. When he relaxed Santos was an extremely handsome man, and his smile held a certain boyish charm. "It's the oldest, deepest and most arcane of all secrets. I almost always spend *Pâques* in Paris. I like to come for Easter Services and stay through the end of May for the feast of the Ascension, although this year that will not be possible. I need to leave tomorrow for a series of business meetings in Taiwan."

Adin blinked in surprise. "You celebrate *Easter* services?"

Santos nodded. "Of course."

Adin shook his head and drank his wine. Why shouldn't Santos still be an observant Catholic? "I guess I didn't realize it was so close."

"Next Sunday." Santos appeared to be reasoning something out in his mind. "I have a place in the seizième. The sixteenth Arrondissement. It's a nice neighborhood."

"I know." Adin blinked at the understatement. It was *the* nice neighborhood in Paris, on the west side across the Seine. It boasted upscale businesses and grand apartment homes.

"If you run out of options, Boaz can take both you and the boy to my home where he can look after you."

"What on earth would make you think I'd take you up on an offer like that?" Adin wasn't entirely over nearly being killed the last time he'd been forced to accept Santos's hospitality.

"Bygones," Santos murmured. "Besides, I won't be there but Boaz will. You'd be safe as a child with its mother."

"In a species that eats its young," Adin snarked.

Santos shot Adin an exasperated glance and then looked down at his untouched wine glass and chuckled. "You really are a handful. I hope someday Donte realizes that by letting you live, I've given him far more grief than I had reason to hope for by killing you."

Adin's muscles relaxed as the wine hit his bloodstream. "Certainly. Wasn't that your plan all along?"

"Well, no, it wasn't." Santos grinned, and it was the first time Adin had ever seen it when it wasn't meant to be cruel. Santos could be attractive, dark like Donte, but with curlier hair and softer features. Very much the offspring of the beautiful boy Adin had seen illustrated in Donte's journal, Donte's dead lover, Auselmo. Even if Santos was far more deadly than he was letting on in that moment. "But I have to take it as a win that he's tearing his hair out with worry over you."

"As long as you're happy."

"I am happy, actually. For now."

"Happy Easter," Adin said over the rim of his wineglass. "A new life awaits."

"I'd prefer you didn't share that information with Donte. I find I'm reluctant to let him relax."

"Fine." Adin watched as Santos's eyes strayed every now and again to the door. "Expecting someone?"

"I estimate I have about twenty minutes before Donte finds you, and I'd rather he didn't find you with me."

"*What?*" Adin nearly knocked his chair over in his haste to rise from the table.

"He may have called Boaz to aid you with your little problem, but I doubt he'll be satisfied to leave your safety to someone else for long. I imagine he's hopped a flight to be here and is even as we speak racing to the rescue in a cab."

"*Shit.*" Adin made for the coat rack even as Santos dropped extra coins on the table for the waiter.

"How romantic you are." Santos caught up with him at the door. "Someday perhaps the thought of seeing me after a respite will inspire some young woman to profanity as well."

"You don't understand. He's only coming here to yell at me and tell me I've proven his point. He'll try to change my mind about being turned and we'll only argue until he goes back to Spain."

"Adin." Santos's brow furrowed as he caught Adin's hand and stopped him. "I hate him for turning me. I *hate* him for it. If it's truly going to come to that, you must accept protection from me."

Adin nearly gaped at Santos with shock. "*Why?*"

"Why what? Being turned is a horror I wouldn't wish on anyone, even those who desire it, although the chance to deprive Donte Fedeltà of his pretty toy is an added incentive. The process is painful and disorienting and the results are anything but guaranteed. Tell me why you refuse him."

"I want to remain who I am," Adin whispered. "I never want to be loved *if only* I were something else, even if who I am gets sick and rots and dies. It's my journey. And without its beginning, its middle, and its end, I'm not ever going to be the man I was born to be. Do you understand that? Does it surprise you so much?"

"Yes," Santos continued, holding Adin's arm. "It's extraordinary, really, but not unexpected from a troublemaker like you."

Adin shrugged and retrieved his coat, then donned it and his scarf before exiting the restaurant.

"Come to my place in the morning. I'll be gone. As for your boy problem," Santos looked around at the darkened street before he spoke again, "I have information that may change things."

"What?"

"Harwiche fears the men he's dealing with, he used you as an intermediary, and now that you have made the monetary exchange, he will either try to trade for him or take him from you."

"That much I figured out all by myself."

Santos cuffed Adin's shoulder again. "Patience, pet," he warned, but without the usual sting. "Boaz can and will get your money back."

"But—"

"Don't ask how. It's confidential but I'll tell him to do it. Or Donte will."

"Donte?"

"Yes, I never know who Boaz is serving from one moment to the next. But there's something Harwiche has recently acquired, and Fedeltà will do anything he has to do to get it. Including giving up the boy."

"What could Harwiche have that Donte will want so badly?"

"My father's letters."

"Your—" Adin's stopped, closing his mouth over an expression of shock.

Santos's eyebrows rose slyly. "I may have told Donte at one time that I burned them."

Adin grasped the lapels of Santos's suit. "Your father's letters? Truly? Donte would kill for those."

"Ah." Santos peeled Adin's fingers from his coat. "If that's the case, it might be wise to turn the boy over to him. Harwiche will ask for Bran in return for my father's letters."

"But I promised to protect—" Adin gasped. "You *bastard*! You knew."

Santos shrugged, then shot Adin a radiant smile. "I suspected. Well… maybe I suggested to Harwiche that the men he was dealing with were unsavory and his problems might be solved by an intermediary. The Harwiche family and I have a history, of sorts."

Adin closed his eyes. "You are *such* a shit."

"It's really a simple matter, Adin." Santos draped an arm around his shoulder and began walking him back toward the Pont Neuf, where they would cross the Seine. "All you have to do is give the boy to Donte—"

"You know I won't do that, I can't. And Donte will try to force me…"

"Yes…" Santos gave Adin's shoulder a hard squeeze, just short of painful. "Well. Eternity isn't much fun unless I'm making some kind of trouble for Fedeltà."

"I have to think." Adin shoved Santos away. "What *is* the boy that Harwiche wants him so badly?"

"That is a very good question."

"All right," Adin growled and looked at his watches. "You've made your mischief, and if you're right, Donte will be here any minute. If you want to add jealous outrage, be sure and stick around."

"Never. That would be too pedestrian for me and he knows I don't share his peculiar tastes." Santos shook his head. "You won't believe me, but it's always a pleasure to see you Adin."

"The pleasure was all yours." Adin headed across the bridge toward the Right Bank but stopped when he'd gotten about ten feet. He sighed and turned back to shoot Santos a cheeky smile. "*Almost*, all yours. Thanks for the drink, Santos, and Happy Easter."

A brief burst of Santos's laughter followed Adin as he crossed over the river. Once on the other side, Adin couldn't help the rush of emotions, the hard beating of his heart at the thought of seeing Donte again. The awareness that—at any moment—he could turn a corner and see Donte's much-loved face quickened his footsteps and compressed his chest with tense anticipation. Adin truly hoped Donte was past his lengthy period of melancholy, because he wanted nothing more than to play.

"Damn you," he said aloud, "come out, come out, wherever you are." He turned another corner and headed down an alley on his way to the hotel. His skin hummed with keen urgency, and he could hear the whisper of Donte's many languages in his head. Adin knew enough to recognize Donte's playful stalking when he felt it. "I can feel you. I know you're here."

Adin passed a fire escape under which a faint puff of smoke curled away from a recessed doorway, redolent with the scent of Donte's expensive cigars.

A tiny flare of light from a rather unusual, nearly original Zippo lighter caught Adin's attention, limning Donte's face, then going out.

Like fucking Harry Lime, there, a briefly lit face in the darkness, and gone again.

"Hello, my lover." Adin went into the sinister shadows to be with Donte, moving with grace into his arms to swap smoke and spit and find skin. Sensation prickled all along the surface of his body when they touched.

"Adin," Donte sighed when their bodies met. He cupped Adin's face in his hands and studied him. "*Più amato.*"

"I've missed you," Adin said between kisses. "Missed us."

"Me too." Donte tossed his cigar to the ground and reached both hands down the back of Adin's pants. "Leather, *caro?* You're dressed like a boy harlot. I have to admit, it has its charm."

"Mmhmm." Adin pulled Donte's shirt from his trousers. He wondered if all vampires had such marvelous tailors, he had only to breathe in Donte's scent and crush the fabric in his fingers to feel a surge of erotic excitement deep within him.

"Turn," he told Donte, uncharacteristically brusque.

"Adin…" Donte resisted, but Adin gritted his teeth and clutched Donte's jacket, spinning him so his face was pressed against the wall. He wasn't thinking too clearly when reached around to unbuckle Donte's belt and undo his zipper. He found the tops of Donte's hips and slid downward to press into the hollows of his pelvis on either side of his cock. Adin dipped his hands lower, cupping Donte's balls and cradling his dick as it thickened and firmed in his palm. Donte protested only slightly when his trousers hit the ground.

"Adin, surely—"

"Shh…" Adin used his upper body to push Donte's into the wall even as he nudged Donte's legs apart as far as they would go, trapped as they were. "Be my man, Donte." He unzipped his leather pants, and his cock dropped hard and heavy against the skin of Donte's ass.

"A—"

"My man and nothing more, right now," Adin told him. "I need you, lover."

Donte's muscles relaxed beneath his fingers. "All right."

"Oh, shit." Adin reached around and stroked Donte's uncut cock erect. "I want you so much. I dream about it every night. Tasting you. Filling you. Lying beneath you as you devour me. Only when I started looking for you, when I realized you were out here somewhere on the street waiting for me, I wanted so much more… I wanted—"

"To hunt me," Donte finished.

Adin jabbed his cock into the cleft of Donte's ass. He hissed, "Yes. And I've caught you, so you're mine." Adin used glistening drops of precome from Donte's cock to tease at Donte's hole, but it wasn't enough. "Shit. We need lube lover. I don't want to hurt you."

Donte held his hand up to what little light there was and tore his palm with an incisor. Blood dripped, viscous and thick, from the wound. "Spit on that."

Adin did as he was told. When Donte reached back and took hold of his cock, the sensation was exquisite. He squeezed through spit and blood, warm and nearly pulsing with life inside the tightness of a thick, cool hand. Adin drew in a shuddering breath and nearly blew right there. Donte played with fire by thumbing the slit of Adin's cock firmly but eased before Adin's balls drew up. Donte pressed his hips backward while he pumped Adin's cock a few more times.

"Pay attention," Donte teased when Adin momentarily lost focus. Adin wrapped an arm around Donte's neck and surged against him, inching his way into Donte's tight channel.

"Ah. So good," Adin moaned when he'd pushed his way in to the hilt and pressed his face into Donte's back, breathing in the scent of him. He could feel Donte all around him as he began to glide and clutched a muscled shoulder for purchase.

Adin wanted flesh beneath his fingers—not fabric—so he kept his dick in motion even as he helped Donte buck off one side of his coat. Together they unbuttoned and slipped his shirt off. As soon as Adin found skin he tasted Donte and teased him with teeth and tongue, nibbling and sucking up marks on his pale skin.

"Adin..." Donte dropped his head back. "You're burning me up."

"Touch yourself." Adin held on and drove into Donte. A+nticipation heightened when Donte shifted to get his hand on his dick. Adin felt the change in Donte's muscles as he stroked himself, felt him tense in satisfaction when he gave himself a particularly pleasurable pull.

Sweat dripped into Adin's eyes, stinging as he buried his face in the thick, dark hair at the nape of Donte's neck. His heart thundered in his chest, and even knowing Donte's heart would never beat for him in answer, he nearly sobbed with relief each time he sank into Donte's cool body. Adin wanted to obliterate the awkward distance that grew so often between them. He pressed his cheek to Donte's back, knowing he shoved him uncomfortably against the bricks on the wall beneath the fire escape, but unable to find the will to let him loose. He pumped frantically, flying toward his release, ready to come apart at the slightest sign or pressure.

Donte's legs stiffened, and he groaned. His body clenched

around Adin's cock. Adin caught the rich, bittersweet scent of Donte's come as it splattered against the wall, then sank his teeth into the meaty muscle where Donte's shoulder met his neck. His legs nearly gave out as his climax hit him hard and he soared, hands skimming over the hills and valleys of Donte's trembling frame, every molecule that touched Donte's skin striking and dancing, sending sensation rippling back through him like a stone skipped in a pond.

Adin collapsed against Donte, who sank, sliding to his knees on the dirty street. Adin draped himself over Donte's back, wrapping arms so tightly around his neck that if Donte had been an ordinary mortal, he'd have died from lack of oxygen.

Where he still had hold of Donte with his teeth, he tasted sweat and salt.

Maybe surprise.

"What the hell has gotten into you?" Donte gasped out as he tried to extricate himself and lunge for his clothes.

"Are you complaining?" Adin slid his hands down Donte's chest and smoothed come across his belly.

Donte dragged his shirt and jacket on and stood to pull up his trousers. "Not really. No."

Adin heard a smile in Donte's voice. He hung on to some part of Donte as long as he could, but finally let go and fell back to the street with a thud. "I claim what's mine, vampire," he said imperiously. "By the power of Count Chocula…and by the gods of breakfast cereal everywhere."

"You're unhinged."

"Shut up. I've had a helluva day." Adin sighed again, tucking his cock into his trousers, then zipping up his fly. "That was epic. We should do that all the damned time. As soon as I get the feeling back in my legs I'll run and you can fuck me if you catch me."

When Donte had his pants done but his belt still dangled he reached down and hoisted Adin up, then wrapped his arms firmly around him.

"*Pazzo.*" Donte kissed him gently, nearly reverently. Adin locked his arms around Donte and pushed so they fell back against the wall again with a *thud*. Out of any human man a burst of air would have escaped, and Adin missed it a little so he voiced it.

"Ooooomph," he sang out, ignoring the shushing Donte was doing in his ear.

"Have you been drinking?"

"I had a glass or two of wine," Adin admitted.

"With Santos," hissed Donte.

"Yep." Adin stepped back and began to pull Donte along toward his hotel, even as he tried to do up his zipper one-handed. "Your immortal enemy."

"Shh," Donte chided. "It's late."

"*To the last, I grapple with thee,*" Adin intoned, giving it all the Moby and a little more of the Dick than it absolutely called for. "*From Hell's heart, I stab at thee; For hate's sake, I spit my last breath at thee.*"

Adin noticed Donte tried to hide a smile. "Come along, Melville. It would be better if you could make less noise and more sense. I thought you might have had enough of the gendarmes for one day."

"Oh." Adin slowed his steps. "You heard about that, did you?"

"Yes. Explain."

Adin sighed. "Come along my lover, I will tell all once we reach the hotel. It's this way."

When they reached the street where Adin's hotel was located, Donte took Adin's elbow and pulled him into the shadows to help him fix his clothing. Adin returned the favor, running his hands over Donte's shoulders and smoothing the wrinkles from his jacket as well as he could. He couldn't stop himself from pulling Donte in for a kiss as he cinched his tie into place.

"It's good to see you," Adin said, hoping Donte could read the truth of his love in his eyes.

Donte stroked a finger over the bruise on Adin's forehead and pressed a kiss tenderly over it. Guilt surged as Adin recalled Santos licking that very spot.

"If I had a beating heart, it would stop whenever I look at you, più amato. You are my life. You know that, right?"

Adin softened considerably. "Yes." Adin kissed Donte's hand and led him into the lobby of his hotel. "My monster." He didn't much care for the look he got from Monsieur Villiers, but when all was said and done, it was an honest mistake. Arguably he'd had plenty of men in his hotel room already.

"Why on earth did the clerk look at us like that?" Donte asked once they were alone in the elevator.

"Why indeed," Adin murmured.

CHAPTER FOUR

Adin wasn't surprised when—after he invited Donte into his room—he discovered that nothing was there. Not Bran. Not Boaz. Not his luggage or personal effects. He sat down on the bed with a sigh and scrubbed his hands through his hair, now just tacky from the gel and product he'd used to style it in what seemed like days before. He stood without saying anything and made his way to the ensuite bathroom.

"Don't bother trying to lock the door," Adin told Donte. "Santos broke it down."

Donte flipped idly through the television channels while Adin scrubbed his face clean of makeup. When Adin returned, Donte opened his arms and enfolded him in an embrace that said as much about the longing Donte had been feeling for him as it did about their present circumstances.

"My things are gone," Adin told him.

"Outwitted by Santos again, were we?" Donte murmured into Adin's hair.

"I don't think so. No." Donte shot him a look but said nothing. "Santos invited me to stay at his home. Call Boaz and ask him if you don't believe me."

Donte's brows knit together. "Oh, I believe you."

Adin straddled Donte and rested his head on his shoulder. "I believe Santos was legitimately offering me a safe place to stay. How much do you know about what happened today?"

"I know you did an extremely foolish thing, going to meet Harwiche in a cemetery."

Adin froze. "How did you know about that?" He jumped to his feet. "You're having me *followed*?"

"Caro—"

"So what, you have me watched when I leave the hotel, you

have Boaz on speed dial to get me out of trouble, and you race here like a biblical angel when you perceive I'm in danger?"

"Yes." Donte turned cold eyes toward him. "What of it?"

"You act like my mother!"

"I do nothing of the sort," Donte growled.

"Well, no actually, you're right. *She* had faith in me."

"I—"

"Admit it, you have not one molecule of confidence that I can take care of myself."

"In the world you knew, yes. You had every right to feel like the master of your fate. In my world…" Donte left his sentence hanging as he pulled the phone from his pocket. He took only a second to check his messages and put it back. "I know where Boaz and your… What were you thinking, Adin? Buying that boy?"

"I doubt it would make any sense in your world."

"Nothing you do makes sense in my world."

Adin frowned. "The boy—Bran—reminded me of my friend Edward. I don't know why. Edward never seemed lost like that when we were growing up. Bran is almost feral. Yet something about him felt familiar. And he was in trouble. I had to do it. You didn't see where they were keeping him."

Donte went to the door of Adin's hotel room. "If you want your things you need to come with me."

"I need to tell Monsieur Villiers I'm checking out so he can fix the broken door."

"The door *Santos* broke. Fine."

Donte waited as patiently as he ever did while Adin accomplished that. When Adin was through at the registration desk, he turned just in time to see two stunning, dark haired women engage Donte in conversation. As usual, Donte was his charming self. He shot Adin an impatient glare when he walked over to join them.

"Ah, Adin. At last. Let's go find out how much trouble you've purchased."

Adin followed Donte glumly out the door and just like that, they were back where they'd begun when he left Spain, silent and separate, walking the streets of the most romantic city on earth without communicating.

Adin slipped his hand into Donte's and they walked a few more feet before Donte stopped and pulled Adin under his arm. They walked the rest of the way to a taxi queue arm in arm like that, laughing when someone honked and shouted the German equivalent of "get a room."

Once inside the taxi, Adin faced Donte. "Let me look at you at least. Are you well?"

The expression on Donte's face softened. "You are positively the silliest man. Of course I'm well."

"Did you get a lot of brooding done while I was gone?" Adin teased. "How's your chair, the one with the leather upholstery? Did you sit by the fire and doodle pictures of bats with little heart shaped eyes? I did."

"I am not in the mood to be mocked."

Adin framed Donte's face with his hands, running his thumbs over the bones of his cheeks and the arch of his brows. "Beloved, I mock you only as a last resort." He leaned in and whispered in Donte's ear, "Do you need me?"

Donte lowered his gaze. "I do. Always."

"Feed," Adin ordered. "I had Thai food for lunch before I met Harwiche. Let's see if you can tell me what I ate."

Donte looked at the driver. "We could wait—"

"I'm sure you can make him believe he dropped Italian nuns off at the Louvre. Now, come to me." Adin's voice roughened. "Maybe I need *you*, lover."

Donte allowed Adin to draw him in. In the end neither of them could fight the attraction they felt. Adin's heart quickened as Donte pressed his lips to the pulse in his neck and a terrible excitement stole over him when he felt Donte's teeth tease the skin there. Donte could tear his throat out with little more than the effort it would take Adin to place a chaste kiss on someone's nose, but maybe that was part of the thrill.

"I wish you didn't like this so much, caro," Donte murmured. "I worry that you'll be indiscriminate."

Adin slapped both his hands to Donte's face and held him away. "You don't mean that." Fury brought a high color to his cheeks. "I am no one's *cheap eats.*"

Donte searched him for any sign of duplicity and Adin wanted to scream. "Promise me? Santos—"

"Santos closed my wound without permission from me," Adin growled. "I will never willingly be with anyone else, in any way, Donte as long as you and I... I don't know what I have to do to prove myself to you…"

Donte struck, his teeth sliding into Adin's neck like ice picks, quick and sure. Adin felt the sudden surge of hot lightning throughout his body that began as searing pain, but brought him almost instantly to an equal ecstasy.

"*Donte.*" Donte had to know that feeding brought Adin a release that was both profoundly sexual and emotionally gratifying. "Don't you know how I feel? Don't you understand what it means to me to nourish you this way?"

Donte used his tongue to soothe away the pain and Adin breathed in deeply, committing to memory the ambiance of Paris as it mingled in his mind with Donte's own deeply masculine scent.

"Ah, *lover.*"

"Più amato." Donte nuzzled him as Adin's head swam. It wasn't unusual for him to get light-headed after Donte fed. He'd grown to count on curling up in Donte's arms afterwards and letting the lassitude take him even as Donte's body warmed and quickened with borrowed life.

After a while Donte broke the silence. "Are you sure you want to go to Santos's place?"

Adin opened his eyes. "Can you think of a logical reason why I shouldn't?"

Donte glared at him.

The familiar argument dragged Adin down far more than the loss of blood. "If he wanted me dead, I'd be dead."

"Who knows what he wants? What if he plans to kill you next week? He could kill you—"

"At any time. So can anything. Accept that or don't follow me next time, Donte. I'm human; I will die. Accustom yourself or walk away." Donte's hold tightened around him and Adin felt unreasonably constricted. He pushed away from Donte who glared at him, hurt and angry. Adin caught the door handle and opened it to step out but Donte held him in place, his jaw tense.

"If I thought you meant that for one second I would have no trouble killing you myself." He gave Adin a shove that sent him sprawling onto the pavement of the road in front of Santos's home and slammed the door, even as Adin heard him tell the driver to go. The cab sped away, its taillights winking back as it braked and surged into the Parisian traffic.

"Bastard." Adin got up and dusted himself off, then walked to the wrought iron gate of Santos's impressive property. While he waited for someone to answer the intercom he muttered, "Time for a new Cosmo poll. Ten ways to tell if you're boyfriend is The One…Question #1. Is he willing to throw you from a moving vehicle…?"

Boaz clucked like a mother hen as he took Adin's arm to lead him down the long hallway. "I settled the boy in the guest suite and put your things in the adjoining room. I take it Donte found you. You reek of jiz and blood and regret."

"I want that for my epitaph, Boaz, please write it down, Adin Tredeger, PhD. He reeked of—"

"All right, remind me later," Boaz said gently as he opened the door to a beautifully decorated but simple bedroom in soothing tones of green and gray.

Adin looked around. "I expected something more… Versailles. I'm delighted to be disappointed. I envisioned Louis XIV gilt furnishings and fleur de lis."

"Santos is a monster, not an American."

"Ah…" Adin allowed Boaz to help him off with his coat. The knob of a door on the interior wall of his room turned and Bran's manacled hands appeared first and then his face. He appeared to be more vibrant; the smudges under his eyes were fainter and the drawn look had all but disappeared from his still-pale face.

"You're back," Bran said carefully, looking Adin over. His nostrils flared and he turned his head slightly, his cheeks pinkening in the light thrown from his room.

"Boaz, can you show me somewhere I can bathe?"

"With *pleasure.*" Boaz shot Bran a look that made him grin.

"Bran, you can wait here, and we'll talk after I get cleaned up." Bran gave him a nod and then entered into the adjacent sitting room where he sat in one of two elegant leather chairs.

Adin followed Boaz back out to the hallway. The hardwood floors were old and rich, the walls decorated with black and white photographs of stars from the silent era of American films. A particularly fetching picture of Garbo as barely a girl caught his eye and he stopped to admire it.

"Not what you expected is it, Dr. Tredeger?" Boaz asked.

"No." Adin couldn't quite put his finger on why that might bother him. "So much nicer to picture the castle with walls that drip blood."

"Santos isn't a monster any more than Donte is, except, they all are. Which makes it difficult to explain."

"You're making my head ache." Adin stopped when Boaz paused near a door.

"You'll find everything you need in here. Can you find your

way back? I left the door to your room open and it's the only green one."

"Is the boy safely locked in? What if he tries to escape?"

Boaz leaned in and whispered, "He has nowhere to go. I don't think he'll leave. Especially not chained."

Adin opened the door to the bathroom and entered it. "My room is right after John Thierry but before Clara Bow. Are you sure that Bran won't try to run?"

Boaz smiled. "Bran and I have an understanding. He's far safer here than he would be anywhere else. Besides, I think he likes you."

"Likes me?" Adin thought of all the different things that might mean to Boaz, and not a few of them involved things he didn't want to contemplate with regard to a boy Bran's age.

"He realizes you saved him from Harwiche." Boaz's voice betrayed his distaste. "And the men who kept him prisoner. He saw how you held your own with Donte and Santos, I believe he thinks you're heroic."

"Spare me." Adin began to remove his clothing. "I'm sure that since he probably saw Donte throw my jiz-covered ass out of that cab he's changed his mind."

Boaz chuckled as he went to the tub and opened the taps. "That was amusing, sir. In a kind of *'can this marriage be saved'* sort of way."

"I'm not in the mood." Adin barely folded his clothes as he piled them on the wide marble counter. "It wouldn't be so bad if he was just angry with me, but I always seem to hurt him in some profound new way."

"He loves you, and he hates himself for it."

"Cool. Just when I didn't think I could feel worse." Adin stepped into the tub and sank into the shallow water. As more water filled it and Boaz added some herb scented oils, Adin's tense muscles began to relax.

"Don't fall asleep," Boaz reached his hand down to slap a

light splash of hot water into Adin's face. "You'll drown."

"I'll be fine," Adin lied, even as he began to let himself drift. He'd fallen asleep in a tub before and didn't think he'd drown. He had a moment of concern that the water would overflow but even that left him as he sank dreamily into the comfort of heat and coriander… maybe juniper berries and lime.

Like hot gin it went straight to his head. He heard Boaz turn off the water, then murmur something before the door closed behind him.

Adin let himself go completely and dreamed of driving an old-fashioned metal pedal car, squeak-squeaking down the dirt road in front of his parents rented home in Pakistan. When his father was working there on geological studies, the families from his small company of surveyors and scientists all lived in a rural outpost consisting of several low homes facing a courtyard just outside of a small village. Crowds of ragged boys waited for their turn, and Adin was ready to relinquish the car as soon as he reached the rusted paint can that signified his trip around the property was over. Dust flew up from the wheels, covering him with grime, and an occasional automobile snorted its way past, forcing him to pull over and wait. Just as he reached the can and began to step out, the Imam called the boys, his friends, to prayer. They scattered to attend to their devotions with their families, and Adin left the car where it was, assuming they'd return sooner or later to begin their play again. He headed for the back door of his house, nearest his mother's kitchen so she or Yasmina, the teenage girl who watched him and cooked for them, could scold him or feed him, whichever pleased them. Adin never knew beforehand which they planned.

As he passed by the window to his parents's bedroom, he heard laughter drifting from within like music. Fascinated, he stepped up to the opening and watched as his father caught his mother against the wall and kissed her. Adin could see her struggling to get away but knew that she was only pretending. Her laughter was low and filled with something he didn't understand. It wasn't anger; he'd never heard his parents angry. They'd argued, certainly, especially about taking more jobs outside the U.S. His mother believed things were changing around the world, and wanted to go back home where she felt more comfortable. His father was a bit of an adventurer and enjoyed travel.

Everyone knew they disagreed. They just didn't let it get angry.

Right now his mother had her arms wrapped around his father, and she lifted her legs up, locking them behind his back. Something about it made Adin smile—like playing piggy back—but it also felt like something he shouldn't be watching. Their kisses were turning more…frantic, he could see, and his father gripped his mother's butt in the palms of his hands where nice people didn't normally touch one another.

It looked hungry, and it felt desperate to Adin, as though they couldn't get enough of each other, as though they devoured each other, breathing each other in like the smoke from water pipes he'd seen in the marketplace in Egypt. Men drew the smoke in and kept it in their lungs as long as they could. His father inhaled his mother the same way.

A hand gripped his arm and pulled him away from the window and Yasmina's voice washed over him as she took him to task for skulking around.

"Don't spy," she hissed at him as she pulled him far away from the window. She held his baby sister Deana in one arm and dragged him toward the back of the house to the kitchen. "Adults need private time."

"My dad had his hands on my mom's butt," Adin told her, wide eyed.

Yasmina shrugged at him, worldly at thirteen where he was only five. "Adults do that. It's disgusting, but someday, oddball, you'll understand."

Adin had private reservations about that but gave Yasmina the benefit of the doubt. "Don't call me that."

"Oddball," Yasmina swatted at him. "Your mother told me it says Oddball on your birth certificate but the doctor told your parents you'd need a nickname so you wouldn't grow up with a psychological complex. This is why you are called Adin." He could see the teasing light in her eyes and forgave her but he knew it was his parents's joke and it would haunt him forever.

"Deana's name rhymes with beans because mom says she gave her gas…"

"True, but she's more than made up for that by being such a sweet and beautiful child, and you are a monster!"

"Am not!" Adin wrenched his hand from her grasp, waiting to see whether she'd chase him, and then ran from her through the open courtyard and past the kitchen. Yasmina called to him to slow down in Urdu, to be

mindful that she couldn't run with a baby in her arms, and he complied. Eventually Yasmina had to return to the cooking, but she left him feeling well looked after and richer by a special ball shaped pastry filled with pistachios and sugar, called a Laddu.

The boys returned and play continued until the afternoon sun found its way to the horizon. After that, when Adin thought it seemed very late at night, Adin ate a meal with his family outside. A billion stars hung overhead while they enjoyed the drop in temperature and the fading of the desert light. They sat in the courtyard on a bench. His father had one arm around him and one around his mother as she held the baby in her arms and sipped her spicy tea. The way his father looked at his mother seemed to make everyone present smile, his mother most of all.

She looked the way she did when she'd figured out the best place to hide Adin's Christmas gifts.

Adin heard a clanking noise and opened his eyes to see Bran sitting on the side of the tub. He grabbed for a washcloth and covered what he could of himself, then shot Bran a killing look. "*Bran.* Generally people like to bathe alone."

"Don't worry. You've got nothing I haven't seen before."

Adin rolled his eyes, still feeling odd. At first, his heart had hurt to be wrenched from that dream. It had been a long time since he'd really thought about his family and how much he'd loved—and been loved by—his parents in return. While he'd dreamed, he'd felt it like a drug, seeping with the heat of the water into his bones. Now the dream still pulled at him, as if the warmth of it dragged him under.

The wetness on Adin's cheeks had nothing to do with the sweat beading on his forehead. He didn't bother to hide the sob that escaped him. Bran sat placidly while Adin wept, one finger stirring Adin's bathwater, the other hand holding his chains up so they wouldn't get wet. When he had no more tears left Bran handed him a small, thick towel and he dried his face with it.

"Thanks." Adin handed it back and began the effort of soaping himself up and rinsing off, determined that if it didn't seem unusual for the boy to be in the bathroom with him, he wasn't going to go out of his way to make it weirder than it had to be. Bran remained silent, and when Adin looked up Bran's eyes shimmered with unshed tears. "What?"

"Beautiful family," Bran said in perfect Urdu. "Much love."

Adin's breath caught. "What are you?"

Bran smiled faintly. "Yes. *Exactly.*"

CHAPTER FIVE

Adin fell into bed and slept. If it was uneventful for most of the night, dream-wise, it more than made up for that in the seconds before he woke, when hundreds of images, mostly faces, flickered like paparazzi flashbulbs going off in his head, *pop*, *pop*, *pop*.

It was as if everyone he'd ever known, every person he'd ever seen, was displayed before him in a lightening round. A PowerPoint presentation slideshow of old love and painful loss, of things that were frightening, and people best forgotten.

"Stop," Adin ground out when he realized he had no control over what he was seeing. Adin heard a noise near him that might have been a sigh, and might have been a smothered laugh.

Adin threw the sheet off his body and swung his feet over the side of his bed. Silk sleep pants clung damply to his sweaty legs. He put his elbows on his knees and rested his head in his hands. The first thing he saw when he opened his eyes was Bran, who lay curled on the floor around a pillow like a cat.

Adin watched the boy for a minute and realized he was pretending to be asleep.

"I can see you're awake." Adin drew his feet back up into the bed, as if the boy was going to chew off a toe or something. "There's no point in pretending. And stop rummaging around in my head, Bran."

"But I haven't gotten to the best bits yet." With a heavy metal scraping noise Bran unfurled himself and sat up. "To look at you a bloke would think that you've never had a moment of anxiety in your life, that it was all pricey and painless—"

"I don't appreciate you fooling around with my memories." Adin leaned back against the well-crafted mahogany headboard. When Bran would have joined him on the bed Adin pushed him back. "Get a chair."

Bran tugged one of the leather chairs to the spot where he'd been sleeping next to the bed and sat in it. He slid back and lifted his legs to rest his feet next to Adin's. His eyebrow rose in defiance, daring Adin to complain.

"Is that why Harwiche wants you? Because you can get inside of people's minds?" Adin asked.

"I don't know why Harwiche wants me."

Adin frowned in disbelief.

"*No.* It's true! I don't know why he wants me. I don't know what anyone would want with me."

"That's probably true," Boaz spoke from the doorway. He entered the room holding a tray of coffee, carefully setting it down between Adin and Bran and then climbing onto the bed. "He doesn't know."

"Make yourself at home." Adin grumbled.

"I am home." Boaz smiled. He handed Adin a cup of coffee then offered one to Bran, who shook his head. "Bran was probably kidnapped for something random. Perhaps someone saw you do something unusual and they put two and two together, yes?"

"For the love of heaven, Boaz. Just tell me what he is."

"That's part of the problem. If I'm not mistaken, Bran isn't any one thing." To Bran directly, he said, "Am I right?"

Bran stayed silent.

"Look." Boaz turned back to Adin. "You have to trust me when I say if I knew more, I would tell you."

"Like you've always done in the past," Adin replied sourly.

Boaz frowned. "Here's the thing. Every culture in the world has a variation on the theme of the changeling, am I right?"

"He's a *changeling*?" Adin chuckled. "A fairy baby switched at birth with a human?"

"Yes, and no. You're so disrespectful, and it ill becomes a man of intelligence. Put aside Disney for right now. A changeling child is believed—in most cultures—to be a magical being that is switched with a human child at birth. Whether it's hell tithes, or mischief, or a way to prevent magical inbreeding. The point is, no one really catches on in most cases."

"Right." Adin sipped his coffee. "And no one has considered the possibility that the entire genesis of these tales is a way for superstitious or hyper-religious people to explain away children with illnesses or birth defects or autism."

Boaz's mouth dropped open. "You *have* studied this."

"I'm a professor of literature, and I vet old documents and manuscripts all the time. Fairy tales are some of the most profound and interesting things people have ever written. Of course I have."

"All right, all right." Boaz winked at Bran. "I told you there would be puffery involved."

Adin sputtered, "I beg your—"

"The point is, even Bran can't tell you what he is, because he doesn't know."

Adin digested this and frowned at Bran. "How the hell can you not know what you are?"

Bran sucked in a breath and held absolutely still for a single second, then burst into tears and ran from the room. Adin heard the nearly obscene *clank* sound of his manacles as he slammed the connecting door between their rooms.

"If you can be any more insensitive, this might be a good time, Adin. After all, I don't completely despise you yet and even though Santos never liked you in the first place he could probably like you less." Boaz got up and then removed the tray from the bed. He reached out and pulled Adin's half-finished coffee from his hand.

"*Boaz.*"

"Think about it," Boaz ordered Adin sternly. "Think about how you know who *you* are and then come down for breakfast."

Adin thought of all the memories Bran had accessed. He thought of his mother and father and their stories of *their* parents.

If he didn't have that…if he didn't remember that, he'd have no idea what he was either. *"Boaz."*

Boaz had gotten to the door, but he turned abruptly. He could be at least as impatient as Donte. "There is folklore suggesting that a changeling child becomes a human child over a period of time. It's a process. At some point, the child in the process of *becoming* is neither one thing nor another. Santos speculates that if the process was interrupted, someone like Bran might be… Well. Certainly he'd be outside the norm."

Adin frowned. "How outside?"

Boaz measured his words more carefully than Adin had ever seen him do, "Entirely new. He's neither. He's not *something*."

"Boaz. Of course he's something. He eats. He stirred my bathwater. He cried."

"He stirred your *bathwater*?"

"It's a long story. The point is he's entirely corporeal. He's very much a human boy."

"Yes." Boaz chewed his lip thoughtfully.

"He couldn't be held in chains if he weren't."

"There is some speculation that iron weakens him."

"It's all conjecture?" Adin entertained the idea that he'd purchased boy who was some sort of magical being with mental Houdini fu.

"I'm making eggs."

"Quel surprise."

Once the door slammed behind Boaz, Adin cursed and ran his hands through his hair. He knew he should get up and put on clothes, clean his teeth, and leave. He should take his luggage and go back to the hotel and leave all the magical machinations to Boaz and his gang of merry monsters, but he couldn't bring himself to leave without saying good-bye to Bran. Then, if Boaz could get his money back as Santos promised, Adin could turn his back and walk away.

Maybe.

He dressed quickly and entered Bran's room and found him face down on the bed. Oddly enough, it reminded him of the many times after his parents died, when he and Deana had been forced to deal with the grief of a sudden shocking loss and he'd found Deana exactly like this. It felt like a familiar thing, sitting on the side of the bed and placing a comforting hand on Bran's shoulder.

"I'm so sorry." Adin smoothed the fabric of Bran's T-shirt over his shoulder blade. "I wasn't really thinking. I'm sorry if what I said—"

"It's all right," Bran sniffed.

"Tell me about what you do know. Maybe I'll be able to understand."

"Everyone's memories are available to me except mine."

"You don't remember?"

"I can remember my name, what I did yesterday, last week. Where I've lived recently and what I spend my time doing, most of the time. Some things from my childhood. A few."

"But the distant past?"

Bran looked as though he were concentrating. "Nothing."

"You remember back how far?"

"It's not like that. It's not like a line I can't pass. It's as if *I've* been nowhere, done nothing. Like one minute I wasn't here and then I was."

"That must be odd." Adin considered it. "It must be horrible."

Bran shrugged with a clink of his chains. "When I figured out that I could share other people's memories and dreams, it seemed strange to me that I didn't have my own."

"Try to think, Bran. What can you do, what have you done recently, that someone might want you to do for them? It has to be something virtually impossible… What is it that sets you apart?"

Bran stayed mutinously silent for several minutes. Adin waited him out. Finally Bran's stomach growled.

"I'm hungry."

Adin sighed, giving up for the moment. "Well, if that's actual hunger and not—you know—the reason people are trying to buy and sell you, go to Boaz and get something to eat, and I'll be down in a minute, all right?"

Bran nodded and got up, heading for the bedroom door.

Adin watched him as he took off; heard his chains rattle and his feet thunder on the hard wood floors. Whatever Bran was, he should never have been made a pawn by Harwiche, nor should he be used in some game between Santos and Donte. He should be free to go to school, to run around with his friends on the soccer pitch, not chained up in dank basements urinating in bins and eating off the floor like a dog. Adin burned with fury at himself that he'd allowed it to continue after their so-called rescue, even though he and Boaz had done better by Bran than his previous captors. Making up his mind, he followed Bran toward the smell of food.

Listening to Boaz and Bran chatter at the breakfast table, Adin thought they seemed like any normal, dysfunctional family. Bran helped himself to food liberally, as though he really were the teenaged boy he appeared to be, and Boaz kept it coming, perfectly shirred eggs, the kind of thick ham called bacon in England, along with sausages and the ubiquitous piping hot bread, with fresh butter and jam. In all it was a very English breakfast—thankfully missing a black pudding—for a French household, and Adin wondered if Boaz made it especially for him. For some reason that warmed his heart a little.

"Boaz, Santos said you have a way to get my money back. I don't suppose it's legal, but then neither is selling adolescent boys, so you won't be hearing a word about it from me."

"He mentioned that. I'll see to it."

"And that only leaves you." Adin turned to Bran.

"What do you mean?"

"I've been meaning to ask you, Boaz. If you don't know what Bran *is*, how can you know he has to be kept chained?"

"Santos told me that it would be unwise to remove his chains until we know why Harwiche wants him. He said specifically—"

Adin waved his explanation off. "I would prefer it if you didn't treat me like an idiot. Santos wants to embroil me in another game of triangles with Donte."

Boaz had the grace to look guilty. "You have to admit it has worked in the past."

Adin finished his coffee and rose to his feet. He pulled all the cash from his wallet and dropped it on the table by Bran's plate. "Only because I didn't see it coming." He pulled the keys to Bran's chains from his pocket and handed them to the boy. "Quick as you can, unchain yourself and go home, wherever that is. Hide from everyone. Make sure you appear to be nothing more than a boy on a school trip or something. I'm leaving."

Boaz leaped to his feet so fast his chair fell over. "Adin, you're making a serious mistake. Donte will *kill* you for this if he realizes that Harwiche has Auselmo's papers and you let his leverage go free. And if he doesn't, Santos surely will."

"It's done. And Bran is a…boy. Whatever he is, he's not *leverage*." Boaz rushed toward Bran but Adin caught him easily and held him fast while Bran worked the chains. "I'm sure you and Santos can figure out a way to turn this to your advantage. I'm done with your games."

The last of the chains dropped from Bran's slight body and Adin half expected a tornado or a mushroom cloud. He anticipated being torn limb from bloody limb despite the apparent unconcern he'd put on for Boaz's benefit. At the very least he expected the kid to get the hell out and not look back. Absurdly, Adin wanted to tell Bran if he was going to do something awful he should get it over quickly. Instead Bran rushed to him and gave him a kiss on the cheek that carried more than a little adoration with it.

"Thank you, Adin." Bran's eyes shone as he poised for flight. "I won't forget this."

Boaz struggled against what Adin realized was a chokehold he'd been trained to use by Donte's minions as they'd patiently tried to teach him to defend himself. "*Run*," Adin insisted. "Hide."

Bran fled.

When Adin finally let Boaz go, the smaller man fell to the floor panting.

"Donte and Santos will have the first common goal in their long lives when they realize what you've done. Both of them will want to see you flogged."

"Excellent," Adin told him. "Time honored. Peace at any price."

On his way out of Santos's house he pulled his cell phone out and made a call. His heart clenched when Donte answered on the first ring.

"I'm a shit." Donte spoke before Adin had a chance to say anything. "Tell me you forgive me or I will be forced to brood in the most beautiful city on Earth."

"I need you," Adin told him. "I just threw away any chance for us, and pissed off about half the underworld in the bargain."

"Did you?" Donte sighed. "Again? You make me laugh to think I used to worry about things like plague…"

CHAPTER SIX

Adin walked in the general direction of the Seine. He was unsurprised when a sedan with dark-tinted windows pulled up to the curb beside him fifteen minutes later.

The driver's window rolled down and Boaz leaned over and spoke. "Get in."

"No," Adin said flatly.

"Donte phoned me and told me to help you get home. *To him.* I take it you didn't tell him what you've cost him."

"That will have to come later."

"I see."

"Why are you here?" Adin asked, still walking along while Boaz crept by the curb—not an easy feat in Parisian traffic, even that early in the day.

"I just gave Santos my notice, and I have not a single doubt that he will peel me like a grape when next we meet. *Get in.*"

Adin glanced around the chic neighborhood then shrugged. He climbed into the back seat and folded his arms. "Whose car is this?"

"Let's hope this escapes Santos's notice until I can return it. He has no need of it in Asia, anyway."

"That home was remarkably free of Santos's usual minions. I can't help but feel I must have reacted exactly as he planned. I hope you brought my luggage, I have an Eiffel Tower pencil sharpener in there for Deana."

"I have no idea what Santos planned. He doesn't share his thoughts with me."

Adin scooted forward and gripped the back of Boaz's seat. "Well, let me share mine. If anything Santos has planned, if anything he has used me for this time harms one hair on Donte's head you had better kill me because I *will* tear you apart, and while

I may not be a vampire, I will *drink your blood*. Do you understand me?"

Adin met Boaz's eyes in the rearview mirror and for the first time in their acquaintance, the insouciant, polite mask dropped from Boaz's face, leaving an undisguised anger. "I understand you. Fedeltà knows where my loyalties lie. I've told you that. Anyway, as I've also told you, you'll be answering to him this time."

"You've told me a lot of things." Adin watched the mask fall back into place on Boaz's dark, sharp features until his eyes held their usual merry light.

Boaz snorted. "Sit back and be silent. *I will drink your blood.* Aren't you simply precious?"

Adin gazed out the window. The sky was overcast; if he looked farther west it was clear they'd be getting some rain. Already he could see a certain yellow cast to the light, which probably heralded a sudden downpour. As they navigated the crowded streets, Adin sighed in contentment. "Where are we headed?"

"Back to your hotel. Donte is waiting for you there."

"I hope you have your own room."

"I'm certain Donte was able to make arrangements."

"I imagine after your little performance yesterday Villiers will find you a place," Adin remarked drily. "If you're a carnivore."

"I'm an *omni*vore," Boaz informed him. "But when I'm working I try not to divide my attention."

"Do you think we'll ever see Bran again?"

"I couldn't say, Dr. Tredeger."

"For his sake, I hope not." Adin decided that if he was going to require being driven through the streets of Paris in April just before a good spring rain, he ought to shut up and enjoy it while it lasted.

When Adin entered their new hotel room he discovered Donte hunched over the tiny writing desk, frowning in the light of a laptop. In a parody of the man himself all the window coverings were drawn and the lights were turned off. Given Adin's curiosity and Donte's fierce concentration, Adin couldn't help but reach into the case he'd brought up from the car to draw out his reading glasses. He slipped them on as he leaned over Donte's shoulder to glance at the screen.

"You smell like sun and rain." Donte's breath warmed Adin's ear.

Adin leaned in and kissed Donte just below the jaw, resting his chin on one broad shoulder. "You smell like home. What has you frowning this fine rainy morning?"

Donte lifted one of Adin's hands and placed a kiss in the palm. "Your hand tastes like iron. Have you ever heard of an *Emere?*"

"No." There was no second chair, and Donte gallantly relinquished his to Adin as he read the wiki article and scrolled down. "Yoruban folklore?"

"West African peoples. They have interesting cosmology and a fascinating language, although I never learned it. An Emere is another type of changeling child."

"Changeling? Boaz talked about changelings. You think Bran is an Emere?"

"I'm just trying to get a read on all the changeling folktales. It's my understanding that changelings are actually fairly common. Sometimes a broader picture, synthesizing an image from a number of different cultures—as many as one can get—will give a better idea of what one is dealing with."

"Look at you getting all research-y. Sexy." Donte turned and Adin tilted his head to taste him, slanting his mouth over Donte's, teasing it open. Donte yielded and they stroked each other with lips and tongue, until between them they could taste the pleasure of homecoming and imminent sex. Donte broke away first.

"So, Emere," Donte hinted, clearing his throat, but Adin

could tell he was pleased to be back to teasing and kisses. "This is a child who can move between heaven and earth at will. They're seen as not quite nice, really, as they are greedy for heaven, even while they experience the joys of earth."

Adin considered this. "I have to wonder if Bran is special somehow even among his kind. The fact that he has powers, but not the first clue what it all means, indicates to me… I don't know what, it's playing hide-and-seek somewhere in my imagination. Boaz said the changeling process turns a supernatural child into a human. What if it isn't the original nature of Bran that's at issue, for example, he isn't valuable because he's a specific otherworldly entity or a changeling human, but maybe…"

"His value lies in the fact that he's neither." Donte frowned. "You realize you said otherworldly entity with no hesitation at all?"

"He isn't human." Adin turned to find Donte gazing at him thoughtfully. "Oh, you mean it's odd that I don't question it anymore?"

Donte rubbed his hand across Adin's back. "That saddens me somewhat. As if I've taken something innocent and—"

Adin ignored him. "I wish I knew why he was so valuable. What do you suppose Harwiche believed Bran could do for him?"

"I don't know. What does he do?" Donte asked. "Have you seen anything out of the ordinary?"

Adin chuckled. "Little prick was in my head all the time, but I hardly think anyone would pay for that. Vampires can do that. He could see my dreams, comment in my thoughts. At the time I thought it was as if he…" Adin frowned.

Donte skimmed a hand over Adin's shoulder and down his chest. "What?"

"This morning I had the rather fanciful notion that maybe he could search my memories and play them for me. As if I were a jukebox. Like he could figure out my greatest hits."

"Yes?"

"Yes, and he could screen them with intense clarity. It was almost as if I could relive them. He seemed to be searching my 'face file' this morning when I woke up. They were all flashing past like—"

Donte's hand stopped moving. "Is there a reason anything you know—*anyone* you know—could be harmful to you?"

"You're kidding, right?" Adin switched off the computer and stood, enfolding Donte in his arms. "There is nothing in my past that Ned Harwiche would pay to find out, if that's what you're thinking. Certainly anyone who wanted to hurt me could find an addict to do it for a few hundred bucks, if that much. I think Bran just wanted to get to know me. Whatever it was, he's gone now, and he's Santos's headache, or Harwiche's or yours, but I refuse to tell you about that until later..." Adin fished around his case for his toiletry kit and tossed it between the pillows on the bed.

"About that? About what?"

"About the fact that after today you will probably, in Boaz's words, want to have me flogged. As if that was anything new." Adin crawled onto the bed.

"You said my headache, Adin." Donte followed him. "What headache?"

"Later." Adin helped slide the jacket off Donte's shoulders and unbuttoned his crisp cotton shirt. "No tie today, how very informal. Were you heading out for a swim?"

"Very funny, I was relaxing at home."

"Ah. And you didn't pack the dressing gowns. Didn't want to sit around in your shirtsleeves like a wanton?"

"Stop making me sound like a gothic novel," Donte told him.

Adin located Donte's belt buckle and undid it without taking his eyes from Donte's. "Don't knock it. Fully half the reason I love you is because of your tailor."

Donte's expression softened. "Still love me?"

Something about the way Donte asked made Adin's breath hitch. "You must know I do."

"When you're next to me, I can feel it." Donte pulled him close. Adin didn't resist. "I can see it in your eyes and smell it on your skin."

"Donte." Adin smiled into Donte's neck.

"Then you leave and it's complicated by time and distance and mortality and—"

"I'm here now," Adin breathed, pulling his shirt off over his head. Donte's fingers worked the fastenings on Adin's jeans and soon they were naked, skin-to-skin, and tumbling into the narrow bed together. "You're magnificent, Donte."

Donte loomed over Adin, who lay on his back against the pillows and smiled up at him like he was a god. "No, you are. *Mio meraviglioso amore. Il mio cuore è per te, caro. Per sempre.*" My heart belongs to you for always.

"*Tu sei la mia vita, Donte, la mia anima.*" You are my life, my soul. Adin felt his face heat. "Which is ironic really, given that you're undead, but there you have it." His lips curved in a smile of welcome, and Donte hungrily found them with his own.

Adin drowned in all the things his senses told him. Donte's skin was soft, velvety, and cool beneath his fingertips and where it pressed against his own, he smelled like cigars and croissants and coffee and tasted of lime and some elusive Middle-Eastern spice, cardamom maybe, but savory. Like a cardamom pod and the bittersweet peel of oranges.

"Donte," Adin whispered, "*lover.*"

Donte lifted Adin's leg, nudging and bumping him until Adin could feel Donte's cock gliding along in its own slickness over his perineum.

Adin's eyes closed. "*Oh.*"

"Must I beg?" Donte asked, but Adin could see he was teasing. "Must I ask permission to enter, as if I were a vampire standing in the doorway of your home?"

Adin felt around over his shoulder and was only a little frustrated by the fastening on his case. He pulled out a bottle of lube and Donte pursed his lips.

"If I believed you packed this just for your trip to Paris, I'd be concerned."

Adin nipped at Donte's chin while Donte slid a slick finger around his puckered entry to prepare him. "I knew eventually you would lose interest in even that most exciting of all undead pastimes—gazing into the dark by yourself—and come to me."

Donte sank into Adin with a sigh they passed between them through kisses and the soft sounds of pain and pleasure. For Adin, the challenge was always how to get closer to Donte, how to be absorbed into Donte's skin, so he wrapped himself around Donte's body and hung on, lurching into a kiss. Hands grasped his ass as Donte's feet found traction, allowing him to drive into Adin again and again.

After a time, Donte's strokes were so fast and short and hard that Adin could barely breathe around the panting half breaths of air forced out of him. He hardly had time to drag air back into his lungs while Donte drilled and held him, punished and cherished him all at once. His head spun. He wondered how he'd ever thought he could live without it – even for a short time.

"Ah, Donte."

Low, throaty groans signaled Donte was on the edge of release, and Adin was with him on the precipice, his heartbeat waiting, his nerves thrumming eagerly.

"*Donte.*" The world tilted and slipped and slid away from Adin as if Donte were rising into the air with him in his arms, taking flight, into perfect, heartbreaking, starry black skies. Adin's cry was both strangled by emotion and smothered by Donte's mouth, which captured his surprised gasp as his heart seemed to burst from his chest.

"*Voglio restare per sempre con te, caro, almeno puoi pensarci?*"

I want to be with you forever, will you think about it? Adin squeezed his eyes shut and clung.

Adin woke briefly to see Donte slip out of their room. He didn't need the windows of the room unobstructed to know that it was night. Donte hadn't fed from him since the day before, and he was no doubt going out to find sustenance. Adin rolled over, content to rest, to let the languor of their lovemaking and his sorrow at their inability to find common ground with regard to immortality, drag him back for some much needed sleep.

"I never could understand why these numbskulls swim here at this time of day," Adin's father said as he set up the tripod. "Think we'll get lucky?"

"This fog should burn off." Adin had been more interested in the coffee his father bought him, even though he'd filled it with cream and sugar so he could drink it without making faces, than the photography part of the outing. "What is it with you and that boat? We've been here every weekend this summer and you still don't have the picture you want."

"Mind your manners Adin. The lady is a ship,*" Keene Tredeger teased. "I freely admit I'm obsessed by it."*

The Tredegers, father and son, peered through the fog at the Balclutha, the three-masted, full-rigged beauty that was part of the Maritime Museum's collection. If the moisture burned off enough, his father would try to get a picture of her, caressed just so by the early morning sunlight. As if the sun would ever shine over San Francisco Bay in the morning. He said he knew what that picture would look like when he got it and until that day, their Saturday mornings would be spent in the aquatic park trying. Adin went with him, mostly for the coffee.

Adin shivered from what seemed like glacially cold, damp air that lay on them like a blanket. San Francisco was like London, only without the charm of age and the patina of empire to hold his interest and get him past it.

"I do not know what you see in this place."

"That's because you're a snob, Adin." Keene's voice was amused. The elder Tredeger practically threw Adin a treat whenever he exhibited his disdain for the commonplace, so naturally, he'd grown to be a quirky little thing. "Your mother loves it here. I've never seen her so happy. It makes me a spectacular hero in her eyes to have brought her home to stay. Your sister

loves her new school, you are doing well, given that you're unhappy to be here, and I have the Balclutha, 301 feet, 2,650 tons of emotional satisfaction. I have never loved anything non-human this way. It's positively obscene. I'm assuming it's a midlife crisis and someday soon we'll grow apart."

Adin said nothing.

"You do like your school don't you?" When Adin grimaced, his father's eyes twinkled. *"Middle school has to be one of Dante's levels of hell. Level 8, I think, the Malebolgia. But you seem to have achieved a singular level of mediocrity in your first quarter grades. Perfectly suitable for a boy in the pit of despair."*

"Actually, middle school is more like Delacroix's painting The Barque of Dante, a horrible boat, ferrying you between elementary and high school," Adin muttered. *"Complete with shit that tries to drown you, and the floating bloated corpses of those who have gone before."*

Keene frowned. *"Adin."*

"It's not that it's not a good school," Adin muttered. *"I get okay grades, people are nice."*

"But you don't fit in?"

Adin closed his eyes and shook his head. *"Not really."*

"You miss Edward?" Keene asked. *"You two were thick in London. It's hard to leave your best mate when you move."*

"I know. We e-mail. We wouldn't have gone to the same school anyway, he would have been sent to prep school and I..."

"You are an American boy whose mother wants him by her side until he's ninety."

Adin bit his lip and rolled his eyes. *"I get that, yes."*

"I needed to bring her home, Adin. It was my responsibility. She was afraid."

"I know."

"The world is changing." Keene took a sip of his own coffee. *"Sometimes I think it gets smaller and angrier every day. Can you imagine the nineteenth century when that ship was built? You're a young man, barely fourteen—your age—and you step aboard the Balclutha with nothing more than a*

canvas sack with a change of clothes, a pocket knife, maybe a tin whistle. Everything you know about where you're headed comes from the images you hold in your imagination and what you can see off her bow: the horizon, in all directions, limitless space, endless possibility, and the great unknown."

"Mother says you grow more and more like a PBS documentary every day."

"I know that. I believe I mentioned I'm obsessed." He looked back and saw the shroud of fog still clung to the object of his desire.

Adin laughed when two of his father's students—attractive college girls—jogged by in short shorts, giggling.

"Hello Dr. Tredeger."

It was as if they simpered in unison. Keene waved. Adin watched his father's face. It seemed safe to say he had no concept of their attraction to him. Even at thirteen Adin knew when he saw the spark of sexual interest in someone's eyes. He'd learned a lot from the far worldlier Edward, whose passion for the Romantic Movement in art was positively exacerbated by his quicksilver moods and an early and fateful reading of the poetry of Walt Whitman.

Gods.

Edward, in whose eyes he saw his own longings clearly and proudly displayed; Edward, who seemed to be an advance scout, a forayer into the hostile territory of adulthood, bringing back information and providing a source of comfort for Adin, who seemed destined to advance at a slower pace.

Edward had already informed his family of what he knew to be his truth, and even though Adin was well aware he'd have to make the same declarations someday, he worried that his wouldn't be met with the same sangfroid Edward's parents and grandmother—who had known before he did—had displayed.

In one of those remarkably perceptive moments that Adin never expected from his otherwise oblivious father, Keene asked him, "Is there anything you think I should know?"

Adin's eyes rose to meet his father's. He hid behind his coffee cup and let the steam from the still hot brew rise between them.

"Did you see those girls run by?" Keene murmured.

Adin grinned. "You know they have a crush on you. They probably don't even jog as far as Pier 39."

"I know," Keene admitted. "But it pays to play the absent-minded professor in these instances. Do you know what? I am a far more keen—no pun intended—observer of human nature than you think. And I think I know when a person is engaged romantically. Although you will never, ever see me look that way at anyone but your mother."

Adin felt uncomfortable with the subject and burned under his father's close scrutiny.

"My brother," his father went on, "died in the early days of the AIDS crisis, right here in this city. He was attending a funeral every week and then finally, had one of his own."

Adin's heart hammered in his chest as his father let out a lengthy sigh.

"I've never told anyone that. Normally when we talked about his illness, or his death after the fact, my family talked about the diseases that were incidental to his diagnosis of Acquired Immune Deficiency Syndrome. The cancer, the toxoplasmosis, the PML, the pneumonia. The reason for his illness became a deep, dark family secret because it was my parents's wish that no one know he was gay or that he was ill with what was then still referred to by the ignorant as the 'homosexual disease'. So we hid it."

Adin could see the regret on his father's face. He swallowed hard. "Why are you telling me this?"

"For two reasons, Adin." Keene looked him directly in the eye. "First, and most important. I loved my brother so much. He was such a wonderful man. Full of life and love, even at the end. A vibrant, beautiful soul. You were barely preschool age when he died, and we hadn't been in the country except to visit briefly, for years. That makes me tremendously sad. He would have adored you. You're very much alike."

Adin remained silent, he turned to the rippling water of the bay. The fog was burning off, barely obscuring the horizon. In only moments the Balclutha would be visible, maybe even perfectly lit by the sun that was beginning to peek through the clouds.

"Second, I want to tell you how terribly disappointed I was in the way my parents handled my brother's death, as if by shrouding his final year in mystery they were preserving his dignity, when in fact, they were robbing him

of it with their failure to celebrate his life. Whatever happened, whatever choices he made, even though tragedy struck, I still celebrate his life. I wish my parents had. I would have."

"Dad." Adin, filled with a kind of rising panic, ducked behind the camera and looked through the viewfinder.

"I feel sure that I would love my children no matter what. No matter what, Adin."

"Dad, pay attention." Adin watched the Balclutha through the camera lens with blurry eyes, even as the mist began to move until the masts were exposed, and in only moments, it went from nearly invisible to patchily outlined, to visible, and kissed by the sun. Adin snapped several pictures in a row, ignoring the weighty feel of his father's eyes on him. Finally he stopped. "I think I got what we came for."

"Me too, son." His father wrapped an arm around him.

Moments later, in the way of dreams, Adin was transported to San Francisco Bay on another day, only ten years later, when it became necessary to hire a small fishing boat to take him and Deana out past the bridge and into the ocean to lay his parents to rest in that same glistening water. Deana held his left hand, squeezing hard as Adin allowed a handful of ashes to sift through the fingers of his right…

Adin's hand hurt. It seemed Deana was crushing it as she clutched it harder than he'd ever felt her hold it before…

Adin swallowed around the stinging in his throat as he opened his eyes. His chest felt all heavy inside, as if suddenly it were filled with wet sand, and dragging enough air into it to breathe was painful. When he could focus he saw Bran sitting next to him on the bed, squeezing his hand.

"Adin." Bran leaned over, crawling toward him. Tears fell freely down his cheeks, and Adin discovered that they were the perfect antidote for his own. He itched to wipe them away from Bran's face but didn't do it. Bran ignored his restraint and clumsily threw his arms around Adin. "I'm so sorry."

Adin pushed at him. "Bran—"

"Your family loved you so much. Your father and mother were wonderful and then you lost them, just like I lost mine..."

"Bran, get off me."

If anything the boy squeezed him tighter. "I'm so sorry Adin. I didn't know. I wouldn't have gone looking around if I'd known it was going to be so awful to watch..."

"*Bran*, I said, *let go*."

Adin heard the door close with a bang, and the atmosphere in the room changed dramatically. The whispering voice sounds that let Adin know when Donte was near buzzed angrily in Adin's head. The noise vibrated, emanating from Donte's whole body and outward into the room like a warning. Adin had only a second to think before Bran was growling as well. Bran responded with an unnaturally feral and uncanny sound, like the roar of a tiger, and he leaped off the bed, crouching by the side of it as if getting ready to defend it.

"Stop." Neither of them paid Adin any attention.

"*Step away from my human*." Donte's voice rolled into the room like pyroclastic flow.

CHAPTER SEVEN

Bran rippled with indignation. "Adin deserves better than to be someone's *human*."

"*Bran*." Adin rose, despite his nakedness and held his hands out to both of them. Tension crackled through the air. Adin sensed that neither of them would move until they were certain to win. He stepped between them. "Stand *DOWN*."

"Back away Adin," Donte commanded.

Bran radiated fury. "He's a vampire. How can you love a vampire?"

"Bran?" Adin said through gritted teeth. "Stay the fuck out of my head."

Donte's brows drew together. "What is he talking about?"

"Adin may seem like nothing more to you than a sack of cells and a ready supply of fresh blood—"

"Hey!" snapped Adin.

"But he deserves to be more to someone than just food and a convenient—"

Donte almost smiled. *Almost.* "You're about to be killed by the man you're defending, boy." Adin noticed he had at the very least dropped his battle stance, and the air no longer rang with his violent intentions.

"I'm not a *boy*," Bran spit, still ready to fight.

Donte shook out his raincoat and hung it up on a stand by the door. He looked tired to Adin. As if he'd been walking a long distance and hadn't fed. "He isn't simply my *human*. He's my life, for lack of a better word. If you can't understand that one, I've got about a hundred terms that are equally inadequate."

Adin's heart did a little flip behind his ribs. "*Donte*."

"Boaz has filled me in." Donte glared at Adin. "You are not

my favorite person right now. Please dress."

"I'm sorry." Adin grabbed his pilot case off the floor and headed for the bathroom. He washed up and dressed quickly, apprehensive that Bran might do something impulsive to get himself into trouble. When he returned to the room wearing a pair of jeans and a button down shirt in Donte's favorite rich shade of blue, Bran and Donte occupied opposite corners of the small room like prizefighters.

"What am I missing, Adin?" Donte ran a hand through his wet hair. "What can Harwiche want with me?"

"Nothing. I'm sure it has nothing to do with you. He just wanted the boy and didn't have the balls to deal with Bran's captors." Adin went to Donte and helped him take off his suit jacket, hanging it for him in the closet, almost on autopilot. "And Santos took advantage of the situation. He knew I'd feel protective toward Bran, and he knew you'd hand him over in a heartbeat."

Donte looked at Adin through his dark lashes and shrugged. "Not my heartbeat."

"The point, if you would please see reason in this one case, is that if the three of us work together we might be able to find a way out of this mess."

"In this case?"

Bran sneered. "Yes, unlike the other case, where you left your 'life' to be eaten by bloodthirsty monsters."

"You *told* him about that?"

"I did not." Adin pulled the chair out and sat on it. "But apparently my memories are accessible to him."

Donte crossed to the wall where Bran stood in less than the blink of an eye. He glared at Bran, but even at Donte's most intimidating, Bran refused to be cowed. Perhaps he'd attain Donte's height when he grew, or perhaps he'd be taller, but right at the moment he came only to Donte's shoulder. Still, he didn't back down.

"If Adin says get out of his head," Donte warned. "Then get out of his head."

"Or you'll what?"

"Stop it!" Adin barked at them. "How do you know you aren't playing exactly into Santos's hands? It's time to act against instinct, and think."

Donte glared down at Bran until Bran's stomach rumbled so loudly even Adin could hear it across the room.

"It's time," Donte said drily, "for food. For something so fierce, you can really be quite human, can't you?"

"You wish!" Bran ignored the offered truce. Adin had had quite enough.

"Bran, even coming from Donte that's not the insult you think it is." He caught Bran by the hand and led the still wary boy to the door where Adin picked up his heavier jacket. "We'll be back."

"Wait!" Donte called out, flipping something small and square at Adin, who caught it neatly.

"I have a phone." Adin frowned at the new touch-screen cell phone even though he experienced a moment of intense physical longing. *Gadget envy.* "Although this one is much cooler."

"It has been modified with a GPS tracker that allows Boaz to monitor where you are. His number is programmed in at speed dial number one. Even though I anticipate a terrible argument, I must ask that you please take that with you and keep it on your person at all times. Argue with me after I've had a chance to think, caro."

Bran leaned over and whispered in Adin's ear. "Is Boaz like Alfred from Batman or something?"

Adin wanted to bang his head on the door. "Donte—"

"Stop." Donte cut him off. "*I* could find you in a city twice this size with no need for such things, but I'm restricted to night and if speed counts..."

Adin said nothing as Donte moved toward him, noticing once again how tired he looked. Adin reached up and brushed Donte's hair back from his face. "Are you all right, lover?"

Donte's half-smile warmed Adin. "I'm fine. You see? You worry about me as well."

Adin lifted Donte's hand and placed a kiss on his knuckles. "Did you eat something that didn't agree with you?"

Donte pursed his lips. "All the time, più amato." He pulled Adin into a hard hug. "I eat something that doesn't agree all the time."

Bran spoke up. "Hey, ew... back off."

Donte turned to him and used Bran's own words to reply, "You wish." And suddenly the air was crisp and tense with violence again.

"Enough," Adin sighed. He caught the collar of Bran's dirty jacket and opened the door, hauling him out into the hallway. To Donte, he said, "We'll eat, and then we'll shop. I'll call Boaz if we need anything."

"Thank you," Donte said quietly as he closed the door. If Adin weren't concerned about him before, those two words, uttered with such simple sincerity would have set alarm bells ringing without the glimpse he'd gotten of Donte's unhappy face.

"Shit."

Bran boarded the elevator with him. "What?"

Adin frowned at the numbers as they descended. "I wish I knew."

Rain continued to fall on the city, darkening the streets and buildings and changing the silhouettes of passersby as they bobbed along with umbrellas. The air was full of everything Parisian, old wet stone and bread baking against a backdrop of diesel fuel and genteel decay. They took the metro to the area around Sacre Coeur in case anyone was watching the cafés and shops around Adin's hotel. Adin didn't see anyone following them, but that didn't mean they were safe. He looked over his shoulder, but relaxed as time passed and nothing happened.

Adin wore a wool pea coat treated to repel rain, so he was unlikely to feel the water soak through to his skin. Bran wasn't dressed for it, so the first thing they did was approach a street vendor selling umbrellas. They bought a large black umbrella to share. Bran had the tendency to carry it off every time he saw something that interested him, and when they arrived at a suitable café Adin's hair was as wet as if he'd stood under a hose. They ordered coffee and rolls, Bran asked for a café crème, which he saturated with sugar.

"It's time you and I had a talk," Adin told him as the waiter left with his payment. "Why did you come back?"

Bran looked away. "I didn't have anywhere else to go. I thought maybe you might have come back or the room might still be unoccupied. I snuck past Villiers. It was easy to break in without the chains. You weren't there so I listened at doors until I found you."

"While I was sleeping?"

"You dream loud." Bran bit his lip.

"I should have given you enough money to get back to England when you left Santos's place, but I didn't have it. That was stupid. Where could I expect you to go? Where were you living when those men found you?"

"Nowhere really. Where do you and Donte come from?"

"I live in the Pacific Northwest. Donte is Italian. I assume by your accent your from Northern England. My friend Edward has an accent very like it when he's not being an art snob."

Bran looked away. "I really can't remember."

"How long have you been with those men?"

"I don't know." Bran's voice trembled slightly as he spoke. Adin reminded himself that Bran was little more than a boy. "A few months."

"Months?" Adin set his cup down with a clatter. "Did you

say *months*?"

"Maybe. I think so. It wasn't very cold when they took me. I was sleeping in the park with some friends. Some men said they needed me for a job, and then... I don't remember much after that. It was hard to tell time because it was always dark."

"And the iron?"

"I don't know about that. It makes me feel sick. Like I'm under water. I lose track of time. I can't remember things."

"Jeez." Adin pushed his roll across to Bran and signaled the waiter for more. Bran continued to eat hungrily. "You were living on the street when you were taken?"

"Yeah. There were lots of us kids. Sometimes people gave us money. Sometimes we'd get odd jobs. The older ones found ways to make money that... I didn't. I don't need much."

"Were they...?" Adin frowned. "Was everyone like you? Did they all have special things they could do?"

"No." Bran shot him a look that said, *duh.* "Not at all. But I always fit in, see, and everyone who lives on the street's a little mental, so you can't really say for certain if a bloke's different like me, or if he's just been on the street too long."

"How'd they catch on?" Adin paid the waiter when he brought more rolls. "How'd you get singled out?"

Bran looked at his plate. "Dunno."

"I need an answer, Bran. Please, it's important to me."

Bran gazed at him, and Adin sensed his hero worship again. That was going to be hard as hell to live up to. "There's this thing, yeah? Sometimes I can tell if someone's about to die."

"What?" Adin leaned in. "You see the future?"

"No." Bran put his roll down and pushed the plate away. "It's nothing like that. If you'd been where I've been, you can tell. I've seen it. There's stages, see. And you just know."

"So what? They think you're psychic or something? Vampires can read minds and sense all human physiological cues, I don't understand, if it's just that you know when people are passing—"

"It's not that." Bran lowered his voice. "I can go with them. Show them things, like I sometimes do for you until it's over."

"What?" Adin tried to imagine how anyone would even begin to realize they could do something like that. "But how—"

"I don't know, alright?" Bran was beginning to fret. "I just know that if someone is going to die nobody can really stop it. It's their time, see? And it's sad for old folks if they've got no one. Worse if—" Bran broke off and looked down at his hands.

"What?"

"I once saw a little girl get hit by a car. The driver didn't stop and she just lay there in the road. I screamed for someone to help, but I didn't want to leave her. By the time anyone got there she was gone. It was only minutes."

"I'm so sorry."

Bran shrugged, but his eyes were moist. "We just looked at things she liked, things she remembered that made her happy while…"

"That's probably the kindest thing I've ever heard about anyone. That you take time. That you care. But…"

"What?" Bran snapped, obviously embarrassed and trying to avoid any praise from Adin. "I know it sounds dumb. I do odd jobs. I live on the streets, I'm… I don't know what I am. And I don't know why anyone cares."

"Is that why you came back to the hotel?"

"I didn't have anywhere else to go. And I thought maybe, if you were still there, I could stay with you."

Adin smiled at him. "Okay."

Bran lit up. "Okay?"

"Yeah." Adin nodded. "So. What? You sit with people who are about to die, and what exactly do you do?"

Bran stared at him. "I don't know. Sometimes we watch their memories. I try to find the best ones. Then we wait until their time."

"Exactly their time?" Adin felt something tease at him. Something he and Donte had been reading. "You know when it's over?"

Bran stared at his coffee. Adin thought the boy might have burst into tears except that he bit his lip. "So?"

"How do you know?"

Bran frowned. "They're just gone and I'm back"

"So you're saying…" Adin asked carefully. "You're saying that you go with them?"

"Yes. No, I don't really. It's like they go, and since I'm in their head…" Bran picked up his coffee and took a sip. For the first time, Adin wondered at the wisdom of giving coffee to a boy with that much energy.

"I see."

"It's not like people say, exactly. The light's there, and sometimes people, but I haven't seen Jesus or the Virgin Mary or anything. People are different so I guess they see what they're going to see, and I'm along for the ride."

"And then you're back."

"Yes."

Adin stared at Bran. He tried to imagine what his life must have been like. He looked out the window and saw an attractive family with teenage boys walk by outside. One of them looked in and frowned at Bran, making a face that carried a familiar kind of Gallic superiority. Adin saw it find its mark. He watched as Bran looked away, tugging at the sleeves of his worn jacket.

"Well." Adin cleared his throat. "I'd like to lose myself in the flea market. Maybe we can find something interesting. I've been looking to buy Donte a gift. Something he doesn't already have, whatever that might be."

Bran's forehead creased. "He's a little…Cold."

Adin sighed. "It certainly seems that way, doesn't it? He's not, though. Maybe I'll get him a red scarf. It might make him look more…approachable."

"Maybe it's not such a good idea for a vampire to appear approachable." Bran pushed the last of their bread into his mouth with a finger even as he gathered up his umbrella. "Will there be artists where we're going?"

"I don't know. Probably. Do you like art?"

"Yes," Bran told him. "And old things, like statues and bones. I went to the British Museum once."

"Really?"

"Yes. When I was young. Someone took me there."

"A relative?"

"I don't think so. I don't know." Bran pulled open the door and walked out into the cool air. Adin was still pulling on his jacket as he took off after him. It was a good thing Adin got regular exercise; he was definitely going to need some stamina. It was only misting periodically by the time they arrived at the market. Soon the sun would come out and dry the streets. Bran closed his umbrella and held onto it in a way that Adin found both sad and a little endearing. Any gifts Bran had received in his life must have been few and far between.

The entrance to St. Ouen had a number of cheap clothing stalls, and Adin noted that Bran passed those by as if they held no interest for him. Clearly, Bran wasn't interested in anything so mundane, finding fascination instead in bins full of doorknobs and drawer pulls, marbles and mechanical tin toys. As they walked together through the tiny crowded shops Adin noticed Bran studied everything from every angle he could without picking anything up. As Adin watched, Bran held his hands behind his back or clutched his umbrella in them as though they would fly all over without his permission if he didn't maintain absolute, rigid control. As soon as Adin realized Bran was *afraid* to touch, he began to ask available sellers if it would be all right for him to pick up an item, and then he'd hand it to Bran, who consented to touch only with Adin's express permission first.

Adin wished Donte could have seen him just then. If Bran seemed impossibly young to Adin how much more so would he seem to Donte. And how much more touched would Donte, whose own centuries-long life had included children, be by the story Bran told?

Bran was clearly growing on Adin, who hung back and observed him, even as Adin's mind raced with more questions. At last Bran found a stall of clothing that attracted his attention, and Adin nearly laughed out loud.

American bowling shirts, suits from the forties with pleated pants, dress shirts with small collars and outlandish ties. Vests that buckled in the back. Adin told Bran to try what he liked, and soon they had a stack of retro clothing and two wool felt fedoras, one black, and one gray. After the fastidious Donte, Adin enjoyed the novel experience of shopping with someone who had no taste whatsoever, and he let Bran purchase what he liked from the used clothing sellers, except for shoes and underwear, which Adin couldn't bring himself to buy preowned.

They searched some more and found inexpensive socks and underwear, new trainers, and two-toned wing-tip Oxfords that made Bran's eyes go goggly with desire when he saw them. Adin finished off the day by bargaining heatedly with a vendor over a double-breasted black military-style cashmere overcoat that brought tears to Bran's eyes when it was understood that it would be going home with them, for him.

"I've never seen anything so nice," Bran murmured when Adin paid, and it was handed over to him. "It's softer than I imagined."

"You're just lucky they made men smaller back in the day or you'd swim in these clothes."

"I sort of do, anyway." Bran's eyes were shining. "A lot of them seem kind of big."

Adin smiled at him as he pulled out his phone. "I imagine you've still got some growing to do."

"You didn't get anything for Donte." Bran looked a little

concerned, as if he thought Donte would pout if they returned with nothing for him.

"Au contraire, mon ami, feast your eyes on this!" Adin held up a small leather case and opened it to reveal a pair of antique opera glasses decorated with dramatic repoussé images of dogs hunting an eight-point buck. "Very sportive, and charming for the opera."

"Vampires don't exactly need binoculars."

"That's where you're wrong," Adin assured him. "It's high time to point out that Donte has been a little shortsighted of late, and I'm thinking this, and a gentle note to that effect, will do the trick."

Bran stopped walking and turned to him. "You really love him, don't you?"

"Yes."

"But he's inhuman—"

"He's nothing of the kind." Adin kept walking so Bran had to continue along beside him, like it or not. "For some reason I find him more human than the men I know who haven't lost their humanity. He... longs for it, when others take it for granted."

"How can you love someone who left you to die?"

Adin controlled his irritation. If he didn't understand it, how was he going to explain it to a young boy, even one who had a window into his head? "Donte is the only person I know—besides my parents—who never has lied to me once."

"But he did, I know he did. About some things."

"He never lied about something important to me." Adin used the preprogrammed speed dial on his phone to call Boaz. "Not once. Even when it would have been in both our best interests."

Bran remained silent while Adin gave their location to Boaz and asked for a ride. As far as he was concerned, Boaz was going to have to earn his trust all over again, if he'd ever had it in the first place.

"Thank you," Bran told him quietly while they waited. "I don't know why you bought me from those men, taking my side and removing the chains. But I'll never forget it. Or these." He indicated the bags of clothes both men carried.

"What happened to you was wrong, Bran. Whatever you are."

"Maybe," Bran agreed. He picked his way along the street next to Adin thoughtfully. Adin saw uncertainty and unasked questions in his brown eyes.

"No maybe about it. There isn't a civilized person on earth who wouldn't have wanted to help you. I was there and I could. That's all there was to it."

Bran didn't look up. Adin wondered what could be wrong for a minute until understanding dawned.

Adin nudged Bran's shoulder. "I'll tell you a secret."

Bran sighed. "What?"

"I'm glad I did it because I like you. You're a terrific kid. I'm very, very glad to know you, Bran. I feel lucky that I was there that night to help you."

Bran flushed with pleasure.

"Just so you know, though… " Bran cleared his throat. "So there's no misunderstanding. I fancy girls."

"Oh, do you now?" Adin laughed until his lungs hurt. When he finally got a grip, he patted Bran on his slim shoulder. "I guess that's a good thing because no self-respecting gay man would go out with you dressed in these clothes."

CHAPTER EIGHT

Boaz opened the trunk of a midnight blue sedan with tinted windows that Adin had never seen before, and helped him and Bran load their purchases. His luggage was already inside it, and Adin guessed that was Boaz's unsubtle way of letting him know he'd been moved from his current hotel. Cars honked and swerved around them. Adin caught a glimpse of Bran, who looked reluctant to part with his purchases, even if only to place them into the trunk. He pulled the bag with the overcoat in it back out and handed it to the boy.

"In case you're cold."

Bran grinned at him. "Thanks."

Adin felt absurdly pleased with himself. He turned to Boaz, who was already heading for the driver's side door of the car. "Are we going somewhere?"

"Is there some reason you shouldn't? Santos and Harwiche both know where you were staying."

"Yes, but they didn't do anything about it for two days."

"Doesn't mean they won't…" Boaz opened the door of the car and got in. "Sir."

Adin gave up and entered the car on the rear passenger side. Bran smiled at him from the other seat in the back. Boaz keyed the ignition, and Bran leaned over to whisper, "Do you think it's all right to go with him like this?"

"It's fine." Adin met Boaz's eyes in the rear view mirror. "Are you allowed to tell us where we're going?"

"You're not being kidnapped. Not this time, anyway. Donte thought we might be more comfortable in a private home."

"I guess that depends on whose home it is, doesn't it?"

Boaz didn't answer. Instead, he took the city streets to the perpherique then found the highway south east, eventually leaving Paris behind. He put in a CD of classical music and continued to drive.

"What about Donte?" Bran asked after about twenty minutes.

"He'll take the train later," Boaz replied. "He keeps a house near Vichy, and the train there will be fast and comfortable."

Adin grimaced. "Is that why we're taking a car?"

"I've truly missed your sense of humor Dr. Tredeger."

"Shit," Adin muttered.

Bran's face held wariness. "Is there something wrong?"

"Boaz is always at his most charming when I'm not going to like the outcome of whatever little adventure we're having."

"You wound me, sir." Boaz said cheekily into the rearview mirror. "I'm merely relocating you and your charge to a rather attractive country home, and Donte will meet us there later, probably sometime before midnight. Did you have a pleasant morning shopping?"

"Yes. It was very pleasant when the rain let up. Bran found a number of outlandish vintage garments he's determined to wear."

"So naturally you indulged him."

"Naturally." Adin grinned at Bran. "They will look very fine on him, and Donte's eyeballs will explode."

Boaz eyed him briefly in the mirror but said nothing. While Adin watched, Bran took out his coat and pulled it over him like a blanket. He turned his face to the window, and soon the motion of the car lulled him to sleep. Even Adin was beginning to drift, so he found a comfortable way to rest his head and just let the motion and the music take over. Whatever Donte had in mind, whatever Santos was up to, or Boaz had up his sleeve, sleep beckoned, so Adin let himself succumb. His last thought—as always—was of Donte's face. The handsome brown eyes, liquid and rich, haunted Adin's dreams and filled his heart with longing. More than anything in that quiet moment before sleep, he wanted Donte's strong arms around him.

Donte would have laughed at that.

Adin held his wineglass and meandered from room to room in the sprawling country house, searching for the face of the man that had haunted his thoughts, his every waking hour since he'd gotten to Princeton. The smell of wine and other, stronger drinks and cigarettes assailed him, even though the host required his guests to smoke outdoors. Most of the guests were men, and nearly all were older. Still, no one said a word when he'd picked a glass of red wine off the tray of a passing waiter. Adin guessed that Charles's crowd played at bored sophistication and the occasional underage young man was more of a cause for celebration than censure with many of them. Adin ignored the predatory and inquisitive glances thrown his way. He was here at Charles's invitation, not merely because he was young or pretty, but because Charles respected his intelligence and was interested in him personally.

People passed by with food as well, with tiny plates of pungent tidbits, cheese puffs and lettuce wraps. Crab Rangoon. Adin ignored them, because butterflies filled his stomach with anticipation. When he finally caught sight of Charles Holmesby his heart soared. Charles's eyes had been on him, Adin could tell. While Adin had been searching for Charles, Charles had been watching him with a pleased look on his face, or so it seemed when he'd finally found him.

Charles came over to talk to him. "I wasn't sure you'd come."

Adin took a fortifying sip of his drink. "Why wouldn't I?"

"I wasn't entirely certain you were ready for what you've been asking me for. I didn't want to presume."

Adin deliberately misunderstood. "Ready to drink wine? Ready to listen to inane party chatter?"

"You know what I mean." Charles studied him as if he were trying to see something written on Adin's skin. Adin was annoyed with it, as though he were looking for a 'best by' date or a tag that said, 'Do not open until Christmas.'

"Stop that, I'm not inexperienced if that's what you're wondering."

"It's not that. I imagine you've had hundreds of lovers." The smile that played on Charles's mouth told Adin he believed no such thing.

"I know, who I am, Charles. I know what I want. From the moment I met you I—"

"Not here." Charles took his hand and led him through the French doors to a terrace where they could speak more freely.

As soon as they were alone in the shadows Charles pulled Adin to him and pressed a kiss to his lips. Adin wrapped awkward arms around his neck and kissed him back hungrily, until his mouth was bruised and he had beard burn from the scrape of Charles's cheeks across his young skin.

"You're the brightest student I've ever had in a class. And the youngest. It says something about you that you lasted when your friend Edward imploded so quickly."

"Edward missed his family."

"What about you?"

"At first I admit I missed my parents. But everything changed when I started working on your research project."

Charles smiled. "You like my ancient smut?"

Adin frowned. "Don't call it smut, Charles."

Charles ran the tip of a hesitant finger along the skin of Adin's forearm where he'd rolled up his sleeves. He turned Adin's arm over to inspect his watches. "You wear two timepieces?"

Adin lowered his lashes. "Before I left for school my father gave me his watch and told me to keep it on Pacific Standard Time so a part of me could always be with them. I looked at it a lot when I first got here."

"How sweet." Charles's smile didn't reach his eyes. "You're blushing."

"You think it's silly sentimental claptrap."

"I said I think it's sweet." Charles's face was a study in flirtation. "It's fantastically consuming, isn't it? To know that men in every age have written of the passion they felt for one another, for comrades in arms. Kings, soldiers, saints, and prophets? How can you be homesick when you know that you and I are a part of something that powerful and permanent? That excites you, doesn't it?"

Adin preened when Charles included him in his work. "Of course it does. It's like peering through a window to history where I can see my deepest *feelings, my darkest fears, my desperate desires, have been shared by men who are long dead. I can see to it they're not marginalized or forgotten. It's my chance to resurrect them."*

"You have bright eyes, Adin. Beauty like yours doesn't always come with matching intelligence." Adin peered at Charles to see if he was teasing.

"You just want me to do your grunt work so you can use your paid assistants for the more glamorous things."

"No, I mean it; you're special. Every bit as unique and deep and thoughtful as the kind of work we seek out." Charles hesitated, his lips close to Adin's ear as he whispered, "I do want to use you. I want to love you, does that make me very wicked?"

Adin's cheeks heated and his body tightened with the first stirrings of real passion. "I don't think so. No," Adin told him breathlessly,

"It has to be our secret at the University. I can't have anyone from the department—"

"Of course I wouldn't tell anyone! It's no one's business but ours whom we love."

"You're a bold boy, Adin. Do you think you're ready?"

"Fortes fortuna adiuvat." Adin's voice didn't quite work.

Fortune favors the bold.

Charles smiled and Adin followed him, wrapped in a pleasant haze of good wine and lively conversation, basking in the warm glow of Charles's regard. Adin watched and went along for the ride as Charles worked the room, his finely chiseled face by turns serious and teasing. He kept Adin by his side, introducing him as his protégé, shooting him speaking glances and knowing looks. Charles could be boyish, even though at forty he bore the first faint traces of silver in his medium brown hair. He had lines near his eyes from laughter, and frown marks from studying. Adin drank in everything about him from his long, thin fingers, to the olive color of his sweater, which exactly matched the color of his eyes, to his easy charm and the way when he grinned one of his front teeth overlapped the one next to it, negating and proving his flawlessness all at once.

Charles was a perfect storm of looks and charisma, a man who had a superior intellect and the sophistication of world travel, even as Adin had, but somehow, fuller and more developed, richer and deeper and riper. Adin reveled in the knowledge that Charles saw something in him; something Charles himself had said was fine and noble and beautiful. Adin was thrilled to be with him. Charles Holmesby's Chosen One. Charles wanted him; he said he wanted to love him.

So yes, Adin had come. And yes, Adin watched Charles like a hungry boy outside a sweetshop, waiting for a signal that the next part of the evening, the most important part, would begin.

Finally, they made their way up the stairs and down a long hallway to a room that seemed enchanted. Warmly lit by a fire in the fireplace it featured fine linens covering the bed, and a bottle of champagne, chilling in a bucket next to a vase full of fragrant, exotic white flowers. Charles unwrapped Adin like a gift, worshipping every square inch of skin as it was uncovered, touching and tasting and breathing him in. Adin's affection for Charles led him to clumsy confessions, trembling hands, and urgency. While not inexperienced he had never been on the receiving end of a seduction of such complete skill. Charles took everything Adin gave him so effortlessly, his demeanor slick and charming, that when the knock came softly on the bedroom door and Charles's lover joined them, Adin simply lay frozen and numb with shock.

"What are we playing with today, Chaz?"

"This is Adin," Charles purred. "He's a delight. Come and share him with me."

Adin roused slightly when the movement of the car ceased. He felt the concussion of the car door when Boaz got out, slamming it shut. It startled him briefly, causing his heart to race until he knew where he was. The first thing he saw was Bran pretending to sleep against the door opposite his. After a moment, Bran stretched and unlatched his safety belt. He glanced Adin's way and flushed when their eyes met. Adin turned away, but not before catching a look of utter desolation on Bran's face.

Intense compassion. True empathy. Was this what the boy had to offer someone? Was this why he was worth so much to a man like Harwiche?

They were parked outside a pleasant two-story chalet style

home, set among fruit trees in a pastoral setting. Neither Adin nor Bran spoke as they left the car and went around to the back to help. Even on an overcast day, like the one they were currently enjoying, the house was a cheerful, whitewashed gem with bright red shutters and matching doors. It had five windows lined up across the ground floor, four on the second, and one centered in the attic under a peaked roof that slanted down over the building like an inverted V. It gave the impression of a face with too many features, pleasing in its symmetry, but disturbing nonetheless. On the whole it looked like a clock Adin's sister had, which featured a little boy and girl who came out of a door, kissed, and returned on the quarter hour. It was impossible to imagine Donte there, gazing out the windows onto the lawns below. Donte had always seemed more at home in timeless buildings made of stone, covered with old vegetation and gargoyles. Donte was a granite fortress, and this was little more than a child's playhouse.

Earlier rain had left the grounds wet and they squelched through grass as Boaz led them around to the back. Adin and Bran followed Boaz past covered patio furniture through a single half-glass door into a spotless kitchen, all white except for a dashing burgundy tile backsplash. Adin tried not to track in mud and grass, but finding it hopeless, he removed his shoes. As soon as he did, Bran did likewise, and Boaz shot them both a grateful look.

"I'll show you to your rooms, shall I?" Boaz led them across knotty pine floors past a sunny dining area with a large rustic table and chairs through a parlor and up a narrow, steep wooden stairway to the second floor. The bedrooms were small. Adin assumed he was being placed in Donte's sleeping quarters, a fact that was confirmed when he opened the clothes cupboard to find two fine suits and one of Donte's trademark silk and brocade dressing gowns. Adin pulled it out and ran a hand over the fabric, surreptitiously breathing in his lover's scent. If he closed his eyes he could picture Donte perfectly, his pride and his ego and his warm dark eyes. Adin put his own clothing away—there was little enough of it—then found his way back down the hall to see about Bran, whom Boaz had settled comfortably at the other end of the hall.

"This is nice," Bran told him as he looked out the window. "It's so green."

"One thing you can always count on is that Donte will live someplace beautiful." Adin began hanging up Bran's new clothes automatically, removing tags and nesting the bags they'd been packed in.

"You'd think it wouldn't matter much; he only gets to go out in the dark."

"If you saw what he sees in the dark, you wouldn't be saying that." Adin pulled out the three ties they'd purchased, each one louder than the one before it, and folded them carefully. "He showed me what it's like for him, the way that his eyes perceive the world at night and how heightened his senses are. It's fascinating."

"But he hasn't turned you?" Bran asked. Adin turned around, still holding the ties. "Hasn't he offered you immortality?"

"Who would want that?"

"*Everyone.*" Bran appeared surprised that he'd ask. "When people die, they all fight it. It's really hard sometimes, seeing them give up."

Adin turned sharply. "You've *seen* that…? Yes, of course you have." Adin sank onto the bed. "I'm sorry."

"Sometimes people think they're going to be just fine, so they don't panic. Sometimes they fall asleep or they don't know what's happening to them."

"Bran. I didn't realize. That must be…"

"It's just the way things are. People will fight to live if they think they'll die. Even if they didn't like living much. Even if they thought they were used to the idea. Sometimes it's shocking to them that they really want to live and it's too late." Bran swallowed hard and sat next to Adin on the bed. "That can be…"

"I can imagine." Adin put an arm around Bran and gave him a hard squeeze. "I don't want immortality, but I don't want to die either. Is there something in between?"

"I don't know."

"I think maybe life is what's in between. My life, anyway. What it is and what it's going to be. Getting old is part of that. Dying is part of it. I don't want to do anything to change that. What Donte offers feels to me like cheating myself out of the things that are important to me. Maybe dying is the price we pay for the things we learn and the joy we feel."

"How does Donte see it?"

Adin grimaced. "He thinks I'm stubborn and foolish and as fragile as a butterfly wing. He worries that I'll trip and fall under a bus because I'm looking at the stars. He treats me like a child he has to watch constantly."

Bran pointed out, "Because he's worried."

"I understand that, Bran. I'd do anything to make him happy, except become a vampire. He wouldn't have chosen it either, so he can't tell me I'm being irrational. We're between a rock and a hard place. Any advice?" Adin waved the tie in Bran's face. "Forget fashion advice because I know you picked this tie."

"What would I know about it?" Bran turned furiously to his armoire to rearrange his new trousers.

Now that they'd spent time together, Adin placed Bran's age at about fifteen, but suddenly wondered what it really was. "How old are you?"

"Fourteen. Fifteen next month."

"Has there ever been a girl?"

"No," Bran told him without turning. "How likely would that be?"

"But someone you liked?"

Color crept up the back of Bran's neck and he tensed, but still didn't turn. "Not like that."

"Liar," Adin teased. "Keep your secrets, Bran, it's fine with me. Unlike some people, I don't feel the need to sort through people's memories and find out every little thing about them."

"I said I was sorry. I don't always do that. I just wondered…"

Adin took Bran's shoulder and turned him. Once they were facing one another it wasn't hard to see that Bran was every bit the uncertain teenaged boy. His brown eyes, usually full of mischief, were troubled and his entire face carried doubt.

"Wondered what?"

"Why you loved a…" Bran bit his lip.

"Go on," Adin commanded. "It doesn't do either of us any good if you don't say it."

"A monster, all right?" Bran leaned against the aging wood of the rustic wardrobe. "Vampires are monsters, they need to prey on weaker beings for food, and they look like people but they aren't human. They don't have human values. Even smart people like you are taken in."

"Do you have a monster story?" Adin frowned. "Did vampires harm you? Hurt your parents?"

"It's nothing like that. I don't remember when my parents died. I know I lived with my grandfather at one point, but he didn't want me, and he wasn't too concerned when I left because he never called the social service people. I heard later he died in a fire."

"But you do have a story."

"You can't live on the streets without a story."

"I didn't even know vampires existed until I met Donte," Adin admitted.

Bran smiled faintly. "Lucky you."

Adin processed that. How long had Bran been aware that there was something different about him? How had he discovered what he knew about the world around him?

How had he survived?

Adin gazed at Bran's wary face and sighed. It was enough for now that both were safe. He'd ask for answers to all his questions when Bran had a chance to process that fact.

"I think we should explore this place starting with the kitchen. I'm hungry, and if it's left up to Boaz we'll be eating an egg dish before we can conceivably find an alternative."

Bran smiled up at him, and Adin thought that maybe he was grateful to leave the serious behind. He was sure of it when Bran found a small cupboard full of board games and lined them up on the table in order of his preference, insisting that they had to play one, and he wouldn't take no for an answer.

By the time Adin and Bran returned to the kitchen, Boaz was already cooking, and they had no say whatsoever in what he made. It turned out to be spectacular though. He'd made use of some pancetta and eggs and some thin dried pasta to create a carbonara that struck Adin as the best he'd ever had. Even in this far outpost, Boaz refused to dine with them, telling him that he preferred to eat alone.

They sat at a long rustic pine table in front of a row of windows. Outside the sky was growing darker. Soon the only light would come from the stars and the moon, as there was nothing beyond the windows but grass and fruit trees.

Boaz had the table set with woven placemats and checkered napkins. He served the food on mismatched transferware dishes, and uncorked a bottle of red wine, putting glasses out for both Adin and Bran, but watering Bran's wine considerably. They ate by the light of two hurricane style lanterns while a strong wind outside caused a draft through the wooden window frames, even though the windows themselves were closed.

"Why does he do that?" Bran asked. "Disappear like that. He too good to eat with us?"

"Boaz likes to play the butler. I think it amuses him to pretend he's in Donte's employ."

"He doesn't take orders well though, does he? For an imp he's remarkably useful."

"He's what?"

Bran paused with a forkful of pasta halfway to his mouth. "You knew he was an imp, right? You can't miss it."

Adin tossed his fork to his plate. "Apparently I can."

"You don't seem much good at identifying otherworldly beings."

"What is that anyway, like gaydar?" Adin snapped testily. "Where would I have developed that? Before or after graduate school?"

"Don't blame me." Bran sulked. "Maybe it's easier to spot one if you are one."

"Ya think?"

Bran's hand tightened on his napkin, a sign he was feeling nervous. "Do you want to know what an imp is or not?"

"I do." Adin sighed and picked his fork up. Whether he liked imps or not, he really, really liked pasta carbonara, especially when Boaz used real Reggiano parmesan cheese and fresh garlic and Italian parsley. And he liked Bran. There was no point in blaming the messenger.

"In the old days, people thought imps were ugly little trolls or that they served Satan or something. They're all over those old buildings, spitting water off the roofs and frightening off demons, but most of the imps I've come into contact with are regular blokes who are sort of small in stature and resent it. It makes them testy. They're marginally magical, like I am, not one of the big cheeses paranormally speaking. They mostly do mischief because they're put out to be so small."

"Really?" Adin had been called an imp more than once. What the hell did that mean? Were imps like some supernatural nerds that got sand kicked in their faces once too many times?

"They're harmless, although you don't want to be around one when his heart's been broken."

"Why not?"

"They're like the Irish aren't they? There's usually singing involved and in the case of imps it isn't pretty." Bran scooped butter onto his knife for yet another piece of bread. The boy could eat. Adin wondered if he'd ever had an appetite like that, and if so how his mother had been able to keep him in food.

"I think you're pulling my leg. I think the only imp around here is you." Bran's eyes lost their sparkle then and Adin regretted teasing him when he had no idea what he was.

"I'm pretty sure I'm not an imp." Bran toyed with his fork.

"I'm sorry; I only meant to rib you." Adin held his hand up in the air, palm out, "You'll be far taller than I am when you've grown, look at your hands, see?"

Bran pressed his hand to Adin's. Each of his fingers was a half-inch longer. "Wow."

"I'm not the tallest man. Donte's called me an imp more than once."

"But he must know Boaz is an imp. Why didn't he tell you? What else do you suppose Donte hasn't told you?"

Adin said nothing, but it was a very, very good question. It hurt him to think that Boaz and Donte had been keeping something like that from him. Santos knew. Probably Edward and Tuan as well. It was difficult to imagine that every piece of information he got about the world he now inhabited had to be dragged out of Donte, or discovered the hard way. Suddenly he didn't feel much like eating.

"I'll just take my plate into the kitchen." He picked up his flatware and made his way to the sink. He called, "Do you want more?"

When he turned, he was surprised by Bran, who stood behind him holding his own plate. "I'm sorry I said anything about Donte."

"It's all right, Bran."

Bran hesitated before he handed his plates over. "I wish you had a human companion."

"I'm with Donte." Adin put the dishes into a bin next to the single sink and asked, "What else do you wish?"

"I wish you'd play chess with me," Bran said quietly, leaving the kitchen.

CHAPTER NINE

"You *bastard*!" Bran spat when Adin placed his king firmly in checkmate. Their first game took Adin completely by surprise. He'd only focused a small amount of attention on playing and before he knew it Bran had him mated and was crowing with triumph. The second game had required his full concentration, and still Bran had put up a decent fight. Adin was no master by any means, but he'd never been a pushover. Yet Bran, was practically homeless, had neatly cornered him once and pushed his limits the second game.

"Tie-breaker?" Adin asked, setting the pieces back on the board. He had no idea what time it was, probably after ten, and he was feeling relaxed, but not yet tired. He'd been working his way through a bottle of Beaujolais L'ancien, loving its rich, peppery taste and red fruit finish. The air was completely free of sound. Not even the whispers of appliances, or Boaz working in the background, marred the quiet of the evening. Bran moved his first piece out, the standard king's gambit, pushing the white king's pawn to e4. Adin began his own game by mirroring but his mind was on other things. His eyes strayed time and again to the window, where he could see the road and the pathway from the door to where the car was parked.

Adin tried to keep his mind on the game but his attention strayed, subtle as a dog waiting for its master to return from work. He sent a wave of longing into the air, and felt a faint frisson of response, like a whisper, almost as tangible as a kiss on the back of his neck, and smiled. Donte was close, somewhere in the darkness, on the road, maybe even on the property itself.

"What?" Bran tapped his finger impatiently. "Did I miss something?"

"Donte's coming."

Bran took Adin's knight. "If you miss him so much, why did you leave him in the first place?"

"I didn't leave." Adin frowned when Bran made the unanticipated move. "Well, I did, but only to get breathing room for a while. We were quite out of anything but arguments, and there were two auctions I'd planned to attend, one in Paris and one in Geneva. Where did you learn to play chess? You're really good at it."

"I watched people play in the park sometimes." Bran held his glass up. Adin pursed his lips and poured a small amount of wine into it, following it up with a big splash of water from a pitcher.

"Donte would frown on me giving you wine, but it's not hurting your game," Adin remarked.

"It doesn't seem to have much of an effect. Maybe that's because of my magicalness."

Adin suppressed a laugh. "Yes, I'm certain your *magicalness* is the very reason that you aren't feeling the wine's effects."

Bran blinked up at him. "I am getting kind of tired."

"Why don't we let this rest until tomorrow then? You've had a big day. I'll stay up until Donte arrives."

Bran stood and carefully pushed the game to the end of the table, where it was less likely to be disturbed. "Do you mind if I stay down here and wait with you?"

"Strange house?"

"Yeah. I guess so." Bran looked toward the stairs.

"I think Boaz's room is on the first floor, unless he hangs by his feet in the closet until Donte needs him again."

"Imps don't sleep like that."

"Well then," Adin teased, "maybe he crouches on the corner of the roof and spits all night."

Bran laughed out loud.

Adin grinned. "Of course, that would probably be one of the more normal things I've seen him do."

"Do you think he's asleep?"

Adin shrugged. "I don't know." Adin heard the door in the kitchen open, then close again. He didn't have to see Donte to know he was there, a breath of *something* inexplicable and marginally enchanting always entered a building with him. Adin had lived with Donte, loved him, long enough to be aware of it now whereas he'd been oblivious when they'd met. That Donte could call Adin to him was pretty standard vampire fare, a trick, a luring of prey using a simple suggestion planted into a human's mind.

That Adin could reach Donte the same way wasn't something either man expected. Donte had once told Adin that—only with him—it worked both ways. At the time, Donte had not been entirely pleased by the fact.

When Donte entered the dining room, Adin was on his feet and moving to meet him. It never failed that his first instinct was to leap into Donte's arms, and he didn't hold back. For Bran's sake, and propriety, he didn't grind and Donte managed not to push him into the nearest wall, but it was a near thing.

"Get. A. Room." Bran growled, disgusted.

"We have a room." Donte rubbed his face into Adin's hair and inhaled. "I felt you," he whispered. "It pleases me that you long for me."

Adin bumped their cheeks together. "I was happy to feel you that close."

"Caro," Donte sighed.

Adin stepped down and cupped Donte's face between his hands. "You look better. Relaxed and nearly pink-cheeked for a vampire. Did you eat someone tranquil? A Buddhist monk? Quick, what is the sound of one hand clapping?"

Donte fought off a smile. "While I love your silliness, I have come a long way to be here, so if you don't mind…"

Both men looked at Bran, who colored but took the hint and headed for the stairway.

"Goodnight, Bran," Adin called out. "I'm only down the hall

if you find you need something."

"Thanks, Adin," Bran murmured. He lurched a bit and Adin thought perhaps he was more tired than either of them realized. He hated to think the wine had anything to do with it, but when he'd poured it, it occurred to him that Bran could use a tiny bit of something to relax him after his ordeal. He only hoped the boy would sleep well.

Adin glanced back at Donte, who was gazing at Bran's back thoughtfully.

"What?"

Donte sighed. "Did you have fun shopping for your unknown adolescent entity today?"

"Yes." Adin took Donte by the hand and led him up to their room. "We bought him some clothes that will scramble your brains. I got you a gift but I'll give it to you later."

"A gift?" Donte brightened. "For me?"

Donte seemed so pleased Adin regretted he'd purchased the opera glasses as a symbolic complaint, and vowed to give them without implying that Donte wasn't seeing him clearly. In fact, given the look on Donte's face, Adin made up his mind then and there to give him gifts far more often. It had been a long time since Adin had seen Donte surprised. He hoped Donte wouldn't bother probing his thoughts.

"Let me get it," Adin said when they reached their room. He walked to the small writing desk and pulled it from a drawer. "I thought…" he began, but drifted off when he turned to find Donte, hanging his jacket in the closet, his tie loose and his collar unbuttoned.

"Is something the matter?" Donte asked when he caught Adin staring.

"I've missed you so much," Adin admitted softly. "I'm so sorry I left. I wish I could make you understand."

"Perhaps…" Donte held his hand out and Adin went to him. "Perhaps I understand more than you think. I haven't forgotten that you love me despite what I am. I haven't forgotten that you've forgiven me the unforgivable; accepted the unacceptable to be with me."

"You're pretty easy on the eye, of course."

"Ah. Certainly. You love me because of my looks. There's little else to recommend me." Donte allowed Adin to help him out of his clothing. He slipped on his dressing gown and a pair of silk pajama trousers and relaxed visibly. A subtle knock sounded on the door, and Donte answered it, allowing Boaz to enter with a decanter of cognac and crystal glasses on a tray.

"I thought you might like a nightcap," he said, leaving the tray on the writing desk. When he turned, he looked satisfied that everything was in order.

"No chocolates for the pillows?"

"I find I'm fresh out of chocolates at this moment, Dr. Tredeger. As you know, Donte doesn't eat it, but tomorrow I will lay in a supply for you and the boy, if you like."

"*Patrick Roger*, if you don't mind. It's my favorite." Adin grinned cheekily at Boaz, as he always did, but now he felt strange, as if knowing Boaz's inhuman status had changed things dramatically between them and not for the better. Boaz left quietly, closing the door behind him.

He turned to Donte. "Why didn't you tell me that Boaz was an imp? *Is* an imp. Why didn't you tell me that more things exist besides vampires?"

"Are you very angry with me?" Donte crossed to the desk and poured them each a drink.

"Not angry, exactly. Maybe disappointed. Unhappy."

Donte sat on the smallish bed and invited Adin to sit next to him. Instead, Adin indicated he should put his feet up and rest his back against the headboard, then straddled his thighs, effectively sitting in his lap. He still held Donte's gift, so he laid it on the bed beside them as he took the drink from Donte's elegant fingers.

Donte met his eyes. "I struggle everyday to decide how much

to tell you."

The anger Adin experienced every time Donte made a unilateral decision about him began to build, but he squashed it flat before it could surge to the surface and ruin their truce. "I wish you'd tell me all of it. Every last thing so there aren't any secrets between us."

"I've thought that would be what I would do if I had a second opportunity." Donte looked at the drink in his hand. "I hoped I would get one."

"Surely you knew you'd have that, Donte." Adin cupped Donte's chin and raised it so they met each other's eyes again. "Surely you knew I wasn't going to—"

Before Adin could form another coherent thought, Donte kissed him, his lips still damp from his drink. Adin licked the strong, strange cognac taste from them and begged for entrance. Donte tasted of alcohol and doubt, and Adin wanted nothing more in the world than to reassure him. He used the palms of his hands to press Donte back into the headboard and part the elegant fabric of his robe.

"As often as I tease, I will usher in the era of full disclosure by saying that I love these dressing gowns of yours." Adin kissed Donte's skin as he unveiled it, starting at the base of his neck, nuzzling at the hollow of his throat. He ran the pads of his thumbs over Donte's chest, grazing his nipples and eliciting a gasp from Donte, who stroked Adin's hair with one hand, and held on to his upper arm with the other.

"I'll have some made for you, shall I? I'd like to wrap you in fine things, and I would quite enjoy peeling them off you."

"I'd like that too," Adin murmured, traveling lower, biting and nipping at Donte's skin, leaving a tiny pinch each place his fingers had traveled. Donte squirmed under him, uncharacteristically playful as he held Adin back and tugged at his hair. Adin caught his hand and kissed his thumb, watching Donte's eyes lose focus as he enveloped it with his mouth and sucked on it, fellating it as thoroughly as he planned to do with Donte's cock.

Donte's head dropped back and his eyes closed. "*Caro.*"

Adin splayed his hands across Donte's chest and slipped lower on the bed until he was a breath away from Donte's hard shaft. He peeled back the silken fabric that bound it and buried his face in the nest of hair there, inhaling Donte's rich and earthy scent as he wrapped his lips around his cock, using his tongue to slick and worry the loose foreskin, teasing the dark, velvety head into revealing itself. Donte thrashed beneath his hands, and Adin gripped his hips so tightly that on any other man there would be bruising.

"By all the gods. *Adin,*" Donte whispered, clutching Adin's hair with one hand as he peeled one of Adin's hands away from his hip with the other. He brought it to his mouth and sucked in two of Adin's fingers, swirling his tongue around them and getting them slick.

Adin took his cue when Donte let go of his fingers. He sought out the sensitive skin hidden behind Donte's heavy sack and stroked his way toward the dark pucker of Donte's hole, teasing it with his damp fingers. Donte closed his eyes and lifted his hips, begging to be inside Adin's mouth even as he gave himself over to Adin's thorough manual exploration. It wasn't long before Donte was rocking, writhing between Adin's mouth and his fingers as they surged and penetrated, sucked and soothed. Until Donte was cupping Adin's head between his hands and fucking his mouth.

Adin bobbed, allowing Donte so deep his nose nestled into Donte's soft thatch of pubic hair then drew off hard. When he lowered his head again he breathed in the earthy, arousing scent that was Donte's alone and his own body tightened. When Donte's fingers tensed in his hair he swallowed, massaging his lover's cock while his fingers of his free hand dug into the hard muscles of Donte's buttocks.

Donte uttered a startled exclamation in Italian, puncturing the silence. The words told Adin everything he needed to know as come hit the back of his throat.

Adin took all Donte had to give him and held him in his

mouth until he was soft again. He pulled his hand from Donte's flesh and drew away, still aware of a gentle hand stroking his hair. He rested his head on Donte's thigh, content to be petted while they recovered. When he chanced a look he found Donte gazing down at him. Something that looked very much like love settled over his features.

Adin regretted getting up and heading to the bath, but he wanted to wash his hands. He returned to Donte with a damp towel to wipe him clean, then settled back into the spot where he'd been, warm and content, lying between Donte's legs.

"There will be times when we are likely to disagree," Adin murmured.

"No doubt," Donte said drily. "Since you are often irrational."

Adin growled, "And you are unreasonable."

Donte sputtered, "Me?"

Adin gave Donte's hand a squeeze and kissed the inside of his thigh.

Donte grunted, but warmly. Adin knew the kiss pleased him. "Times when you are entirely too human."

"Mmhmm." Adin moved up and kissed the crease where Donte's torso met his leg and then the hollow of his pelvis. Donte's muscles jumped when Adin's lips brushed the sensitive skin around his navel. He crawled up until he sat astride, resting on Donte's strong thighs. Donte moaned when Adin bit his nipple. "I imagine you're going somewhere with this."

Adin reached for Donte's gift and sat up, still astride Donte's legs but relaxed and happy, even though his own cock was a knot straining under his jeans and it felt like a rock. "Here."

Donte reached out and took the leather case, examining it, running his fingers over the stitching and fastenings before opening it.

"Well made," he remarked as he opened it to reveal the black cloth interior and the tiny silver opera glasses within. "Opera glasses?"

"Yes." Adin smiled and reached for them, pulling them out of the case.

"Ah, a hunting scene, how appropriate," Donte murmured, putting them to his eyes. "The optics are good."

"Yes, but I'm well aware that yours are better." Adin pushed Donte's hand down so that he could look into his eyes. "The point is, my lover, that you sometimes need to look at things differently. Even when I'm not right by your side, I'm yours. Irrevocably, irretrievably lost in love with you." Adin peered into Donte's eyes, wishing he could see through to his thoughts, maybe his soul.

"*Sciocco.*" *Foolish.* If Donte could have blushed, Adin was certain he would have. He seemed pleased with Adin's declaration. Donte's cock twitched under Adin's thighs, coming back to life.

"Promise me that before you believe the worst you will try to see me clearly?" Adin pushed the glasses back to Donte's eyes, and found he was quite satisfied with the message they sent, even if it wasn't the one he'd originally intended. "See the man who loves you, and look at me past time and distance and mortality to my heart, which *belongs to you.*"

"*Adin.*" Donte pulled him close and rolled them both until Adin was beneath him and the hard bone of Donte's thigh pressed deliciously on Adin's cock. Adin sensed what was coming and tendrils of arousal and fear wrapped around his spine. He hooked one hand around Donte's neck and pulled him in, even as he clutched Donte's ass with the other to press more firmly against Donte's thickly muscled leg.

Donte growled and took Adin over. He shifted slightly and trapped Adin beneath him, every inch the predator. Adin let out a sigh that was more like a moan and succumbed, melted, as Donte struck. His hips jerked at the exquisite pleasure/pain of Donte's mouth on his throat, as first the sharp sting of the bite, and then the lapping, sucking sensation pushed through his body and down his spine.

"Ah, *Donte.*" Adin jerked again, spasming as his cock spit

come inside his jeans and his spine zinged again and again with pleasure so indescribable that he could only hold on and claw at Donte's back. "*Lover.*"

After, when Donte pulled his teeth from Adin's torn flesh and licked the wound closed he didn't let go, but clung to Adin, burying his face into the junction of his neck and shoulder while Adin held him, stroking and whispering soft love words as he rocked Donte in his arms. Neither man moved for a long, long time.

"What's all this?" Adin asked. "Donte? Are you all right?"

Donte shook his head against Adin's neck but said nothing.

Adin listened to the sound of more rain pattering lightly down on the roof of the chalet. He'd been roused by Donte's restlessness at first, and awakened fully when he pressed a kiss against Adin's forehead and told him he was going to take a walk.

Adin had muttered, "How Heathcliffe," and rolled over, turning a tired back to his lover-who-didn't-sleep.

Now he frowned into the darkness. He couldn't quite put his finger on what exactly was wrong, but as surely as he knew his own face in the mirror, he knew that something bothered Donte, and it wasn't simply the usual inability to predict Adin's behavior or control it this time. In the past, Donte had been content to draw while Adin slept. To write in his journal or read. Yet now his wakefulness manifested itself into a restless desire to get away by himself.

Adin had never seen him quite so concerned, and the nagging worry that—once again—something important was bothering Donte and he wasn't going to discuss it, coalesced in Adin's mind and heart.

Adin threw the covers aside, unwilling to wake Bran or Boaz if he could help it. He donned a T-shirt and flannel pull-on pants before creeping downstairs, where he grabbed his pea coat on the way out the back door. He smiled to himself as he walked out into the rain and called, "Ollie, Ollie, Oxen Free," in a breathy whisper.

Adin wasn't surprised to feel a playful push of energy rock him back, as though Donte were right in front of him, giving him a teasing shove.

Within the blink of an eye, Donte stood before him.

"Ollie *what?*"

Adin smiled. "Ollie, ollie oxen free," he said patiently. "That's what you say when you're playing hide and seek. When you're done looking and you can't find someone. I came out to walk with you."

Donte still frowned. "But what does this Ollie—"

"Never mind, Donte, it's nonsense. A children's game."

"I should think they'd rectify that," Donte took Adin by the hand. "Children have enough nonsense to deal with. You'll get soaked if you come with me."

"I won't melt."

"No, we've established you won't melt in the rain." Donte attempted to hide a smile.

"What's wrong?" Adin stepped off the cobblestone patio and onto the grass in his bare feet, following wherever Donte led. "I can tell you're worried about something. Don't lie to me anymore Donte, and don't obfuscate. I've more than earned your respect. If I haven't…" Adin let the sentence hang, but he knew Donte understood. If he hadn't earned Donte's respect then all the love in the world was futile.

"I've been trying to make sense of a series of things, caro. I haven't mentioned them because I don't yet understand what they could mean."

Adin froze. "Please tell me if we're in some sort of danger."

"I believe we are, yes. Or I am, as always. This is nothing new." Donte swiped at a tumble of wet hair that had fallen into his eyes as they meandered along the path that led to a small orchard.

"But you're more concerned this time?" Adin pressed closer to Donte as he began to feel the cold.

"I am," Donte admitted. "Because of you. You'll be unsurprised when I tell you that nothing is more precious to me. Therefore if anyone wishes to harm me, they will strike at me through you."

Adin kept silent but gave Donte's arm a squeeze. It didn't help being reminded of their past; of how Santos had attempted to use Adin to harm Donte over old vendettas.

Adin made the decision to tell Donte everything he knew. If he was going to expect the same from Donte they had to begin somewhere. "Harwiche has Auselmo's papers. Santos sold them to him to spite you. He'll want to trade for Bran and he knows I won't allow it. I don't want to go to war with you on this but I'm prepared to protect that boy," Adin said in a rush. He wanted to get it out into the open, in case Donte either didn't understand or Boaz hadn't shared that information. "I'm sorry. I should have told you. I should have said exactly what—"

"Hush caro." Donte lifted Adin's hand to his mouth and kissed it. "I know what Santos told you, but he was playing with you. Harwiche has nothing that belonged to Auselmo. Santos only told you that to cause trouble between us. I think when he saw you in Paris it occurred to him as a parting shot. I told Boaz to reassure you. Did he not?"

"No he didn't."

"That is troublesome." Donte frowned.

"Santos. *That prick.*" Adin felt foolish and angry.

"He's been manipulating men and women for centuries, try not to take it personally." Donte walked between the still barren fruit trees, ghostly skeletons reaching spindle-fingered for the night sky. Adin followed him, stepping carefully in the loamy soil. "I did check it out, after Boaz indicated I should look into it."

"I wonder why Santos thought I wouldn't tell you, at least eventually. That I wouldn't ask you to help me protect Bran, and find another way to get Auselmo's things back."

Donte chuckled. "Because, più amato, he has completely underestimated you. *Again*. I can't tell you how happy that makes me."

"Really?"

"Certainly. He expected you to be jealous at the very least. Or angry that I would once again put my love for Auselmo on the scales and weigh it against what I feel for you." Donte turned and put his hands on Adin's shoulders. "He expected you to take Bran and run from me, fearing that I would sacrifice the boy for mementos from my one true love."

"I see." Adin didn't have to share that he might have preferred if Donte didn't refer to Auselmo as his "one true love."

"But because you love me and trust me, you came to me for protection instead. Santos completely underestimated your faith in me." Donte appeared delighted with his conclusion.

"I wonder if you know how particularly annoying you're being right now."

"I beg your pardon?" Donte's fine features slackened with surprise.

"While you're congratulating yourself because your human came so quickly to heel, are you aware that I've been feeling terrible about the whole thing?" Adin punched Donte's arm. "The thought that—once again—I might cost you something valuable and important to you has been preying heavily on my mind. Not to mention your apparent willingness to sacrifice me in the past. It isn't the best recommendation."

Donte rubbed where Adin had landed his blow. "I did notice you didn't explicitly mention that Harwiche had Auselmo's papers at first, did you?"

"Because you had an *imp* in Santos's employ!" Adin spit. "Did I need to be explicit? And anyway, I alluded to it straight away and I just *did* mention it."

"Well. It was a lie. And despite my past behavior I intend to help you to protect the boy." Donte gazed at Adin seriously. "If you ask it of me."

"You'd do that?" Adin hardly dared to breathe.

"For you, caro, yes. If the boy is precious to you then we will keep him safe." Adin was about to argue when Donte raised his hand. "I can foresee no need to break my vow to protect Christiano. Other than his little lie to you, Santos is uninvolved. And as for Harwiche… he hardly matters now, at any rate." Donte took off back the way they'd come, walking briskly. "The rain will come down in buckets any minute. You must go back inside. I shouldn't like you to become ill."

Adin went after him, reduced to practically leaping from place to place in his hurry to catch up and not harm his feet. "What do you mean, Harwiche hardly matters?"

"Harwiche was injured," Donte muttered. "Someone broke into his home and stabbed him with a letter opener. They… played with him first."

Adin stopped in his tracks. "*What?*" he cried out. "Wait. *Stop. What?*"

Donte turned and met Adin's eyes. "I found him or he'd be dead. Someone nearly killed Ned Harwiche last night, and I believe… It's likely they were looking for Bran."

CHAPTER TEN

"Boaz will be in bed, I expect." Donte spoke in low tones once they'd entered the kitchen. Adin was soaked through and shivered with the cold. "Do you know how to use this?" Donte pointed to a simple electric kettle. "You should have something warm to drink."

"You're joking," Adin accused.

"What?" Donte picked up the pot and pulled off the lid, gazing earnestly into the interior of the white plastic appliance. The cord slipped off the counter and dangled, hitting the cupboard with a thud. "You're shivering. If you make tea I'll change and bring you my dressing gown so you can remove your wet clothing—"

"You don't know how to use an electric kettle?"

"Think, Adin. When would *I* ever have occasion to employ one?"

"That's true enough." Adin took the pot from Donte with a nudge of his shoulder and watched as he left the room. He poured water into the vessel and plugged it in before searching the cupboards for tea. When he found what he liked, he turned his attention elsewhere.

Removing his clothes, peeling them off until he wore nothing but goose bumps, Adin opened the door and dropped his wet things outside. Only then did he realize that if the footsteps on the stairs belonged to anyone other than Donte he might have some explaining to do. Adin turned just in time to see Donte in the kitchen doorway.

If vampires had to breathe other than to talk, Adin would have said Donte held his breath. As it was, it looked like Donte was certainly moved by what he saw. He halted in his tracks, put a hand on the door frame, and smiled warmly. Adin felt devoured by Donte's eyes. His face heated as he stood there, fighting the urge to cover himself with his hands.

"You are utterly perfect, più amato," Donte practically purred. He stepped forward so slowly Adin was mesmerized by every move he made. It had been months since they'd done a home-y thing like having tea in the kitchen while the household slept. Adin wanted to savor and prolong the moment, so he remained cautiously still. "I found you handsome when we first met on the plane. I planned to steal my journal back from you, and when we spoke, I decided to play with you a bit. You were so cheeky; I thought you deserved to be pulled down a notch or two."

"I am Donte," Adin teased, the familiar refrain singsong and silly, "apex of the food chain on this planet…"

"*Enough.*" Donte stood behind Adin and draped the robe over his shoulders, holding it so Adin could push his arms into the sleeves. "Will you never tire of mocking me?"

"Probably not." Adin bit his lip to keep from laughing.

Donte wrapped the robe around Adin as he pulled him back into an embrace and kissed his neck. "I was going to say I thought you were beautiful when we met, but I had no idea how truly extraordinary you were, nor how much you would come to mean to me."

"*Donte.*" Adin's heart sped up.

"I had the opportunity to think while you were in Paris without me. I was engaged in some rather difficult business negotiations, and I realized I had practiced some of those most unpleasant tactics on you. It's no wonder you left me."

"I didn't leave you, Donte."

"You left our home," Donte reminded Adin. "You didn't say when you'd return."

"But I would have returned." Adin leaned his head back on Donte's shoulder, finding it exactly the perfect height, as always. "I believe you know that."

Adin felt Donte's lips twitch on the skin of his neck. "Perhaps I did. I grew impatient, caro, can you forgive me?"

"Always."

"Do you promise me? Always?" Donte's voice was urgent.

"My always," Adin replied. "But that's not what you want, is it? Is that going to be enough?"

Donte pressed kisses on Adin's nape then, so close the breath he didn't really need to take lifted Adin's hair and ruffled it. "It will have to be."

Thick curls of steam indicated water boiled in the kettle, and Donte let Adin go.

They sat together at the long table as Adin brewed their tea in an old ceramic pot. The air seemed to hang thickly, shivering with possibilities. Adin automatically poured two cups, simply for show. Donte might take a few sips, but that too, was a façade. Even as Adin sat across from his lover, he knew they were playing at domesticity, knew he was kidding himself.

Reminded of the Japanese tea ceremony, Adin tried to imbue his every movement with something symbolic and beautiful. Something memorable that revealed his emotions, which he wasn't completely comfortable sharing. When he took his first sip he sighed with contentment.

"What?" Donte lifted his cup and idly looked over Adin and Bran's chess game.

Adin captured one of Donte's hands. "It's nice to have you here beside me. Does that sound lame?"

"I assume lame is being used as an insult these days?" Donte allowed Adin to keep his hand but his attention remained on the chessboard.

"Do I sound foolish to you?" Adin pressed.

"No more foolish than I am, trying my best to tie you to me forever when that's the last thing you desire."

"Being tied to you is not the problem, Donte, I thought you understood that. I don't want to be—"

"Turned into a monster, yes." Donte circled a finger on the rustic table, but wouldn't meet Adin's eyes. "I understand. I'm sorry. It's late and I'm tired."

Adin frowned. "Tired?"

"Yes." Donte took up his teacup. There had been something about Donte that seemed different to Adin and he wondered how he'd failed to noticed it. A shadow against Donte's skin, under his eyes. A slight hollowing of his cheeks. "I'm feeling rather more of my years than usual, caro. I thought a bracing walk might help but I'm still a little fatigued."

"Does this happen often?" Adin asked, frowning. "I thought you were immortal, immune to things that make humans sick. I thought you never—"

"I can't become diseased, Adin. But I can be fatigued. Often the fault is my own. Either I don't eat enough, or I choose unwisely."

Adin grew worried and offered himself. "Then take what you need from me, lover, you know you don't need to ask."

"I will be fine, Adin." Donte shook his head. "I took enough. Your tea will be just what I need. Or maybe we can retire, yes? I'll draw your portrait while you sleep. It's true that I haven't let myself rest lately."

"If you're certain…"

"I'm sure." Donte looked back to the chessboard. "Who was white?"

"Bran," Adin told Donte. "That's the tie-breaker; he's a strong player. Surprisingly good for someone with little formal education."

Some expression Adin couldn't read crossed Donte's features. "You've grown very fond of him."

"I have." Adin grinned. "But you have nothing to worry about, he told me he 'fancies girls'."

"What a relief," Donte teased. He was still gazing at the board. "You realize that if he recognizes his advantage here he'll have you in eight moves? Like this?" Donte reached out to touch the queen's bishop; the one Bran had advanced to take Adin's knight, but drew his hand away as though it burned. He stood up quickly, sliding his chair back with a scrape against the tile floor that sounded thunderous in the quiet house.

"What was that?" Adin jumped up so fast he nearly knocked over his teacup.

Donte glanced at the chess set and then back at Adin. "Nothing," he said crossly. "It's nothing."

"That was *not* nothing," Adin pressed. "What happened just now?"

"Just now—" Donte shook his head and resumed a casual tone of voice. "Just now I remembered what a foul temper my older brother had if I moved any pieces of a game he planned to finish later."

"That must have been quite a temper, to be worried about it five centuries later." Adin sat back down. "You scared the hell out of me, bolting up like that. Donte…Tell me what's wrong. I'm beginning to think—"

"I'm sorry, caro. It's really nothing you need to worry about. Your heart *is* beating very fast." Donte's smile widened.

Adin sighed. Apparently Donte felt like playing the tease. "I'll bet you could make it beat faster."

Donte didn't reply but the way his gaze slid over Adin's body while he sipped his tea told its own story. Adin returned the favor and catalogued the many things he found attractive about his lover. Donte's face held a deep kind of beauty. Hooded dark brown eyes under uniquely handsome brows. Prominent bones in his cheeks and jaw, a cleft chin and dimples when he smiled. His lips were full and luscious. Adin could lose himself in the contemplation of that face, and had, on many occasions. There was something mysterious about Donte beyond being inhuman, a part of himself he always held back that showed up as a conundrum on his familiar countenance. Each individual feature was attractive yet unremarkable on its own. The alchemy that brought them all together and the man behind it were captivating. Adin would never tire of looking at him.

"You're fascinating," Adin told Donte. "Did you know that?

I wish I could draw you. Maybe you'll let me have the journal tonight and you can model for a change."

Donte's lips curved up in an enigmatic smile. "That would please me, caro."

Adin drank the rest of his tea and they went up the stairs together hand-in-hand. Adin sketched Donte for close to an hour, trying to get the face just right. He drew Donte's hands as well, capturing the long fingers with their slightly square tips, drawing them palm up and open, powerful and gentle at the same time. He would never pose a serious challenge to Donte's artistic ability, yet he felt absurdly pleased when Donte remarked more than once that he was quite good.

Every so often he stroked Donte's palm to let him know he wasn't too immersed in his task, just as Donte had often reached for him when he worked. It wasn't hard for Adin to imagine at times like this one that whatever their differences, they could overcome them with silence and mutual physical attraction

Adin shaded the hollows of Donte's cheeks and the area under his eyes, wondering again what it was that made him seem drawn. Had he always been vaguely gaunt? Perhaps it was the color of the bed linens. Adin was frowning at the sketchpad when a mischievous thought pushed into his mind.

Donte tried to look innocent.

Image after image of Donte without clothing on appeared inside Adin's head like a lascivious slideshow. Donte posed and preened in impressions like snapshots, ranging from flexing his pecs to riding a mechanical bull.

Adin's dick showed more than a passing interest, but he wasn't finished drawing Donte's left hand. Playfully, he shoved Donte backward hard enough that he tumbled to the floor. How had he caught Donte unaware?

"Are you all right? I'm so sorry." Adin leaned over to make sure he was unharmed and glared at him a little. "How am I going to draw you if you keep that up?"

Donte's laughing face appeared as he crawled back up onto

the small bed. "Keep what up?"

"You know your vampire mind games don't work on me." Adin gasped when Donte grabbed his growing cock.

"It seems this one is working perfectly."

Adin tossed Donte's journal onto the floor next to bed and gave in to the pleasure swamping his brain. "Come here, you."

"Pleasure yourself on me," Donte drawled, placing his hands behind his head. Donte whispered the suggestion, accompanying it with a dizzying visual image of Adin astride him, riding his cock.

"Well." Adin rose to the occasion and reached to the bedside table for lube. "Aren't we just a perfectly convenient and fuckable vampire this evening?"

"I live to serve." Donte gasped when Adin dropped a line of cold gel on his cock like icing.

"Except the living and serving part, I completely agree." Adin looped a dollop of lube onto his hand and readied himself. When he closed his eyes, he got a bright picture of how he looked. He could see himself as Donte saw him, complete with a stupefied fingers-up-my-own-ass facial expression, and he nearly collapsed with embarrassed laughter.

"Ah *shit*, Donte. Is that what I really look like?"

Donte threw him the same image, but with a ridiculous bronze-age helmet on his head. It framed his eyes, and had a piece that covered and protected his nose. He resembled Alexander the Great in a cheesy porn flick.

"Now, that has possibilities." Adin sighed with pleasure as he sank onto Donte's cock, filling himself until his balls rested onto the nest of hair that crowned it.

"*Adin.*" Donte's voice sounded like he'd been swallowing gravel.

Bracing his hands behind him on Donte's thighs, Adin leaned back into a full, mind-blowing stretch. Heat suffused him. "Oh, lover... *So good.*"

Donte's eyes seemed to both widen and darken. His tongue darted out to wet his lips, but he didn't move his hands from behind his head. Adin slipped his hand between Donte's legs, fondling his balls and sneaking behind them to circle a finger around more private places. He could feel every twitch of Donte's cock inside him. Adin rocked his hips and his vision blurred a little.

"What shall I show you, Adin?" Donte asked. "Shall I pelt you with the world's greatest art? Fireworks? Stars? Film noir movie classics?"

"Shut. Up." Adin sucked in a deep breath, then leaned forward and braced his hands on Donte's chest. His hips began to move, undulating, scooping and lifting, as he rubbed his cock along Donte's firm abdomen. Sweat and a glistening trail of precome slicked his way, and hair tickled his skin until he hummed with pleasure.

"I want to see us like this. Show me how I look riding your cock."

The images in his mind crystallized until he could see himself leaning over Donte, hips rising and falling like pistons in a machine. His jaw hung slack, his eyes rolled nearly back in his head with pleasure. Adin shifted his hips until Donte's cock was hitting his sweet spot and he shivered with pleasure. Every single stroke was a deep, twisting pleasure under his skin that spread to his heart. He flushed all over, but it still wasn't enough.

"Touch me," he begged Donte. "I need you to put your hands on me."

"*Adin.*" Donte pulled his hands from under his head and complied, first gliding his hands softly up and down Adin's arms, then rubbing his chest. "Like this?" Donte stroked Adin's nipples to stiff peaks, thumbing them in a way that drew invisible lines taut between them and Adin's dick.

"Yes," Adin hissed. "*Yes.* Let me feel your touch."

Donte's muscles bunched beneath Adin as he used the strength he rarely displayed to push himself up to a sitting position with

Adin still riding his cock. He turned so his legs dangled off the side of the bed. Adin locked his ankles behind Donte's back in an intimate full-body embrace, kissing him passionately.

Adin panted as they strained together, dizzy until his hands found purchase on Donte's strong shoulders. From there, he slid them up to wrap around the back of Donte's neck, under the slightly too long hair.

Donte held him tight and surged within him, rising and subsiding in waves, going again before Adin could catch his breath. Adin felt the first tight flutterings of orgasm in his balls, the electrifying zing, which traveled up his spine and down his legs. He wanted to kiss Donte, needed to connect to him before his whole body jerked like a puppet in Donte's arms and he flew apart, before he lost his words and the ability to share what he was feeling in his heart. He pressed his lips to Donte's, then drew back to meet his eyes.

"Caro." Donte's smile warmed him.

Adin swallowed hard and pressed his mouth to Donte's again and again. He surrendered to light kisses, nips and soulful, thrilling explorations of Donte's teeth and tongue. The sweetness of those kisses spread warmth to his toes as his body dissolved around him, flying apart, held to earth by Donte's strong arms, pinned by his cock. Adin lost himself completely to his senses. Donte clutched at Adin's ass and stiffened with his own release. Adin clung to Donte, who pulsed deep within him.

Donte represented strength and love and *home*. Adin brushed his lips over Donte's face and murmured endearments. "Ah, lover."

"Cuore mio."

Adin leaned into him, spent and shivering. "Always yours. Sempre, amore mio."

Donte held him close. Silent and still. Adin gave in to nagging doubt and looked at Donte's face. His eyes met deeply brown irises, which looked almost purple in the dimly lit bedroom.

"Tell me again," Donte implored.

"Always yours, Donte." Adin took his lover's face gently between his hands, even as the evidence of Donte's passion softened and slid from his body. "Always yours. As long as I have breath."

In an odd reversal of roles, Donte laid his head on Adin's shoulder and allowed himself to be cradled in his arms. Adin was touched and humbled by it. "Good vampire." Adin rubbed his cheek against Donte's. "Good, good vampire."

Donte went boneless in Adin's arms, limp and sated, and for the first time since Adin met him, he slept like a simple human man.

Adin lay on the single bed in his Holder Hall dorm room and allowed the answering machine to pick up. His own voice came over the speaker, his outgoing message, and it startled him. His voice was always higher on a recording device, and he seemed younger on tape than he sounded inside his head. When he heard it he wanted to hurl the machine into the wall.

"Adin, pick up if you're there please." Charles's voice broke the silence. "I've not seen you for a few days, and I'm concerned. Surely you're not going to let some vague sense of personal outrage get in the way of the work? That's not like you. You believe in what we do here, Adin. The work needs you. I need you. I need the translations on those last three Mary letters, and I'm going to need you to test the inks…There isn't anyone else, and if you don't step up we'll be late with the paper."

Adin held his breath, swirling his roommate's favorite red wine around in a plastic tumbler. His roommate might be old enough to buy wine, and therefore had an advantage over Adin, who had just turned eighteen and wasn't even supposed to be contemplating drinking it, but he had a terrible palate, the wine was thick and too sweet for a red. Something about it spoke to Adin of turnips, and it was going to give him a headache.

"Adin, I know you're young but you're not naïve and I didn't take you for a prude. I thought you were far more sophisticated than that. You're acting like some freshman coed who lost her virginity to a drunken prank. Where's the intelligent boy I fell in love with?"

Fell in love. So Charles could pass him around like a party favor? There wasn't enough cheap red wine in the world.

"Shit," Charles hissed. "I'm going to talk and you're going to listen. I don't know what you want from me but you can't seriously expect some 1950s idealized version of happy families. I'm a man, I'm highly intelligent, and I can have anything I want. I do whatever I like. I thought you were mature enough and smart enough to see that the archaic notion of monogamy simply for it's own sake is useless to people like us, Adin. I thought you were more like me. I should think you'd want a relationship where your lover feels free to leave or to explore what someone else has to offer. I should think you'd want to be chosen, and not live like an anchor around someone's neck. There are no fairy tales. Why would you even want one?

"I have my work to do, and then Shep and I are heading to Vermont. You could come with us; we could ski during the day, and work on Shep's book at night. I don't have to tell you how grateful he'd be for your knowledge of Greek and Hebrew. I'd hate to think you're the kind of person who just quits when he's not gotten his way. The work is here, and it's important. And if you're half the student I think you are and half the man I think you are, you'll suck it up, get with the program, and do it. I don't have to tell you there would probably be a line of undergrads just waiting for the opportunities you have. Don't disappoint me over something stupid like love, Adin."

Charles finally hung up.

Adin closed his eyes. He was at least as intelligent as Charles said. Probably more so, because he saw exactly how they planned to use him for their own gain. He saw how Shep enjoyed watching his lover with a young man, the younger the better, and he saw how it made Charles feel like a god to think he was molding Adin into his acolyte. He imagined they toasted the beginning of each semester by choosing someone on whom to lavish their attentions; a careful seduction with the most perfectly crafted blend of praise for their chosen's academic achievements and admiration of his physical form. Adin wasn't stupid. He'd been naïve, but he wasn't clueless.

At some point Adin had believed he'd fallen in love. But love was for fools and teenage girls. He wouldn't make that mistake again.

Adin finished the rest of his wine and packed. He liked to ski, and his Greek was very, very good.

Adin didn't know what woke him, but he rose, startled from sleep and the deep dream that brought back a clear and painful moment from his time at university. At first he looked for Bran, wondering if the boy was playing tricks again, digging around for memories and using Adin's dreams to probe his history. He turned to find Donte on the bed beside him, deeply unconscious.

Adin leaned over. His heart seemed to stop completely, then rocketed around his chest erratically, frantic with fear.

"*Boaz!*" Adin ran to the door too afraid to worry about nudity. "Boaz, I need you. It's Donte!"

Footsteps thundered up the wooden stairs, even as Bran emerged from his own room, rumpled and looking younger than his fourteen years.

"What's happening?" Bran asked as Boaz raced past him to get into the bedroom.

Adin ignored Bran and followed Boaz, who moved to the bed without hesitation, and peered down at Donte.

Donte was pale, even for a vampire. His eyes were closed and profoundly shadowed. The faint dark smudges Adin had noticed the day before now gave way to thick, etched circles which hollowed out the area under Donte's eyes and created trenches under his high cheekbones. There wasn't the faintest doubt that something was very, very wrong. Even Donte's wavy hair, once so lustrous, so dark and rich, was now threaded with silver at the temples.

Boaz's eyes met Adin's, and what they conveyed was nothing less than terror.

"Boaz," Adin ground out. "What the fuck is going on? *Help him!*"

Boaz shook his head, his brow furrowed. For the first time since Adin met him there was nothing but honesty in his words. "Adin, I have no idea what to do."

CHAPTER ELEVEN

Adin shivered in the predawn air. Boaz and Bran seemed to be watching him carefully as he shoved their belongings into the car.

"I'm trying to understand, Boaz," he hissed. "I thought you knew about these things. What's happening to Donte?"

"I really can't say." Boaz pressed his hands together until the knuckles were white. Adin thought that was to keep from doing anything as melodramatic as wringing them.

"Can't or won't?" Bran asked. He was concerned for Donte, and Adin found it touching. Together, they'd packed and readied Donte to move him back to Paris where there was a chance they could find out what was happening to him.

"Can't."

"Who would know? Who can tell us how to help him?" Adin reined in his temper and his frustration, but his patience was a thin thread, ready to snap.

"I put in a call to Santos. He's checking into things. He said he'll help if he can."

"I'm sure he'll just jump right on that!" Adin shouted. "How could you call Santos? You've effectively notified Donte's oldest enemy that he's in a weakened state." He turned and went back into the house.

Boaz followed him. "Santos isn't what you think, Adin. At the very least he's not as…black and white as you believe. He's not just going to send someone—"

"But he could. And that's why we're not going to sit here waiting for him to do it. Bran, get dressed quickly so you can help me and Boaz get Donte to the car."

Bran spoke, "Won't the daylight burn him?"

Adin ran to the stairs and took them two at a time. "The

windows in the car are tinted. We can cover him until he's inside. If we leave early enough it will still be overcast."

Boaz argued, "Adin I promise you, you don't need to move him. We can figure this out. We—"

Adin entered the bedroom and found Donte with his eyes open, struggling to sit up.

"Donte!" Adin ran to help him. "*Here.* I'm right here, let me help you. We're going to go back to Paris, all right?"

Donte caught Adin's hand and forced him to sit. "Stop, caro."

"Donte…"

"Sit with me for a moment, will you? You wake the dead with all your shouting. What a fishwife you've become."

"I'm sorry." Adin took Donte's hand in both of his and pressed it to his heart. "I'm so scared, lover."

"I can tell…your heart races." Donte sighed and reached out to pull Adin into a tender hug. Adin helped him to a sitting position, then together, they stood. "I must look dreadful for you to react like this. Before you become completely unhinged, let me get my bearings." He walked slowly toward the mirror on the wall, but not without grimacing as though he were in pain.

Donte gazed at his image for a moment without visibly reacting while he inspected his face. He turned his head, peering at one side and then the other. Even though he seemed mildly shocked, he grinned. Adin saw nothing, regretting that for him Donte's mirror image would only appear in his peripheral vision as a trick of the light.

"What?" Adin asked.

"So this is what I would look like were I to grow old. I still have my hair."

"Yes," Adin rolled his eyes. "It's rather dashing really. I hope I keep mine."

Donte turned to him, the light of old argument in his eyes. "You know very well that I can see to it that you do."

"In your current state, you couldn't blow out a birthday candle." Adin impulsively cupped Donte's face in his hands and kissed him. "Let's get you sorted before we argue again, please?"

Donte's eyes softened, all the love, all the exasperation there for Adin to see. "Yes, caro. Let's. It hardly makes sense to ask for forever if I'm going to shuffle off my mortal—"

"Adin," Bran called from the stairway. "We have everything packed and ready, but we also have company."

"What the hell?" Adin strode to the window and saw a second dark sedan parked next to Boaz's car. *Tinted windows.* The driver's side door opened and a man emerged. He wore a dark hat and gloves and carried an umbrella. "Friends of yours?" he asked when Donte came to stand at his side.

Donte held his hand up to block the light. "Not that I know of."

Adin pushed him back gently, away from the window, surprised that Donte yielded, and then dismayed, because he probably couldn't resist. He watched as their guest raised an umbrella over his head beneath the overcast sky, even though it wasn't raining. A momentary glimpse of his face sparked recognition. "That looks like one of Santos's men. *Fuck.* Does he clone them? Why do they all look alike?"

"He likes to keep it in the family," Boaz spoke from the door. "They're related."

"You brought them here!" Adin turned to Donte. "How could they get here so fast?"

"I suspect they've been watching Donte from a safe but still adequate distance. Just as Donte has someone watching them." Boaz looked to Donte. "Am I right?"

"Yes," Donte agreed.

"Vampire games," Adin hissed. "Do you keep weapons here?"

"Before you arm yourself—"

"Shut up and figure out a way to keep Donte safe or I'm going to research the worst possible way to kill an imp. I should warn you, I'm very good in the library."

"I can attest to that," Donte said drily, then caught Adin's arm. "However, there's no need to arm until we see what they want, caro. They can't come inside unless we invite them."

"You stay here then," Adin ordered. "Bran?"

"Here," Bran called from the stairs.

Adin walked to the bedroom door. "We won't invite them in. You and Donte stay inside no matter what. Boaz, come with me."

"All right." Bran entered the bedroom and went to the window.

Donte spoke as Adin turned to leave. "Adin, I quite like this side of you. Very nouveau-martial. Remind me to tell you sometime why your concern for my safety is so ironic."

"Shut up." Adin walked to the stairs. "Do you keep a sword here, Donte?"

"Why? So that you might lop my head off with it by accident? Sorry, no."

"At this point if I lopped off your head it wouldn't be accidental." Adin shot a look back up as he descended. "Stay inside."

Boaz stood in front of the kitchen door with his arms folded. "We're going to listen to what he has to say."

"All right." Adin stopped before him. "Do you know why he's here?"

Boaz turned to open the door to step out onto the patio. "Unless I'm mistaken there's more than one person visiting." Adin followed behind, stepping on the cobblestones in Boaz's wake as he made his way around to the front of the house. Coming from the side offered ample opportunity to assess their guests. The man they'd seen from the window, the driver, now opened the rear door to assist another passenger from the vehicle. Someone so extraordinary that Boaz—and even Adin—stopped where he stood to watch as she emerged.

No taller than four and a half feet, and unutterably ancient, the newcomer was dressed all in black, from the long, lacy shawl at the top or her sleek silver hair to the tips of her narrow, booted feet. She was reed thin and gave an imperious wave as her driver held the umbrella over her head. After her, a man emerged, not a great deal taller but younger than she by half. He wore a fine vintage suit and a bowler hat. They both had deep-set brown eyes that seemed to broadcast merriment—and maybe a little cruelty—at Adin's discomfort.

Adin stared, dazzled by them. Their clothes were fine, their features perfect and pale. They had the odd appearance of porcelain dolls made for a funeral vignette. They strolled up the pathway toward Adin and Boaz, trailed after by their driver, who slipped and slid along the damp stones to keep up.

"Okay," Adin murmured to Boaz. "Not what I expected."

Boaz was silent until the odd party made their way to him.

"Boaz." The woman inclined her head regally. "I understand someone here requires assistance?"

Adin whispered, "You've got to be kidding me."

The man in the bowler hat donned a pair of rimless glasses that were tinted an inky black. "You must be the *Adin* we've heard so very much about."

Adin rippled with indignation. The man said his name like "odd un," and it appeared to be entirely on purpose.

"Donte…" The tiny woman raised her voice as though she intended to be heard inside the house. "I know you have better manners than this."

Adin watched the man who held the umbrella, unmistakably one of Santos's men.

"You came here on Santos's orders?" Adin asked.

He nodded. "At his request."

"To do what, specifically?" Adin looked at each of the three in turn. Boaz had remained oddly silent and respectful. He neither looked directly at the couple, nor ignored them. He seemed to keep his eyes down and held his hands at his side as if he would be expected at a moment's notice to fetch a bag for them or open a bottle of wine. His demeanor very clearly said, *servant.* It was so unlike his behavior with Adin or even Donte that Adin wondered about it. With them, he *played* the servant although everyone seemed to understand that he was nothing of the kind. With these people, however, he was determined to remain invisible, and Adin wondered why.

As usual, there was an entire dimension of information involved in the exchange that Adin wasn't privy to. It made sense that Adin wouldn't enter Donte's life and learn everything immediately, but just *once* he'd like a heads up when he was going to receive a visit from what was obviously vampire *fucking* royalty.

"I came for Donte."

The way she said it gave Adin chills. She couldn't possibly know—or maybe she could—how much she sounded like the witch in *Snow White* to Adin.

"He's inside." He moved in front of them. "You can't go in."

Boaz leaned over to hiss in his ear, but he held his hand up.

The tiny woman in black eyed him critically. "I could have Peter tear you apart like fresh bread."

"Right." Adin didn't move. "Like you're the first person who's ever said that to me."

Adin heard Donte's rich laughter behind him. Donte stood in the doorway silhouetted by the light from inside. "Isn't he marvelous? Look what I found, mother. May I keep him?"

"*Dios mio*, Donte, you look as old as I feel." She shoved Adin aside none too gently, and left him behind her.

Adin turned to Boaz. "His *mother?*"

Boaz shook his head. *"Not so loud."*

They watched as the odd little couple walked forward toward Donte who came out of the house to welcome them. He kissed the woman's hand and warmly embraced the man, all the while standing in the shade of Peter, the driver's, umbrella. Adin watched as Donte made small-talk, for all the world like he was greeting long lost relatives.

"What the hell?" Adin asked Boaz.

"*Adin*. You've never had a talent for wait-and-see, have you?" His lips lifted in a tense smile as Donte casually ushered the trio into the house.

"No, Boaz, I would say I have no talent for that whatsoever."

Boaz turned to face him. "That woman is an elder. She's a shaman, of sorts."

"He called her *mother*."

Boaz shrugged. "He probably did that just to annoy you. She isn't his biological mother. Everyone calls her that."

"I see."

"She's old as the hills and a highly skilled healer. You should consider yourself lucky that Santos sent her to you. I imagine you're responsible for that. Since you forced Santos to read his father's memoirs he's softened toward Donte considerably. He's most unhappy about it actually. I think he preferred to hate his father's lover and blame him for the catastrophe that befell his family."

"Yeah, I got that." Adin couldn't help the shiver that came over him.

"If anyone can discover what is causing Donte's weakness, she can."

Adin glanced up and to his complete shock, Bran flew out of the doorway, literally and figuratively, to land on his ass on the hard cobbled stone path. He still wore his sleep pants and clutched a ball of what Adin thought was wrinkled clothing. It was clear even from a distance that he'd been roughed up, blood dripped from the corner of his mouth and nose and there were deep scratches on his arms and bare torso.

"What the—" Boaz rushed forward and knelt beside him, slipping his arms around the boy.

Adin ran for the door, where Peter stood, implacably blocking the way back into Donte's home.

"Get out of my way," Adin growled, but Peter effortlessly gripped him around the shoulders to hold him fast. "*Donte!*" Adin cried.

Peter poked a finger in the general direction of Boaz and Bran as they stood by the car and spoke in Adin's ear, "*That's your problem, human.*"

"What?" Adin couldn't comprehend.

"That boy. He's what's killing your lover." Peter shoved Adin so hard that he sprawled next to Bran. He still didn't understand. He reached over to where Bran leaned on Boaz's arm and gripped his shoulder.

"Bran? *You* caused this?"

"No!" Bran shrank from him. "No. I never… Donte's… *No.* I didn't. I couldn't have."

"Tell him what you are, *boy*," Peter demanded.

"I don't know what I am," Bran shouted. "Adin, you know I don't know…"

Adin got up and ran at Peter again, trying to get inside to Donte. Why was Donte allowing them to be treated like this? In his mind, the only thing that made sense was Donte was too ill to intervene, or… Adin couldn't bear the thought. Powerful anger and fear gave him more strength than Peter expected, and he almost, *almost*, got by him. At the last minute, Peter grabbed him by the arm and jerked it so hard he felt the bones above his wrist crack. Searing, astonishing pain stopped him and he stood motionless with shock.

"Donte!" He screamed, appalled by the sound of his own voice. If Donte didn't answer him… then it meant Donte *couldn't* answer him. Fear twisted his gut, and the pain in his wrist made him nauseous.

"*Adin*," Boaz commanded, his voice suddenly inches from Adin's ear. "We need to leave."

"I can't leave Donte." Adin wanted to rip Boaz to shreds.

"*You* did this."

"Adin, you need to come with me."

"Donte's in there. At their mercy… He…"

Boaz led him to the car without saying anything. He noticed that Bran held himself up stiffly and was following painfully along after them. He carried what Adin now saw were clothes and shoes, and Adin wondered if he'd been interrupted trying to dress when their guests arrived.

It hurt to see him like that, clutching the clothes he'd chosen so proudly the day before. Something about it tore Adin's heart in two. From what he could tell Bran had lived with little and suffered a lot in his short years.

"I'm sorry," Bran whispered, when Adin finally coaxed him to lift his head. "I didn't mean you harm or nothing. You've been so—"

Adin's heart gave a painful squeeze. "I know," he spoke hoarsely. "I know you never meant to hurt Donte."

"I don't even know what I did!" Bran ran an arm under his nose, the gesture so childlike Adin couldn't help pulling him closer. "If I did I'd have run away. I never would have—"

"Donte told me he wanted to protect you." Adin told Bran firmly. "He said he wanted you to be safe. *We* want to keep you safe."

Bran buried his face in Adin's chest, pressing closer, until one of his shoes dropped onto the damp ground. Adin waited while he picked it up.

"We need to get out of here," Boaz said grimly. "They're considering this vampire business and Bran—whatever he is—appears to be some sort of a threat to them."

"*Shit.*" Adin used his good arm, thankfully his left, to usher Bran into their car. He was grateful they'd packed before the outsiders arrived anyway. At least they had their clothes. "I'll get in back with you." Riding in the back with Bran could serve two purposes: it would reassure Bran and keep Adin from killing

Boaz.

When Boaz keyed the ignition, Adin rolled his window down and put his head out, tilting it so he could see the window of the room he'd shared with Donte. He opened his mind and his heart. All he got back was silence. Boaz waited. He seemed to understand that Adin needed time.

Finally, Adin pulled his head back in and pushed the button to raise the window. He felt Bran's hand reach out and clasp his, giving him strength. He would not cry, although he was experiencing the deepest grief he'd known since his parents passed away.

"Drive," he told Boaz quietly. As they rolled away from Donte's house, he took one look back, trying again to feel his lover's presence.

Nothing. All Adin felt was silence as deep and empty as the life Adin had lived without him.

CHAPTER TWELVE

Adin's arm throbbed and swelled on the ride back to Paris, becoming almost unbearable within an hour. Rain had begun to patter down onto the roof of the car and Boaz switched the wipers from intermittent to low. They made a slow and languorous *swish-swish* sound, almost perfectly timed to the music—Mendelssohn—Boaz played in the background. Soon, Adin's eyelids grew heavy. He could hear Bran humming, a soothing, almost otherworldly sound that called him into sleep and then to dreams. He went with little or no fight to escape the pain of both his broken arm and frantic heart.

Adin put down the slide he'd prepared when the phone rang and got it, tucking his pen back into the pocket of the lab coat he wore. "Hello?"

"How's my favorite minion," Charles practically purred.

"I don't know who your favorite minion is," Adin replied, "so how could I possibly know?"

"Don't be pithy. Of course you're my favorite. Didn't I make that clear enough in Vermont? Shep was quite put out to be placed on the back burner. Ordinarily he doesn't ski much and he rarely drinks the way he did that weekend."

Adin closed his eyes. Shep had indulged entirely too much on their ski trip. They'd ostensibly gone for a ménage à trois but their mathematical equation ended up being more of a fractal containing three couples than a balanced love triangle. He couldn't help it; he just didn't feel as strongly about Shep as Charles wanted him to. Shep sensed—rightly—that Adin didn't find him particularly attractive, and it was this, Adin thought, more than jealousy that caused their problems.

What started out as a simple weekend away turned into a poorly staged road show of some sordid Albeesque drama, with Shep in the agonizing role of aging gay man pitted against Charles's bitter recriminations over what he called bourgeois romantic fantasy, with Adin playing the part of hapless ingénue. In the end, no one was spared.

Shep and Charles were like children fighting over toys in a sandbox. The whole academic community knew it, and he who died with the most acolytes would win. Since they collected undergraduates like ceramic figurines, boys—and to be fair—plenty of girls, lined up for the honor. Adin had felt less honored than used by both men when he returned, and he didn't intend to allow them to play with him anymore.

He was hard pressed to keep the bitterness from his voice when he spoke. "I'm just finishing the tests on the ink now. I wish I had access to electron microscopy."

"All in good time, my thorough friend. Did you get your tux from the cleaners?"

"Yes, I did. I'm still not happy about celebrating this before we're absolutely certain that it's—"

"You worry too much, Adin. Everyone who has seen those letters agrees that they're legitimate, and I've only assigned you these tests to broaden your horizons and expand your authority."

"Thank you," Adin managed. He was aware Charles had everything riding on these letters. So many experts in the field had already handled them; he was certain what he would find.

That Charles was giving Adin this chance, placing his trust on Adin's slender credibility, was more for Adin than to vet the items in question. Adin felt heat creep up his neck. He truly didn't want to be singled out this way, certainly not because of his relationship to Charles. On the other hand, Charles assured him he'd been chosen for his scholarship, not their affair.

No matter; both he and Charles knew how others saw it.

"Don't be late, Adin," Charles admonished. "I'd like to have you there when they toast our success. The department chair will be wanting to thank the man behind the man, as it were, and I'd like you to be by my side."

"I won't be late," Adin reassured him, although he knew that Shep, not Adin, would be by Charles's side, or there would be serious hell to pay. Adin hoped Charles would see that. He glanced down and found the slide he'd been examining and frowned. "I'm following up an interesting aberration in the text, and I'd like to document it, though, before I leave."

There was a palpable silence. A pause before Charles spoke. "What kind of an aberration?"

"Just some scratches on the vellum. I know they represent erasures, the scraping off of ink from the surface with a knife, but I like to hypothesize what's been erased. It's a thing of mine. Wanting to know what the writer has taken out, or as I suspect in this case, what mistake they made in spelling or whether the ink got out of control."

Another pause.

"I guess that makes me a dork, huh?"

Charles laughed subtly. "It certainly does. Are you finding many of those?"

"No, just a letter, here or there. It hardly matters. I promise I'll be along and looking my very best in time for everyone to toast your success. Really, this is a terrific find, and you're to be congratulated. The find of a lifetime."

"Thank you. You make me very happy. Don't dawdle."

"I'm on my way." Adin hung up and went back to work. He really did enjoy the work in the lab. Photographing a document and preparing it for analysis. The careful scraping of the ink and the parchment for testing. Disturbing as little as possible but enough to determine the artifact's age. Guessing who wrote it if it remained unsigned, and building a picture in his mind about their daily lives.

Charles told him he'd found the documents on a recent trip to England, where he'd had to pester a family named Hodgkins to let him look at some papers before they sold them at auction, ostensibly because he'd overheard one of them in a pub talking about them. In the case of these letters, no one knew where or how the family had obtained them, but they'd appeared to be the genuine article, and Charles's reputation as an astute document hunter had been further cemented. As fantastic a story as it was, it had turned up a number of letters in French signed by Marie Stuart, later to be known in England as Mary Stuart, first in the line of succession for the crown, after Elizabeth. Mary, Queen of Scots.

In the final letter, the one thought to be of most value, Mary discusses the restitution of Havre de Grace, and signed it, "Votre Bien Bonne Amie, Marie R." Again, Adin noted the strange scratched out bits of the letters, under the last part of the word Marie, and he thought it odd only because *it was a signature. Possibly, she'd had an ink mishap, and scraped of the excess. It certainly could have happened, given that she'd have been working with a quill. He held a jeweler's loupe over the tiny letters, and froze.*

Unlike the earlier incidents of this kind of erasure, these letters had been neatly excised with nothing less than —possibly—a surgical instrument. If he hadn't seen the others and hadn't been looking for similar erasures, he'd never have seen it at all. The cut was clean and the paper that filled it exactly, flawlessly fit it. The glue that bound the edges in place couldn't be seen, it was absolutely, positively perfect.

Perfectly fraudulent.

Excited to be the one among them to see the discrepancy, and completely naïve, Adin ran to the phone and picked it up. He dialed Charles at his home, knowing that he'd been there when they'd spoken only minutes before. Adin assessed that placed Charles less than five minutes away, and it would therefore be entirely possible to figure out the whole of the mystery before the party where his find would be announced to the world.

"Charles, it's me, Adin." He doubted Charles knew his voice well enough to distinguish it from all his other disciples. "Listen. I've found something important enough that I think you should get down here right away..."

Adin heard the door open behind him and turned to find Charles and Shep, resplendent in black tie, entering the tiny lab together.

"Oh, thank heavens." Adin waved them over to his workspace. "I've found something—an anomaly in the third letter that I think you need to see right away."

Charles looked closely at Shep, and Shep shrugged.

"That's all right, Adin. I've seen it." Charles nodded to Shep. "We both have."

Adin woke with a start when the door he was resting against unlatched and Boaz opened it, leaning into the car to help him out.

"Sorry, sir," Boaz murmured as he accidentally jostled Adin's now-swollen arm. "I thought it best we have that looked at immediately. He'd brought Adin to a modern-looking clinic at the outskirts of Paris. Over the course of the next several hours, he and Bran helped him through the arduous and interminable process of getting his fractured arm examined, x-rayed, and wrapped in a soft cast. He planned to travel home to the States and once there, he'd have to have it examined further and address the possibility of surgery.

They'd discussed the probability quietly and rationally, that if they didn't hear from Donte, all three would fly to the United States, the most difficult aspect of which would be obtaining papers for Bran. Numbly, Adin accepted Boaz's assurances that within a matter of days, maybe even hours, he could procure what they needed, and they could be on their way.

Bran watched Adin with sad and curious eyes.

"What?" Adin finally asked the silent boy.

"I'm so sorry I brought this on you, Adin. If it weren't for me, you would be with Donte right now."

Adin sighed and wrapped his good arm around Bran, gathering strength from the solidity of his caring attention if not from his small, thin frame. "If it weren't for you Donte would have continued to brood and I would never have had these last few days with him. He would have stayed in Spain and I would have been alone. Who can say what might have happened?"

"But—"

"No, Bran, I know you did nothing to harm Donte. We should simply drop it now."

Boaz returned from getting Adin a paper cup of tea that tasted like brackish fountain water. "We just need to wait for the last of the paperwork, then you're free to go. I have your medications right here."

"Thank you, Boaz."

"I went outside and made a few calls."

Adin's heart raced. "Donte?"

"I haven't heard anything. I'm sorry." Boaz gave him time to process it. "We should be ready to leave in two days, no more. In the meantime, I suggest we go someplace and lay low."

"Fine." Adin rested his eyes but a thought caused him to jump. "No. Wait. I have to go see Harwiche."

"*What?*" Boaz and Bran stared at him as though he'd lost his mind.

"I have to see Ned Harwiche before we leave Paris. Donte told me he'd been attacked. If it weren't for the fact that Donte showed up when he did, Harwiche would have died. How could I forget? I need to go see him and ask him to tell me everything he knows about Bran. He got me into this mess… He owes me."

"Do you have any idea where to find him?" Boaz asked.

"No." Adin closed his eyes again. "But I have no doubt you do, and you will take me as soon as we're done here."

"Dr. Tredeger," Boaz began.

Adin only opened one eye. "For Bran. Take me there for Bran. All right? Maybe if it's not too late…I can learn something."

Boaz remained silent for a long time. "All right."

CHAPTER THIRTEEN

Ned Harwiche looked awful. Adin fought back the urge to cringe when he was ushered into an unrelentingly stark white room and his eyes found the man, broken and bruised, sitting uncomfortably on an ultra-modern chair. The entire scene, including Harwiche, was straight out of Austin Powers—a parody of über hip sixties spy films. Adin tried not to laugh when he pictured Donte coming here. Harwiche was bandaged and stitched in several places that Adin could see and heaven knew what was hidden from view by his clothes. Since Adin's arm was bound in a soft cast, held close to his body in a canvas sling they looked like embattled bookends.

"Adin." Harwiche had the grace to look ashamed. "I think I have you to thank for my life."

Adin fought hard to keep from saying, *I hope not*. Once again, Adin chafed at ever having been confused for this man. They shared—maybe—height. Or lack of it. Adin guessed they were both about five feet nine inches tall, but Adin was svelte. He had small bones and a diminutive, distinctly planed face, high cheekbones and deep set eyes, while Ned's chubby face lacked discernable structure. That the men at the cemetery took him for Harwiche still rankled.

Adin merely shrugged.

"Your vampire arrived exactly in the nick of time." He said this with a pout of thick lips that was almost a sneer. "I must say he wasn't what I expected at all. He kept me from bleeding to death, and called the paramedics."

Adin took an uncomfortable seat across from him. "Did he? Now you have the chance to return the favor. What the hell did you get me into here, Harwiche?"

"I don't know what you mean."

Adin narrowed his eyes. "I could break the remaining bones

in your body to see if it helps your memory. Boaz has been very resourceful when it comes to getting me out of trouble with the police—"

"All right, although I should warn you, I'm no longer unprepared to deal with the threat of physical violence. I'm sorry about duping you in the cemetery. I just thought…" Harwiche waved his good hand impatiently. "I don't know what I thought. Maybe that I'd get a chance to see the men I was dealing with before we met formally for the transfer of the boy. I never imagined you would go with them."

"They had guns, Harwiche. They didn't give me a choice."

Ned's eyes closed. "I'm sorry about that."

"You need to tell me about Bran. What the hell did you think you were doing, trying to buy a *boy*?"

Ned's face remained impassive. "He's not a boy. He's not human."

"I can't argue that, but he is—at the very least—a fully sentient, intelligent being. You still can't buy or sell him. *Chain him.*"

"There's always been a war between humans and… for lack of a word, inhuman entities. I descend from a long line of men and women who knew how to make the world of the non-living run smoothly, much as your imp Boaz does for Fedeltà. We've been richly rewarded, and a number of my ancestors chose to become like them. In the last two centuries those Harwiches, living and undead, have made it their business to find out everything we can about all the worlds around us. Believe me, Fedeltà and his kind are the tip of the iceberg."

"So you know what Bran is?" Adin sat forward. "Then tell me. Bran needs to know."

"What he is? You mean what he was before he was exchanged for the human child?"

"Yes. I understand he's a changeling."

"You don't understand at all. There are a million changelings.

You can't swing a dead cat without hitting an ordinary changeling child or a man or woman who started out as something else. The *changeling* isn't an entity. It's not a type of otherworldly being like an imp, for example, your Boaz. A changeling is a part of a process. A magical contract, fulfilled when whatever entity has been entered into it becomes a human."

"Yes, Boaz told me Bran never made the full transition to human, that his contract was interrupted somehow."

"Yes, but you need to understand that the contract is bound by the blood of all participants. Bran's original, magical family and any living human grandparents, parents, and siblings from his human family."

"I see. Everyone is bound by the contract?" Adin frowned.

"Everyone living. You can see how exceedingly rare it would be to find a magical being whose entire original nominal family line was dead, say, to find an orphan entity with no living relatives. And then to add in the extremely unlikely event that one might find a child who had been exchanged with someone whose human family was in the exact same boat. To be adopted by the one family with few or *no* living relatives at all…"

"Shit."

"It's one in a million. One in a hundred million."

"How would you know? Who's to say there's not a cousin or something, still alive who—"

"The only person who would know all the facts of the transaction would be the person who oversaw the original contract. Genealogical studies would have been made…"

"But the odds of everyone dying are astronomically high. Someone, *somewhere* must still be—"

"Not if one helps it along." Ned waited for that to sink in, and when it did, Adin flinched.

"That's monstrous!"

Harwiche shrugged but wouldn't meet Adin's eyes. "I didn't *do* it. I merely put the word out that I meant to purchase the end result."

Adin wanted to wipe the look of satisfaction from Harwiche's fleshy face. He rubbed his temple, trying to prevent the headache building behind his eyes. The very idea Harwiche advanced twisted something inside his gut like a knife. "You should be *locked up*. What a terrible...will we *never* learn what Bran was?"

"Probably not, no."

"But why do this? What can he possibly be that you—"

"Bran's unique condition makes him very, very special."

Adin waved a hand in the air. "I know about his ability to probe my memories and screen them in my dreams, I know that he can be in my head." Adin suddenly wondered if that was how he'd been so good at chess. "He told me once that he can accompany a human into death, as if he were some sort of spirit guide, and return once they...acclimated. What the fuck does any of that matter? What can be so important to anyone that they'd eliminate—"

"Bran was meant for me," Harwiche growled.

"See here," Adin sputtered. He grimaced when he realized he sounded like Winston Churchill or something. Stodgy. "Bran is an underage boy! I won't allow—"

"Dear heavens, you're obtuse." Harwiche shook his head and *giggled*. "Fedeltà even told me so in a roundabout way, but I had trouble believing him. It's not what you're thinking."

"Donte *never* discussed me with you." Of that, Adin was certain.

"No, but he did say you wouldn't allow him to turn you." Harwiche settled more comfortably in his chair, at home at last, making Adin squirm. "Which is very wise, considering the limitations placed on a vampire's lifestyle. I for one would miss fine dining and wine."

Adin bit back the sharp reply that *he could see that*. "What has that got to do with Bran?"

"*Everything*. It's time to think outside the box. "

"That's—"

"That's the answer to your question."

Adin shook his head. "I don't understand."

"Bran's magical contract was interrupted, and therefore he isn't entirely, functionally human and he never will be. Each and every cell in his body has the potential to differentiate into human cells of any kind. He doesn't have a blood type. But he still has blood. He makes bone marrow. He's a walking, living, breathing stem cell donor."

"Oh, my G—"

"*Yes!*" Harwiche seemed pleased with himself. "It's a lot to take in isn't it?"

"He doesn't have a clue—"

"No one does."

Adin pulled back. "You bastard," Adin ground out. "How is it that he didn't come with an outrageous price tag? Surely he'd be worth more to a billionaire than a trip into space, which costs, what? Twenty million? What are you leaving out?"

Harwiche reached for a button in the table beside him. "We'd like whiskey, please. Are you still a Bushmills man?" Adin nodded. Harwiche leaned into the intercom and clearly said, "Jameson's." He smiled pleasantly from his odd modern chair, giving Adin time to take it all in.

"I don't suppose it will come as any surprise that I absolutely loathe you," Adin said finally. He couldn't believe he'd been civil at all. His upbringing, his conscience, his tendency to think before he spoke, all of that finally snapped. "You're Dr. Ned *fucking* Frankenstein. This is all speculation isn't it? You know absolutely nothing. You've pasted together ideas from medical mysteries and cultural myths and you've caused an impoverished *homeless* teenager to be kidnapped and held in chains for months on the off chance that it might be true. How the fuck are you going to get a doctor to listen to your nonsense?"

"You really have no idea why this might be important to me?"

A servant came in with a tray bearing the makings for drinks. She didn't speak, but with hand gestures and eye contact asked Adin if he wanted ice. He declined, and she poured each man three fingers of whiskey and served them. Afterward, she left the room as silently as she came in.

Adin wondered if Harwiche required physically mute servants. The drink wasn't Adin's usual choice, but it went down smoky and delicious. He thought about everything he'd learned from Harwiche until something teased at him and puzzle pieces finally began to fall into place. His heart sank.

"You're dying."

"I am." Harwiche deflated. "I had a malignancy and it spread. There's only so much the doctors can do."

Adin looked more closely at Harwiche and realized he wore a wig. A very fine one, but once he looked...

"Ah, Ned. I'm so sorry." Adin found he almost meant that. He finished his drink, downing it more quickly than he'd intended. Boaz would have his head, given it had only been a few hours since he'd taken pain medication. "But you have to see that using the boy that way is wrong. What do you plan to do? Force him into a marrow donation? Use him as your own personal Petri dish? That's the stuff of horror novels."

"We'll have to agree to disagree. It's possible a bone marrow transplant will kill me. It will require destroying my immune system, and doctors aren't convinced I will survive that. If I do an autologous transplant there is no guarantee that the cells from my own body will be free of the cancer, so replacing them is risky. Of course, Bran has no cancer and if I make it through the preliminaries...a bone marrow transplant from your Bran comes without with the risk of rejection. It could be done more than once. Blood transfusions. Organ replacement. Virtual immortality if one were able to set aside the moral implications. And I can... However it seems that once again, you got there first."

Adin put his whiskey aside, dropping it sharply on the table in the silence. What Ned was saying nauseated him. Had he intended to keep Bran forever, like some living farm of human cells? Harvesting organs and tissue and blood and bone marrow until such time as one or the other of them died?

"And they call Donte and his kind monsters. I warn you, I'll kill you if you come after him again. If I don't, Donte will. Bran is under our protection now."

"I won't." Harwiche struggled not to cry. "He might have said something to that effect."

"Who else will be looking for Bran? Who else knows?"

"No one knew why I wanted him, if that's what you mean. It's possible the men who sold him will come after you for the money now that they realize it wasn't me who bought the boy. It seems to have disappeared from their coffers very mysteriously."

"Imagine that."

"And…"

"What?"

"It's possible they might have put all the pieces together. Maybe they've realized what I conjectured and will try to get him back to sell him to the highest bidder. I don't believe they fully understood when I began making my inquiries. If that's the case, they'll be difficult adversaries. They'll kill anyone who stands in their way."

"Who are *they*?"

Harwiche smiled. "Oh, hell no." He chuckled. "That would be more than my life is worth."

Adin pursed his lips. "Your life is worth nothing to me, Ned."

"Suffice it to say that if they realize that they can name their price for the boy, and the world will come knocking at their door to meet it, the only thing left for you to do will be get to get out of their way, or die." Harwiche shook his head. "If they were to kill me that would only make the time fly. See him out," he said to no one in particular. A panel in the wall opened and a beefy blond man came to stand by Adin's chair.

"Ned, you never fail to amuse me." Adin rose and held his hand out to stay Harwiche's Bond-film minion. "You don't have to, I can see myself out."

The blond shadowed him until he was on the sidewalk heading for the car, and Boaz and Bran, who waited for him. Both of them watched as he entered and slid into his seat. He remained silent long after he buckled his seat belt. Eventually, Boaz took his cue and keyed the ignition, pulling out into the damp traffic of the sixteenth arrondissement, ironically close to Santos's Paris home.

"What did he say?" Bran appeared to have used up his patience. "What did he tell you about why he wanted to buy me?"

"He told me…" Adin searched his mind for a way to put it. "He told me that because your changeling process was interrupted you're able to move between this world and the next at will. He told me that was the reason he wanted you. He didn't know what you were before."

Bran looked crestfallen, but tried to hide it. Adin realized he'd hoped for some definitive answers about what he was before he'd been switched with a human child, and it occurred to Adin that Bran might wonder about his real family.

"He also told me you're the last of your line. Your real family is all gone. I'm so sorry."

"My biological parents? Everyone is gone?"

"I'm afraid so, Bran." He'd never considered whether Bran had biological parents per se. He hadn't realized the boy might be looking for his true family, a place where he belonged among those who placed him with humans to begin with. And yet that made perfect sense.

Except the entire world made no sense to Adin at all anymore. He reached out to take Bran's hand. He understood grief. Leaning way over in his seat, impatiently pushing aside his shoulder belt, he gave Bran a firm, one-armed hug. Everything hurt, yet he felt better.

"You know, you have a family here if you want it. With us.

With me."

Bran shook his head. "I hurt Donte. I made him sick, that old woman said so."

Adin admitted the prospect looked bleak but held on to the hope that Donte was still alive and that together, they'd be able to find a solution. That he'd be all right eventually. "We'll figure something out. I know Donte wanted to help me protect you. He told me so, and he won't have changed his mind."

Bran sighed unhappily but clung to Adin, even when he sat back up and replaced his seat belt. Adin saw Boaz's eyes in the rear view mirror. They were unreadable but he knew Boaz liked Bran. The boy would always have a home. He and Boaz would see to it.

"Thank you." Bran pressed his face into Adin's shoulder.

Adin continued patting Bran with his good left hand, thinking hard about what he'd learned from Harwiche. It was all speculation, but enticing enough for a dying man to gamble on it being true. *If* Bran was what Harwiche believed and *if* he was some sort of Universal donor, then… Yes. That would make him very valuable indeed. And the feeding frenzy would only end when Bran was some greedy man's experiment, because that would be the only way to find out the truth.

Bran's breathing grew deep and even as he fell asleep trustingly against Adin's good arm.

"We've got company." Boaz interrupted his thoughts.

"What?" Adin didn't understand.

"We're being followed. I've been driving around for a while, wondering if this person is following us or if we're experiencing a phenomenal coincidence."

"I don't believe in phenomenal coincidence."

"Neither do I." Boaz sped up a little, trying to find a way to dodge around the cars in front, and put a cushion between them and their tail. He was doing a magnificent job, one worthy of any Parisian cabbie. Adin got a tighter hold on Bran. The late-afternoon traffic was thick, the air punctuated by the constant staccato blasts of horns.

Well, *shit*.

"Who do you suppose they are?" Adin asked.

"If I had to guess, I'd say they were the men who sold Bran. Seeing as how they probably watched your money disappear from their bank accounts like magic the next day."

"I could have you put the money back," Adin suggested. "If it means we'd be safe."

"I think that comes under the heading of too little too late at this point."

"I see."

"There's one place we could go…" Boaz reminded him.

"Boaz," Adin warned.

"Hear me out. Santos has men at his compound who will help us. All I have to do is call and they'll open the gates and deal with anyone who's following."

"How can Santos be so helpful all of a sudden when—"

"Eventually, I will run out of gas, Adin. I can't keep driving forever. Currently we have nowhere to go. Unless you made arrangements for a hotel?" Adin shook his head. "From Santos's place I can get papers for Bran, and make travel arrangements. Please, Adin."

Boaz had never, *ever* said please to him before. The car was stopped momentarily at a traffic light, but whoever followed them was only three car lengths back. He met Boaz's eyes in the mirror again. Boaz was worried. He cared a great deal for Bran, who looked up to him. Plus he was something equally not human, and he made Bran feel less alone. Without Boaz, Adin didn't have a prayer of taking Bran back to his home in the States.

"All right," Adin agreed. "Make the call."

Ancient iron gates closed behind the sedan as Adin looked

back to see how close their pursuers had been. Five men emerged from Santos's home, their height and coloring all similar to that of the man who had evicted them from Donte's. They wore dark overcoats and black leather gloves against the chilly spring air, and hats pulled over their brows. They moved with precision and power, their faces covered by blank white Venetian carnival masks, giving them the look of exquisite, if merciless, marionettes.

"He does clone them," Adin whispered, waiting for a signal from Boaz that it was safe to emerge from the car. "He must. Why are they wearing masks?"

"It's intimidating isn't it?" Boaz murmured. "Mostly it's to keep the sun from harming them, but it serves the dual purpose of frightening off the unwanted."

"How come I didn't notice them before?" Adin shuddered. "It's like a Jean Cocteau film."

Bran stuck to Boaz like glue. The older man put his arm out to comfort him. "You came as a guest last time and it was late at night. This time they're here to see to any trouble. Santos says they know to stay away from us though, especially Bran, until Santos finds out why the hell the healer's men reacted that way."

Adin watched as the car that had been following them sped past. "Do you expect further trouble?"

Boaz glanced at Bran then back to Adin. "Yes, count on it."

CHAPTER FOURTEEN

Adin pushed his fork lazily around the dish placed before him. It appeared to be a blue cheese soufflé accompanied by some sort of spring mix of greens, topped with Bosc pears, more blue cheese, and candied nuts. He stared at it listlessly. He'd called Donte's cell phone and the farmhouse repeatedly but no one answered. Donte must know he needed reassuring. Something had to be terribly wrong. It drained him of his strength and his desire for food, although he was trying to act naturally for Bran's sake. But even Bran, teenage boy and bottomless pit, seemed to have little or no appetite.

Whatever immediate threat the men following them posed, Santos's minions had neutralized it. Now, nearly night, they'd seen nothing of their host's private army for hours. Boaz had managed dinner and disappeared as well, leaving Bran and Adin alone to dine. Adin poured himself a second glass of wine.

Bran finally broke the silence. "May I have wine?"

Adin shot him a tired smile. "Pour some water into your glass first."

Bran did as he was told and Adin added some of the deep red cabernet to it. "You're worried I'll become a drunk."

"For the record, that's the least of my worries." Adin leaned back in his chair. Unbidden, a horrible thought occurred to him. "Can you tell me, do imps lay eggs?"

"Excuse me?"

"The only thing Boaz ever cooks is eggs. He's very inventive, but it's always eggs." Adin pushed his plate away. "Donte once pointed that out. Suddenly, I'm not hungry."

"These are chicken eggs. I saw the carton." Bran looked at him thoughtfully. "You're still worried."

"Of course I'm worried. Donte is…"

"He's what?"

"He's my happiness. I know that's maudlin drivel. I'm a grown man, and I don't believe in fairy tales, but—"

Bran's eyes widened. "Why not?"

"What do you mean?"

"Why don't you believe in fairy tales? It seems to me that once you learn how the world really works, fairy tales make a lot more sense. There *are* fairies. And imps. Things that are dark and dead scary and sources of magic that ordinary people never find out exist. Undead people walk the earth."

"I never thought about it that way." Adin frowned a little.

"I've seen your dreams Adin. I know why you don't believe."

Adin stiffened. "And why is that?"

"Come on. Do I have to spell it out? Do you know how many blokes try it on with a boy living on the street?"

"I certainly never—"

"Charles used you Adin, as much as any pimp who ever picked up a runaway boy at the station. He had to change the way you saw the world to get you to go along with his schemes, and then he used you. In your dreams you see that clearly."

Adin picked up his glass and drank. "I know Charles used me. But in no way did he change the way I saw the world."

"No. He just made you feel like the worst fool that ever lived."

Adin didn't know what to say to that.

"So you think Donte is…?" Bran asked.

"I can't bear to think they couldn't help him. I don't like not knowing," Adin admitted.

"It must be nice to have a connection to someone." Bran's face twisted. "I wish I knew what it was that I did to make him sick!"

"I'm sure you didn't do anything. What could you even have done? You saw each other for a brief moment before you went upstairs. I'm certain there's been some sort of—" Adin's cell phone rang and he motioned to Bran that he was going to take it in the kitchen. He answered as he walked. "Tredeger."

"Adin." Santos's voice sounded concerned. "My man confessed he was rough with you. How is your arm?"

"Broken." Adin heard Santos curse.

"You have my sincerest apologies."

"Thanks for that." Adin paused. "Is Donte—"

"Fedeltà is perfectly safe in Madame's hands, which is more than I can say for Peter once Donte finds out he manhandled you until you broke. Peter said you fought like a man possessed. I'm impressed."

"I was distraught. They made me leave without him. Without saying good-bye. I think that was the worst I've ever felt," Adin admitted. "Can you tell me what the hell happened? He aged overnight."

There was a palpable silence on the line. Adin knew Santos weighed his options. He'd been, at times, an implacable enemy, at times charming, almost kind. One never knew where one stood with Santos. Adin held his breath.

"It's the boy," Santos said finally.

Adin rested a hip on the kitchen counter and glanced back to make sure Bran couldn't hear him. "How can that be?"

"Mme. Restieaux conjectures that the boy manifests a powerful natural energy very similar to that which is given off by the sun. We're simply allergic to him."

"That's absurd; he's as flesh and blood as I am."

"Is he?" Santos asked. "Things aren't always as they appear. Nature's process is relentless. All living things are part of its cycle. The vampire is its antithesis. We represent the manipulation of nature. The avoidance of death. These require deep magic—for lack of a better word—that is as old as nature, and in opposition to it."

"If he were made of sunlight why am I not affected? I would be irradiated. I would be burned. *I* would be growing older—"

"I said it was similar to sunlight. It's as if he's made of life itself. At any rate, it seems the undead are unsafe within his sphere of influence."

"He has no idea of that." Adin peered into the dining room where Bran sat, eating his salad and finishing his watered wine. "What should I tell him?"

"Tell him nothing Adin," Santos warned. "When you took off Bran's chains, his strength grew and it impacted everything around it. He'll only get stronger. More dangerous to those of us who must not face the sun. You cannot protect him and Donte both. You'll need to choose."

"No."

"Madame said that Bran's nature is older than time. I am sorry." Santos's voice held real regret. "Truly. I had in mind to twit you with hard choices, but not... never fatal ones."

Adin took the apology to be sincere. "Thank you Santos."

"Odd to hear you say that."

"Nevertheless." Adin swallowed hard. "Thank you."

Santos disconnected the call.

What a clusterfuck.

Adin tried Donte's number and once again, it rang straight through to voice mail.

Bran spoke from behind him. "If you want, you and Boaz can go to Donte. I'd have to borrow some money, but—"

"There is not a chance in the world that I'd leave you alone to fend for yourself," Adin told him tiredly.

"I've been alone most of my life, Adin."

"Donte has been fine without me for centuries. He's with friends. He'll come for me as soon as he can."

"What if he doesn't? What if he decides he can't risk being

around me?"

Adin gave Bran a smile that was probably as weak as he felt. "It's his call to make. His survival. That's as important to me as my own." Suddenly, Adin felt the cold in a new and more profound way. He left for his bedroom to find a sweater and a little privacy. Once there, he removed his sling and paused in front of the wardrobe drawers, allowing himself to consider what it might mean to him if Donte wrote him off.

He reached into his suitcase for an Aran wool pullover that he'd had for years and slipped it over his head, painfully pushing his soft cast through the worn, loose cuff of the sleeve.

There were others, surely, who could care for Bran. With the correct papers, he could be placed with a family in Washington, somewhere Adin could be a regular part of his life. Tuan would know about otherworldly immigration and they could all come up with a suitable solution together. Bran could be happy and live a semi-normal life. Maybe even find a family that could love him as much as…

Boaz appeared behind him in the mirror as he pulled his sling back on. "I found a place to go for documents. It could be tricky because we'll have to deal with people we would normally avoid. We won't be able to go to the usual forgers because Bran can't be around the undead."

Adin turned. "Why does putting myself into the hands of criminals feel so much worse than being around people who want to eat me?"

Boaz shrugged. "If you'd rather stay here, I could take him."

"No." Adin followed Boaz from the room and down the stairs. "I'd feel better if I went with you. I don't know why, really. Of all the players, I'm definitely the weakest link."

"He trusts you," Boaz said quietly when they walked down the stairs together.

"Yes. I know." Adin sighed.

"When you're finished eating then?"

"Yes." Adin stopped on the bottom step, already tired. "I'm exhausted and my arm is throbbing. How far is it?"

"Not far. I'll get your meds. It's nearly time for you to take them."

"Thanks." Adin leaned against the railing at bottom of the stairs. "I want to go home."

"Where? To Washington or your sister's in Los Angeles?"

Adin shook his head. "Maybe San Francisco. I want to see Edward, and ask Tuan for help. If I go to Los Angeles I'll have to explain Bran to Deana."

"I'll make the arrangements."

"Thank you Boaz." Adin wanted to ask him if he'd heard from Donte, but discovered he didn't want to know the answer if it was *yes*.

Boaz appeared to read his mind. "He hasn't called me either. I'm sure he's taking his time to make certain he's well. It's far more dangerous than you can imagine for someone like Donte when he's in a weakened state. Not just for himself, but because no one is safe around a weakened vampire. There are those who would take advantage of it."

"Santos is in Taiwan, isn't he?"

"Santos isn't the only vampire who would like to see Donte Fedeltà taken down. Men with the kind of power Donte wields will always have enemies."

"*Perfect*." Adin picked up his plate, no longer even pretending to be hungry. He walked to the kitchen and placed his food in the trash. Bran followed him quietly, having finished his dinner, but no less unhappy. "Let's head out. The sooner Bran has papers the sooner we can go home."

Adin's fears with regard to getting Bran's papers turned out to be fairly unfounded. All it took was the right word in the ear of a clerk at a specific camera store. They were led behind a set of dirty curtains and down a flight of stairs into a basement filled with high tech digital imaging equipment. A photograph of Bran was placed into a highly official-looking US passport along with other papers, a birth certificate, and an identification card for the state of Utah. When Adin asked why Utah, the girl there simply gave him a Gallic shrug, but apparently a highly detailed identity had been constructed for Bran, including a social security card, school and health records, and family ties. Adin was even provided with a signed and notarized permission from Bran's very fictitious parents to see to his care while he was in Adin's custody.

Adin had to wonder—or worry, really—how often adults took children illegally into the United States and required such documents. Boaz's expression told him not to ask.

They headed back to Santos's place where they dropped off the car and then had a taxi pick them up. Boaz lugged their baggage from inside, gave the driver instructions to take them to Roissy/Charles De Gaulle, and off they went.

Adin checked his phone obsessively, giving in to the urge at smaller and smaller intervals. By the time they were getting ready to board, he was fully beginning to panic.

Bran stopped him from rising so he could pace for the third time. "Adin. You need to go back and find Donte."

"He's a big undead boy." Adin stopped his hand when it crept toward the cell phone in his pocket again. "He can take care of himself. I just wish I knew why he isn't answering his phone."

"I'm sure it's nothing. Maybe he's not getting a signal or the battery is dead."

"I'm sure that's it," Adin replied absently. It wasn't as if the battery could go dead on Adin's internal sense of Donte, and that's what had Adin most worried. Since they'd been together he'd never had a loss of connection of this magnitude.

Bran caught Adin's good hand between his. "*Adin.* I'll be fine. Boaz and I can leave on this plane, and you can follow when you've found Donte. I hate that you're leaving without knowing he's all right because of me."

Adin shook his head. "It's important to get you someplace safe, Bran. Trust me, if I didn't know this before, then my visit with Harwiche nailed that right down for me." Adin pulled his hands back. "Donte lived for five hundred years without my help. He can go another few days."

"But what about you?"

Adin bit his lip. Donte—all vampires—would see his concern as a weakness. They'd pull at it like a snag in a sweater to see if they could exploit it. Vampires didn't think like humans. Selfless devotion was an unknown quantity in the vampire world. Even Donte's desire to turn Adin, as nice as it felt, wasn't really based on seeing Adin live forever, but on the very real and painful loss Donte would endure when Adin died.

And therein lay one of the reasons that Adin fought it.

Just as surely as prolonged sunlight would burn out every trace of Donte's existence, being turned—if he allowed it—would eradicate the human side of Adin. Adin didn't want that. Protecting Bran, caring for anyone, even Donte, required that he be human for it to have any meaning at all. Donte might throw his considerable power into taking care of Adin, might accede to his whim regarding Bran and back him in a fight to keep the boy from Harwiche's schemes, but he did so only because Adin asked him to.

Adin's thoughts were too difficult to explain to Donte, much less to Bran who stood before him with earnest eyes, sharing that very trait, his own humanity, by putting Adin's need to see Donte before his own desire to feel safe.

Adin took a final look at the busy airport. He was leaving France, and Donte, behind. But not forever. Wherever Donte was, whatever he was doing that Adin couldn't be a part of, Adin *would* return. They would be together again.

That had to be enough.

CHAPTER FIFTEEN

Once the plane was aloft, Adin took his pain medication with a bottle of water and settled in as comfortably as he could. Bran sat on his right against the window and allowed him to pillow his soft cast on the armrest between their seats. Across the aisle, Boaz flipped the pages of a magazine.

Adin tried to get a sense of Donte, but came up with nothing except the guilt he felt for leaving Donte behind. The soothing motion of the plane and the medication wiped out even that, until he was drifting, floating off to sleep.

"This is a very, very serious accusation, Adin." In Adin's experience among department chairs they fell into one of two categories, the Machiavellian and the hopelessly obsessed. As department chairs went, Historian Evangeline Chandler fell neatly between the two. No one doubted her sincerity, but everyone trod carefully around her desire for acclaim. Even knowing this, Adin had pulled her out of a cocktail party designed to give her just that.

Adin's ears were still ringing with the scorn Charles and Shep heaped on him.

"I'm well aware of that," Adin replied. "I'm trying to prevent a huge embarrassment."

"I see." Chandler looked at him thoughtfully. "It will be very difficult, if not downright impossible to prove that anyone is perpetrating a fraud."

"I know that." Adin's heart thudded painfully against his ribs.

"At the very worst, Shep and Charles will claim ignorance. They'll act the outraged consumer, and blame it on the seller."

"Yes, they will." Adin told her. "And of course, that could certainly be true. If, right now, they reveal it to be a fraudulent document even as they're accepting a cocktail party in their honor for finding it. So many experts said it was the genuine article that this all goes away if they tell the truth now, before they announce their find."

"You say that Charles was aware of the problem when you confronted him with it?"

"Yes."

"But they found the problem after they purchased the documents?"

"That's what they said, yes." Adin didn't meet Chandler's probing gaze. He wasn't sure he believed that anymore. He didn't know what to believe.

"I doubt we'll ever know."

"I don't suppose we will. They'll know I spoke to you, though. They saw us leave the room." Adin tried to get Charles's angry glare out of his mind. Charles would hate him for this. Irreversibly.

"What a mess."

"If I try to go public with what I know on my own they'll find a way to fail me. Accusations of cheating or plagiarism or some such thing. I'll be an object of scorn for my disloyalty. Tossed from academia forever for my lack of tact and everyone will think it's because of some sexual melodrama between happily monogamous gay men and a boy who has a hopeless crush."

"Is that what they told you?"

"In a nutshell. I left out the part about never getting a job at MacDonald's. I don't care that they used me. I saw that coming and let it happen. But I do care about the truth. About letting people think that I looked the other way and allowed them to pass off a forgery for a grade."

Chandler didn't speak for a very long time. Adin knew she was calculating the odds, going over all the possible outcomes as if she were playing chess. It took her a little time to decide which way to spin the situation, but when she had her answer he could see it on her face.

"That's not true," she said, finally.

"What?" Adin blinked in surprise. "I know those papers are fake."

"Of course they're fake, but truth isn't the only thing you care about. You're angry that they're trying to make a fool of you, reacting quite naturally, I think, to their blackmail, and outraged by their callous treatment of you, both within the boundaries of your education and outside of it, in bed." Adin blanched but didn't deny it. "There was a moment when they treated you as an equal. And you liked that. They treated you as a peer, a person *with a brain and a heart and value, and that's over. It makes you sick to think you allowed any of this to happen. It makes you sick to lose that cachet."*

Adin blew out a long held breath. When she put it that way it was a heady kind of freedom to blow it all up behind him. "Fuck, yeah."

Chandler smiled at him for the first time, and it was a genuine, indulgent kind of thing. As if she had simply waited for him to say the secret word. As if confetti were going to fall on him along with the warmth of that smile. He followed her back into the ongoing soiree with the sure and certain knowledge that she would do whatever was right. That would be enough for him.

When Chandler reached the podium, Adin held his breath. Charles and Shep remained together, holding cocktails, pressing the flesh. If Adin didn't know them so well he would say they hadn't a care in the world. But when Adin looked closely, a muscle bunched beneath Shep's high cheekbone. Charles held his drink in a death grip, his knuckles white, and there was a sheen of sweat on his upper lip. They'd avoided looking at him when he'd returned to the room at Chandler's side, but now the promise of terrible retribution animated both their faces. Adin knew he had only a few more days to enjoy this particular institution, then he'd head home during the winter break and look for another. Or make plans for something else entirely if another university was truly out of reach for him. Only a few more very tense days, and he could go home.

Chandler could project her voice, and did, silencing everything in the room but the footsteps of the wait staff and the rattle of ice. "As many of you know, our visiting professors Dr. Holmesby and Dr. Edgerton are the guests of honor this evening. Their dedication to finding and preserving documents from the past has been admirable to me since I arrived here. Their passion is obvious, their delight in making each new discovery has always been based on the principle that it provides a snapshot of the past and sheds light on the players of history, and not their own aggrandizement. We are so lucky to have such devoted professionals affiliated with this university. Likewise during the time that it's been my pleasure to preside over this department, I've seen some fine students come and go.

"That's why it's with mixed emotions that I have to announce that the papers that Drs. Holmesby and Edgerton purchased for the university have

been found to be forgeries." Everyone looked at Charles and Shep whose faces never gave up their frozen smiles. No sound could be heard as Chandler continued. "Doctors Holmesby and Edgerton asked me to postpone this event, or to cancel it altogether under the circumstances. Their disappointment has been profound. Naturally they came to me to explain the situation fully, highlighting the participation of one of their students, Adin Tredeger, in the discovery and I must say, all three men stand as beacons of integrity in a truly difficult situation.

"So tonight, instead of congratulating Charles and Shep on their discovery of the Mary Stuart letters, I'd like to congratulate them on their passionate pursuit of truth, and their mentorship of a young man who is a credit to this University and to the study of history in general."

At this, Chandler motioned Charles and Shep to join her. She placed her arm around each of them. The three of them seemed to wear the mantle of academic pride. Only Adin knew the reason for her carefully blank smile and their nervous acceptance of her praise. When they invited Adin over for a photograph of the four of them, he went reluctantly, half expecting Charles's eyes to bore holes in him like lasers when they shook hands. Chandler cleared her throat for silence again and Adin no longer felt all the eyes in the room on him.

"As a special announcement, though, I thought this would be a fine time to reveal that Adin Tredeger will be leaving us as he's privately discussed with me his desire to attend, and his acceptance by Williams College, where he hopes to become part of the Williams/Exeter program. As disappointing as this is for me personally and for this institution, we wish him all the best.

"I thank you all for coming, please enjoy the evening."

Adin stepped away from Chandler and watched as Charles and Shep moved back into the crowd. When they walked past, Charles bent his head as if to kiss Adin on the cheek and growled, "Don't carry hard feelings, Adin. The first cut is always the deepest," into his ear. Adin pulled back, his pasted-on smile still beaming. Right then, Adin's heart froze around the vow that he would never allow any man to make that second cut.

When Chandler finished answering individual questions, she looked neither right nor left but made a beeline for Adin, taking his hand and pulling him from the room. He followed her quietly, saying nothing. It was fairly clear that she was in control of the situation. She'd handled the possible *scandal with the tact of a Medici prince, and she would tell him in her own time what would happen next. He didn't ask, for instance, how she could praise him for his honesty in one sentence and then utter the obvious lie that he was headed for Williams in the next.*

Adin heard the tapping of leather dress shoes behind him and turned to find Charles and Shep following, hot on their heels, obviously determined to have an audience with Chandler to tell their side of the story. When Chandler and Adin reached her office, she unlocked it and entered, pulling Adin inside.

The last time he saw Charles Holmesby's face was when History Department Dragonslayer Evangeline Chandler snapped the door shut firmly on it.

A jolt of awareness hit Adin when the drink cart rattled noisily next to his ear as the flight attendant pushed it toward the back of the plane. Turbulence. His lashes rose as Bran turned his head to stare out the window at the dark sky. Although in the months just after leaving Princeton Adin had dreamed of Charles quite often, he hadn't had that dream in years.

"Are you messing around in my head again?"

Bran looked at his lap. "Maybe a little."

"I promise there's nothing terribly interesting in there, Bran."

"Did you go? To Williams?"

"Yes," Adin replied. "Eventually. After I fled home for a while. Professor Chandler helped me greatly, and I went to Williams the following fall. I spent a year at Exeter, one of the Oxford colleges, later, which was very nice because my friend Edward was there, and he helped me to fit in."

"You trusted them and they were just using you. They threatened you." Bran lowered his voice and looked around him at the other passengers. "They should have paid for what they did."

Adin shrugged and tried to explain. "I had a choice, Bran. They never tried to force anything on me, except to look the other way when that letter came to light, and in the end I believe I did the right thing."

Bran pressed his lips together.

"What?"

"You thought you were in love, and they knew that. They treated you like shit, and told you they did it because you were special. They told you if you were smart enough, you'd see things the way they did. There's a fairy tale right there, if you ask me."

It was Adin's turn to be surprised. "And what does that make you, the boy who says, 'Look, everyone. The king is bare ass nekkid?'"

Bran grinned. "Not everyone is like them. Not even Donte, and he's a monster."

"He's not a monster," Adin said impatiently.

"Yes, he *is*." Bran put his hand on Adin's soft cast for emphasis, momentarily forgetting that Adin was injured. Adin tried not to wince as he disengaged Bran's hand. "I'm sorry."

"It's all right. Donte isn't... He's not what you think he is. Not everything, anyway."

"Donte *is* a monster. He's *your* monster. I think he knew it was me making him sick, but he didn't say anything."

"Why on *earth* would he do that?" Adin asked. "Vampires are hard-wired for self-preservation. It would go against his nature."

Bran raised his eyebrows. "But he promised you he would protect me, didn't he?"

Adin looked across the aisle at Boaz to see what he thought about the matter, but the man was fast asleep, leaning heavily on the shoulder of the woman next to him. She didn't seem to mind. Adin turned back to Bran.

"I never wanted that. Surely he knew if he'd told me what was happening I would have let him out of his promise."

"Maybe he didn't want you to have to choose?"

Adin's heart sank like the Titanic. "Maybe he was afraid of

what I would choose."

"Maybe," Bran said carefully, "every once in a while you should give Donte a hard squeeze so he can feel you there, because I'm starting to think he's not what you think he is either. He's not like me, he can't see everything that's in your heart."

"Stay out of my heart," Adin muttered. "And my head."

Bran didn't reply. He turned back to the window and the night sky.

"Do you really think that?" Adin asked a few minutes later, after the drink cart finally stopped next to his chair and the flight attendant handed him a couple of nip-sized bottles of whiskey and a plastic cup.

"I think he loves you."

"You said it yourself, you can't read Donte the way you can read a human," Adin reminded him quietly.

"But I have eyes." Bran shot him a look.

"How'd you get so wise?"

Bran took time before he answered. "In the end, no one thinks about what went wrong, Adin. They just long for the people they love."

Adin swallowed hard. "What a mess."

Adin stayed silent for the remainder of the long trip, then led Bran off the plane to get their bags and grind through customs. He held his breath when Bran's passport was checked, but no one gave it more than the cursory look they gave Adin's. Boaz had to be fingerprinted for his entry to the United States, because he carried a British passport, but everything checked out cleanly for him as well.

As soon as they were through the official business, Adin phoned Edward and left a message. He'd made arrangements to stay at his favorite hotel, but wanted to see Edward as soon as he could. The sooner he could speak with Edward's lover Tuan about their situation, the better he would feel. In Tuan's official capacity in the government agency dealing with the paranormal world—what Tuan jokingly referred to as "undead management"—he might have far more insight into Bran's situation than any of them did. Adin was wholly new to this esoteric world, but he knew how Edward and Tuan would feel about the kidnapping of what appeared to be a very human young boy.

Adin hoped Tuan would be able to provide answers for Bran as well. As they left the airport he wanted to put an arm around the boy's shoulder, but couldn't because he had to pull his bag with his good arm. Bran looked so young. Maybe he was anxious from his first plane ride or intimidated by a new city in a foreign country, but the events of the past few days were taking their toll. He had smudges under his eyes, and his usual bravado seemed faint. He went wherever Adin and Boaz led him, fairly quietly, following along like a baby chick. Once they'd piled their luggage into the trunk of a taxi, he sat next to Adin in the back while Boaz chatted up the driver in the front passenger seat.

Adin continued to observe him in silence until he heard his cell phone ring. Both Bran and Boaz watched him when he pulled it out. "It's Edward, calling me back," he told them, far more disappointed than they were that it wasn't Donte.

"Finally," he answered, gazing out the window as San Francisco seemed to fly by.

"You're here?"

"Yes. We'll be at the hotel in a few minutes. Did you get a chance to ask Tuan about my new friend?"

Bran raised an eyebrow at him.

"I did," Edward answered. "Tuan wants to see you right away. Can you come straight here?"

"I can." Adin leaned forward and gave the driver Edward's address. He might have wanted to go to a hotel first, maybe get cleaned up, but he'd learned recently that Tuan's expertise in a situation like this could save his life.

Boaz turned around in his seat and shot Adin a curious stare.

Adin shrugged. To Edward he said, "Boaz is here as well as Bran. Should they come too?"

"Absolutely. Tuan wants to talk to everyone. What have you gotten yourself into this time?"

"I haven't got the faintest clue."

"How's Donte? Have you heard anything?"

"No." Adin clenched his teeth. He would *not* blow his cool.

"It's going to be all right," Edward said gently.

Adin swallowed hard. "I know. I'll be there soon." He ended the call and leaned his head against the window.

Edward opened the door of his attractive Victorian row house and immediately enveloped Adin in a hard hug. Adin clung to him, pressing his face against the colorfully inked skin of Edward's neck, inhaling the familiar scent of the best friend he'd ever had.

"*Fuck.*" He tried not to cry, but the emotions of the previous days and the fact that Edward was crushing his soft cast between their bodies got the better of him. Edward rocked him for a second, soothing Adin until he couldn't help but wince from the pressure. Adin pushed him gently away.

"I'm so sorry. I forgot about that." Edward put an arm that jingled with the music of multiple bracelets over Adin's shoulder. "I'm so glad to see you."

They ushered Bran inside while Tuan stepped out to greet Boaz and help the driver with the luggage.

Adin watched them briefly from a window in the vestibule, as always admiring the fluid grace with which the bookish-looking Tuan moved. His jacket stretched across his back as he easily lifted Adin's case from the trunk of the car.

"Oh, my man." Edward sighed. "Isn't he the bees's knees?"

Bran appeared to be stifling a laugh as Adin nodded.

"Right then." Edward turned to Bran. "Let me get a look at

you. Bran, yes?"

Bran nodded, running a nervous hand through his hair. Under the long, elegant coat Adin had purchased for him he wore a vintage suit, one of Adin's crisp, colored dress shirts, and a spectacularly horrible tie. Adin knew Edward, who still flogged the bad boy vibe in a tight T-shirt and low-slung jeans, would love Bran on sight. Bran stared open-mouthed until Edward—who was pierced and tatted everywhere, which lent him a somewhat fierce air—gave him a playful growl.

"What are you looking at?" Edward folded his thin arms and grinned.

"You look exactly the same as you do in Adin's dreams."

Tuan walked in the door at that precise moment. "Adin dreams about you?"

Bran flushed. "Not like…you know. *Dreams*, dreams."

"Careful, Bran. We don't know if Tuan's the jealous type."

Edward answered for Tuan. "He's got no reason to be."

He carelessly grabbed Bran's hand to pull him into the parlor. Adin's eyes were on Tuan at that moment, but he felt a shudder all around him, a shockwave that rocked his body back like a light earthquake. His muscles tensed, and he put a hand to the wall. Everyone fell silent for a minute, waiting, Adin thought, to see if the quake would turn out to be a big one. When nothing further happened, Adin looked to Tuan again.

"Did you feel that?"

Tuan frowned. "Yes."

Boaz's face held surprise as he too, looked to Tuan. "Was that a quake?"

Tuan shook his head. "I don't think so."

Adin glanced from the vestibule into the beautifully furnished room. Not an ornament was out of place. "What could it have been? Nothing seems to have fallen…"

Boaz whispered, "Look," and nudged Adin's good arm,

focusing their attention on Bran and Edward. They simply stared at one another, hands linked, oblivious to the people watching them or the time that passed.

"Edward?" Gently, Tuan placed his hand on Edward's shoulder. "Come back lover."

Edward dropped Bran's hand and shook his head as if to clear it. "*Tuan.*"

Bran was pale and dazed. He stared at his hand for a minute, saying nothing.

"What just happened?" Adin touched the small of Bran's back. "Do you need to sit down?"

"No." Bran continued to look at his hand. "Not really."

"What was that?" Adin asked Edward.

Edward shook his head again, this time looking to Tuan for an explanation.

Boaz, standing forgotten in the hallway, asked, "Did that shockwave happen when you touched Bran?"

Edward nodded.

"But he's not a vampire." Bran frowned. "I know I'm bad for vampires, but he's human. I can tell he's completely human."

Edward's and Tuan's eyes met and they communicated something without words. Tuan nodded.

"I am *now*," said Edward.

CHAPTER SIXTEEN

At Edward's house, no matter what else the situation called for, there would always be tea. He poured graciously from an ornate ceramic teapot into paper-thin china cups, depositing them—on their saucers—in front of each guest while everyone else sat around the elegant dining table in a room that smelled newly painted.

A dazzling chandelier hung from the ceiling above them, throwing light onto the perfect gloss of the mahogany table below it. Framed art decorated the walls. Due to Edward's work as an art dealer and his family connections to a number of well-known artists, the collection was stunning. It always intimidated Adin when he found himself sipping tea under a genuine Chagall, or a Picasso line drawing of Edward's maternal grandmother.

Edward cleared his throat. "Tuan and I wanted to talk to you before you took Bran to the hotel. I thought... well. We thought..." His eyes met Tuan's again.

Tuan continued for him. "When you called us about Bran, Edward told me that everything you described was familiar. Eerily similar—in a way—to his own experience. As near as we can tell, Edward is a changeling."

Adin sighed. "Well, that explains a lot."

Edward ignored him. "In my case, the process reached completion on my eighteenth birthday as it was intended to." Edward didn't look at all happy about this. "I'm entirely human."

Tuan's hand fell on Edward's, and he continued the story. "When we met, the more Edward told me about himself the more I realized there was something unusual about him."

"What was your first clue?" Adin asked drily. Edward's appearance, from his short, spiked blond hair to the Doc Marten boots he tied with rainbow laces, was so thoroughly *different* that he was a one-man traveling sideshow. Edward shot Adin his trademark sweet smile, and Adin's heart melted a little.

Boaz ignored Adin and asked Edward, "What seemed familiar to you about Bran?"

"Certainly Bran's ability to read your dreams. When I was young, I thought all children could see each other's dreams. I could search through their memories and learn about them. I could push thoughts into people's awareness. I learned young to hide everything that singled me out as different."

"Then you abandoned that on principle?" Adin asked.

Edward cuffed him playfully. "I've always been able to sense the difference between types of entities. I still can. I knew, for example, that Boaz was no more human than Donte from the very beginning."

Adin wanted to smack him. "What the hell? And you never told me?"

"What was I going to say? You obviously didn't know anything and I wasn't sure —at the time—that you needed to." Edward pulled at the hoops in his ear, a nervous habit of long standing. "I had no idea why I was different when we were kids, for years I thought it was highly evolved gaydar."

Tuan snorted.

"I learned never to speak of it because people didn't understand. Whenever I tried, even my own family thought I was a liar or disturbed or both. Except my grandmother, thank heavens. She simply told me to keep my mouth shut. Then later I met Tuan and he told me things I'd never known about the true nature of the world, about the vampires and other entities who inhabit it. When the supernatural world caught up with you, Adin… It seemed like too much to tell all at once. Where could I even begin?"

"We're going to have a long conversation very soon," Adin said darkly. "Do I need to worry about werewolves and other things too?" Tuan didn't meet his eyes and Edward shrugged. "Well, *shit*..."

Bran asked, "What's different about you, Edward? Now that you're human?"

Edward put his hand on Bran's and even though he expected it, Adin was still surprised to feel the shock when it came. It was considerably less intense, but palpable, as if some sort of energy—or magic—escaped into the world when they touched. They tried it several times, and the effect appeared to be diminishing. Edward took his hand back and picked up his tea.

"I'm restricted to my own head," Edward said quietly. "I used to be able to come and go from...other places."

Bran nodded tightly. "I understand."

Edward heaved a deep sigh. "Adin, Tuan and I think Bran should stay with us."

"What?" Adin looked to Tuan, who nodded his head.

"It's a real solution," Tuan told him. "They have a connection, whatever it is. And we can protect him. There are no vampires here, nor are there likely to be any in the near future. As soon as Donte arrives..."

Adin nodded. Tuan had left the words hanging but Adin knew if Donte followed him he would need to keep his distance from Bran. Maybe he was already staying away for that reason. Adin looked to where Bran sat, his tea hovering between his saucer and his lips, forgotten.

"What do you think, Bran?"

Bran frowned and looked over at Edward. "Would you really want me to stay?"

"We talked about it before you came because it seemed like a good solution to your vampire allergy problem. But now..." Edward nodded and took Bran's hand again and this time Adin barely felt it. "You feel like a part of me. Something I lost and found again. Maybe you give me a little of my magic back."

"Do you think we're related?"

Adin shook his head. "I doubt that, Bran. Harwiche said you had no living relatives. He was fairly certain on that point."

Bran nodded. "But maybe we're the same type of being, right?"

Edward grinned. "I think so."

"It's possible that's why I felt such a strong urge to protect Bran. He felt familiar. I guess I saw Edward in him." Adin thought about it. "He does remind me of you at that age. Did you see my dreams in those days?"

Edward blushed and looked at his hands.

Adin gave him a shove. "*You bastard*. How embarrassing."

Bran's lips turned up in the beginning of a shy smile. The first real smile Adin had seen on his face since they'd arrived. "It might be nice to stay here for a few days." Bran looked to Adin for permission.

"You can stay where you're happy," Adin told him sincerely. "I promise you, Boaz and I will be around if you need us."

Boaz agreed. "We'll need to get him a phone like yours, Adin. But if he wants to stay here, it seems like a fine idea. Tuan?"

"Perfectly fine." Tuan nodded. He watched Edward—and Bran now too – with an oddly satisfied look on his handsome face. "It's like they're brothers and even if it's not by blood, that makes Bran my brother too. He'll be part of my family now. We'll take good care of him."

"Then it's settled." Edward clapped his hands like a child and turned to Bran. "I suppose you like all sorts of junk food and sweets that are bad for you?"

Bran blushed and mumbled, "I suppose so."

"Thank *heavens*." Edward pulled the boy from his chair, "I have a ton of menus. Let's go pick something awful and have it delivered." To Tuan he said, "We'll be in the sun room."

Tuan wore an enigmatic smile as he watched them leave. His glasses reflected the lamplight. The glare, coupled with his conservative dress and how he sat holding his cup and saucer made him look like an accountant more than ever. "I don't know what I'm going to do with *two* of them."

"Are you certain it's what you want? You have to think of the long term."

"If it makes Edward happy then it's fine with me. We have plenty of room. It will take a little getting used to."

"As long as you're sure." Adin smiled at how tired Tuan already sounded. "I was hoping you'd be able to tell me more about Bran."

"There's no real way of knowing exactly what he is. When I met Edward, it was clear he was an elemental entity who'd been exchanged for a human child, so that's as good a guess for Bran as any."

"How was that clear to you? I've known him forever. Edward is just… Edward. I mean he's impulsive and a little wild…"

Tuan grinned. "I saw right away that he wasn't entirely human. He had earth magic in spades. He was a tremendously gifted empath when wasn't all about himself, but more than that, he was able to discern the occult nature of others. Which is distinctly uncomfortable if you're hiding something." Tuan grimaced and cleared his throat. "That is… I would imagine."

Adin felt more than a little angry. "He's my best friend. Why would he tell you, and not me?"

"Remind me to tell you exactly how we met sometime. Suffice it to say that Edward has gotten himself into a situation or two where he required rescuing." Tuan flashed his white teeth in a predatory smile. "And I have awesome ninja powers."

Boaz interrupted. "If Bran's an elemental that wouldn't explain the effect he has on vampires. Elementals are only marginally magical. They're not even like imps."

"Unless he's an earth elemental like Edward." Tuan looked toward the door where Edward and Bran had disappeared. "They stand as a harmonizing agent, stabilizing the possible destructive powers of the fire, air and water elementals."

"Ah. *Earth.*" Boaz nodded. "Santos said Bran was made of nature itself."

Tuan sighed. "That would explain why the vampire aged. The Earth elementals are tied to time and seasons. They're a part of the very force that makes things grow and ripen and die. A vampire in proximity to Bran is a peach in a brown paper bag."

"No wonder Donte looked tired."

"He would have felt it. He might even have discerned its cause." Boaz lifted his eyes to Adin.

Adin sighed. "Oh, man. I *suck* as a boyfriend."

"You didn't know."

"Because he thought he couldn't tell me."

"You don't know that," Tuan told him.

Adin rubbed his face tiredly. "But I do. So much makes sense now. Boaz, you know Donte. I think he was afraid I'd be forced to choose between being with him and protecting Bran."

"You might be right," Boaz agreed. "It's just the kind of—"

"Ridiculous, harebrained, poorly thought out, *didn't even bother to ask me first* kind of thing he'd—"

Boaz snorted. "It's odd how he's always using the same words to describe you."

"Well, *shit.*"

Tuan laughed. "Be that as it may, that doesn't explain Harwiche's plan, or who else might be after Bran."

Adin lowered his voice. "Harwiche said the changeling process was interrupted, and that makes Bran a walking stem cell donor. I don't even think he knew for certain. I think it was all conjecture and wishful thinking…"

"*Harwiche.*" Tuan made a face. "He's little more than a pimp. He's greedy and amoral, and his wealth comes from the suffering of innocents over centuries. It's not any surprise to me that he thought kidnapping Bran was nothing more than another business deal."

"He's dying," Adin told them.

Boaz shrugged. "He's clutching at straws. He had a boy kidnapped on the off chance that he could prolong his life. There's no downside to him for trying it."

"How could he find a physician who would go along with it?"

"Money?" Tuan suggested. "He's got boatloads of it."

Adin suddenly felt the weight of the world on his shoulders. "It seems as if each day brings something unfathomable. Like Alice in Wonderland if it was written by Jack the Ripper."

"Sometimes things happen like that, I'm sorry." Tuan's sad smile was sincere. "Where will you be heading from here?"

"I don't even know. We were on our way to the hotel when Edward called so we had the cab bring us here."

Boaz stood. "If it pleases you Dr. Tredeger, I'll call a taxi to take us to the hotel, and then in the morning we can make plans to rent a car. We can head for the estate Donte uses when he's in the area. I telephoned Donte's friend, and it's unoccupied and available for use at any time."

Adin smiled with gratitude. "Thank you."

"Excuse me, then," Boaz said, taking his phone from his pocket and heading to the foyer where the luggage sat waiting.

Adin sat, subjected to Tuan's intense gaze for a while. "Do you love Donte Fedeltà?"

"I do. Very much."

"That's highly interesting to me. You don't seem the undead groupie type."

"It's complicated." Adin frowned.

"Believe me, I understand." Tuan glanced down at Adin's tea. "Do you want something stronger than that?"

Adin shook his head. "I'm taking pain meds for my arm."

Boaz returned to the room. "I made the call. The cab will be here shortly."

The three of them headed for the back of the house where

they could hear soft music playing. When they got there, they found Edward and Bran on a small window seat full of overstuffed cushions overlooking the garden, fast asleep. Edward had slung a careless arm around Bran, who snored softly. Even as they watched, the climbing vine outside the window seemed to grow and twine around the window frame, draping down to shade them. Maybe Bran was right. It seemed that fairy tales carried more than a kernel of truth. Adin's throat tightened.

Brothers.

"They look like brothers," Adin whispered.

Tuan sighed. "Ah, *damn*. This is going to require a lot more gardening than I have time for."

CHAPTER SEVENTEEN

Adin dropped his key card on the tiny desk and wheeled his luggage into the closet, where he automatically emptied its contents and hung up his suit bag. He eyed the newest of his belongings, an elegant, shiny black walking stick with a silver skull handle and a lethal sword hidden inside that he'd received as a gift from Tuan. It was so much like the one used by Moriarty in the Sherlock Holmes television series that he'd annoyed Tuan and Edward by laughing out loud. While it was true he knew how to handle a sword without killing himself—from spending the time with a Kendo master at Donte's home in Spain—it wasn't likely that he'd survive against even a moderately experienced opponent.

But it made him look so very cool.

Adin stood in front of the mirror, holding it, playing with it a little a la Fred Astaire, until he heard a knock on the door. He called out, and when he heard Boaz's voice on the other side he opened it.

Boaz entered and looked at the cane in his hand. "You are going to get yourself killed with that thing."

"That's what I told Tuan, but he seems to think I should have it. Maybe he realizes that I'll throw it to you and run away."

"See that you do," Boaz ordered.

"Dinner?" Adin asked. Boaz was silent for so long that Adin peered closely at him and asked, "What?"

Boaz let out a heavy sigh and dropped into the lounge chair next to Adin's bed. It was as if his spirit just left him, all his masks dropped away, and he was wholly and completely unguarded. Adin had the uncomfortable feeling he was seeing the real Boaz for the very first time. "*Gods.* I'm tired."

"I could order in…" When Boaz didn't answer for a while Adin frowned. "Do you feel as if you're affected by Bran as well?"

"Of course not," Boaz snapped.

"Then what's wrong?"

"Would it matter if I were affected by Bran?" Boaz asked him roughly.

"Yes it would matter. Of course it would. What do you mean? If you couldn't be around Bran I certainly wouldn't ask you to be. I certainly wouldn't—"

"Since when do you ever *ask*?" Boaz rose and turned to him with the air of a man who needed to get something off his chest. "Since when does it matter to you what anyone else wants or needs?"

"*Excuse me*?" Adin stepped back

"You always do whatever you want. If we don't like it, if it's dangerous or stupid or just plain inconsiderate, you dance out of reach, move on, go home to your sister or your friends or your little house and your books."

"What are you *talking* about?"

Boaz gave Adin a shove that nearly knocked him over. "*You are Donte's weakness.*"

When he regained his footing, Adin grabbed his key card off the desk and shoved it into his jeans pocket. "Then Donte is safe because I would never, ever hurt him."

"The hell he's safe. That's just exactly *it*. The Donte Fedeltà who has survived for nearly five centuries can be broken as easily as your arm, Adin. He willingly undertook the care of a boy who is toxic to him, for *you*. He sends his bodyguards away from his side to watch out for *you*. You don't have to hurt him. All you have to do is continue on as you are, and the inevitable consequences of your existence will *kill* him."

Adin drew in a shocked breath. "That's a hell of a thing to say, Boaz."

"That doesn't make it any less true. You leave him open to attack by his enemies, you bring something poisonous into his home, you refuse to commit to him, to be his partner in every way—"

"Because I don't want to be turned? Because I don't want to lose my humanity?"

"Humanity is vastly overrated. Donte adores you. He's beyond loyal to you. If he allowed anyone—even you—to see how much he loves you, he'd be completely vulnerable to his enemies. He's a true prince among ordinary men. I don't know how you define humanity, Tredeger. I truly don't."

"He has no faith in me," Adin whispered.

"That's right. He doesn't. Why would he?" Boaz turned on his heel and headed for the door. He opened it and then looked back. "What have you done that didn't require one rescue after another since the day you met?"

The door closed behind Boaz with a metallic snap. After that, the silence was the deepest Adin had ever known.

Adin woke the next morning before dawn. He wasn't surprised at all. Even when he was a kid, if something preyed on his mind, worry, or guilt, his eyes snapped open right around four a.m., and he could never get back to sleep.

It didn't help that he felt spacey and jetlagged. His circadian rhythms were all messed up. It would be hours before the hotel staff would lay out the coffee and Danish that comprised the continental breakfast on his floor, and he was still hungry from missing dinner.

Even with Boaz's ugly words from the night before—or maybe because of them—he couldn't help dressing warmly and heading out the door. It meant putting himself in possible danger. It meant annoying Boaz once more, by giving him the slip if he'd really come along simply to be his bodyguard.

Adin couldn't help being a little annoyed as well. He hadn't signed on for the lifestyle of a mafia princess. He didn't want to live like the offspring of the American president. He was using a walking stick with a sword in it. He had both a phone, which was also a GPS tracker, and a light device that worked like a less pyrotechnic flash grenade to stun an enemy so Adin could make an escape. If he had human enemies he was certain Donte would insist he carry a gun on his person.

As each one of these things became necessary, he lost a little more of himself. He'd never imagined, even with all his traveling, that he'd ever have the need for anything more lethal than a pair of reading glasses. But Boaz had railed at him the previous night about his stubborn behavior *hurting* Donte. As if by remaining human he was costing Donte time and energy and resources that he needed to protect himself. As if he were costing Donte his health, and his well-being. Even his—for lack of a better term—life.

Was Boaz right?

He was right about one thing. Donte Feldeltà *was* a prince among men. And maybe it was past time for Adin to broaden his definition of humanity.

Adin took the elevator down to the lobby and exited out the front door. The doorman, dressed for the chill, misty weather, gave him a tired smile.

"Morning sir." His breath puffed out in wisps of fog. "Can I get anything for you?"

"I thought I'd take a walk," Adin peered at the man's nametag. "Kevin. I figured I'd head over to the wharf. By the time I get there it should just be coming to life."

"Yes sir, be sure to warm up with some nice, hot coffee and sourdough bread. Nothing like it."

"That sounds heavenly." Adin took a few steps and turned. "Thank you."

Adin first headed toward the embarcadero from the hotel on Post. From there, if he took Hyde Street into the Russian Hill area, through the neighborhood where Edward's painted lady Victorian stood, he would eventually come to the bay at the Hyde Street pier near his dad's beloved Balclutha, a short distance from Fisherman's Wharf. It was a long walk, hilly, and taxing, but his heart soared as he gorged on the unique smell of the city and he treasured the feel of fog on his skin.

Being back in San Francisco again more than made up for the energy he needed to expend. He drew its ambience to him like a cyclone. Out of all the places he'd lived, San Francisco and his tiny cottage in Bainbridge Island were the only two he'd ever really called home. San Francisco still held his heart like no place ever had because he'd spent the happiest, most carefree years of his life there while his family was still intact.

Maybe that was his problem—the word, *carefree*. He never expected to spend his life carefree, yet he'd done a considerable amount of racketing around the globe, putting one mile behind another, satisfying his intellectual curiosity without ever touching down and taking on any personal obligations. His home was cared for in his absence, his job—on hold since he'd purchased Donte's journal—had never required the commitment of a true academic career. He had no wife or family and no one to answer to but himself, and occasionally, his sister. His relationship with Donte was new enough that he was still trying to understand what it would mean.

Adin very much feared that Donte would be happy to substitute the word *reckless* for the word carefree. He treated Adin as if he'd travelled the globe, pleasing himself, unattached, free from the distractions of a normal life, free from worries of an economic or domestic nature, daring fate to throw what it would at him, *because he had*.

As if Adin were spoiled and thoughtless, *because he was*.

Maybe Boaz was right. Adin knew he didn't always think things through, and he rarely asked permission because he'd never had to make decisions with anyone else in mind.

When he'd first seen Bran, the horror of the situation so completely eclipsed everything else for him that he made the decision to get him out of there before he'd taken his next breath. A young boy—a child really—chained in a basement, fed like an animal, kept in the darkness, and left there for months to wonder why. *No*. Taking Bran out of that basement had been the right course of action whatever the cost.

But to keep him? To make promises? To adopt him like a pet?

Adin should have asked—not informed—Donte. He should have weighed his options before he charmed the boy, and bought him clothes, and made any assurances to him. What did he think? That they'd be one big happy family, two gay men still working out their *arrangement* and their slightly mysterious son? However sincere he'd been, he could never have taken care of Bran without the protection of both Donte and Santos, without Boaz's cooperation. He'd been foolish, and taken everything for granted. And now Donte was ill, Boaz was angry, and Edward and Tuan had become involved, all consequences he hadn't begun to consider.

Ah, shit. Boaz was right.

For some reason, maybe because of past disappointment or maybe from a lack of confidence that he'd hidden from even himself, he'd been deliberately keeping himself out of Donte's reach. Keeping his heart untouchable. Sure he'd been saying all along that he loved Donte—that Donte was his happiness—and yet he'd held himself aloof and apart because he believed *true love* was for suckers and fools.

He could almost hear Charles mocking voice. *We're above all that Adin. We're sophisticated men of the world. We don't need to tell ourselves lies to get what we want.*

Was that simply some shit Charles told him to get him to accept being treated like a toy? And when had Donte EVER treated him with that kind of casual disregard?

Adin frowned. There *was* that whole leaving-him-with-Santos-to-die affair. Thank heavens Tuan had arrived in the nick of time.

Tuan.

How had Tuan known to be there at all?

Adin began walking at a ground-eating stride and eventually he came to the end of the trolley line and turned, not toward the wharves and the food but in the other direction, heading for

Aquatic Park on the San Francisco Bay trail, toward the beach and maybe Golden Gate Bridge if his feet held out, and he didn't need to stop for food.

His mind was reeling.

By the time he got to the Palace of Fine Arts buildings, the sun had come up and the fog was dissipating. The seabirds could be seen wheeling overhead, looking for food. The city was waking up and so was Adin. He checked the time on his watches. Six-fifteen a.m. that meant three-fifteen in the afternoon in Paris. He hesitated before taking out his cell phone. While he was making up his mind whether to try Donte again, or to phone Boaz or get a cab, it rang in his hands.

"Tredeger."

"Are you *sightseeing?*" Boaz's voice held undisguised contempt.

Adin closed his eyes. "Thinking," he answered.

"It's about fucking time."

"I'm at the Palace of Fine Arts and I need—in no particular order—a ride home, breakfast, and to visit Bran at Edward and Tuan's."

"Anything else?"

"I'd like a pedal powered airplane," Adin told him. "Or a zeppelin."

"*Adin,*" Boaz growled.

"Oh, all right. I'm sorry, Boaz. You were right and I was wrong and I'm so very, very sorry." Adin swallowed. "I presumed a great deal. Maybe I don't have *relationship skills*. I only hope I'm able to say that to Donte in person sooner rather than later, and to make up for allowing him to wonder whether he comes first with me."

Boaz hesitated. "In that, you may be in luck."

"*What?*"

"It's possible that he might be on his way."

"Don't be cryptic. When?"

"I'm not being cryptic, it's just something Santos told me, that Donte might be well enough to be on the move again. I have no idea if it's even true."

"Does he know where we are?"

"Yes."

"Then why hasn't he called, damn him?"

"We'll have to ask him when we see him." Boaz hung up.

Edward ushered Adin and Boaz into the kitchen where Tuan was already sitting with his coffee, reading the paper. He looked up, owlish in his glasses, and grinned over a vase of freshly cut Irises. "Morning."

"Good morning." Adin dropped into a chair, still pathetically grateful to sit after his long walk. *Thank heaven he hadn't had to walk back to the hotel.* "Boaz and I brought donuts and I'm ravenous."

Boaz handed a bag to Edward, who opened it and exclaimed "*Zeppole!* I love these."

Adin sighed dramatically. "I asked for a zeppel*in*."

"Technically, you asked for a ride, breakfast, to come here and see Bran, a pedal powered aircraft, *and* a zeppelin." Boaz seemed in a much better mood.

Adin took one of the still-warm, eggy fritters. "These are delicious."

"How's Bran?" Boaz asked.

Edward grinned. "He's brilliant. A terrific kid. Asleep like a stone still this morning."

Tuan rolled his eyes. "Edward is already scouting private tutors to get him up to speed for school, and I'm going to have to fabricate a number of documents for him. His current identity is already proving to be far too pedestrian for Edward."

Adin peered at Tuan as if his earlier conjecture might be discernable on his face. Did Tuan and Donte know one another before Adin introduced them? "Is that going to be a problem?

Will it conflict with your job?"

Tuan hesitated. "Actually, documentation of otherworldly immigrants seeking asylum is part of the job. There are restrictions on travel and special requirements for foreign entities. Someone like Bran will be easy to document, and he'll sail through the restrictions because he's a minor, an orphan, and he has a family here to sponsor him."

"Namely, us." Edward grinned.

"Dear heavens." Adin raised his eyebrows.

"We talked about it last night," Tuan said. "Well, I listened mostly."

Edward cuffed Tuan lightly on the arm.

"Have you thought this through?" Adin asked.

Boaz coughed, and it sounded a lot like *look who's talking*.

"As much as we can in such a brief time," Edward answered.

"I can't think of anyone better suited to care for someone like Bran, but have you really considered what it will mean to foster a teenage boy?"

"We don't plan to foster him, we plan to adopt him," Edward explained. "He needs a *family*."

Adin couldn't stop himself from asking, "Tuan? Is that what you want?"

"I like him," Tuan said carefully. "I've always wanted to have a family, but I'm not as confident as Edward is that we're Bran's best choice."

Boaz spoke. "This doesn't have to be settled right away. What's important is that we keep him safe. Adin and Edward are both impulsive, and now isn't the time to allow that to dictate our thinking."

"Do you know something I don't?" Tuan frowned.

"Not for a fact." Boaz returned Tuan's grim expression. "But from what little Adin has told me, I doubt Harwiche will go gently into that good night. Nor will the men who sold Bran to him, if they realize where Bran has gone."

"Adin, when you saw him, what exactly did Harwiche say?"

Adin tried to explain that Harwiche set out to locate a changeling whose process had been interrupted and whose contract went unfulfilled, and how he believed the boy could somehow be a universal donor for bone marrow and organs that wouldn't be rejected by his body. "I got the feeling he meant to keep him prisoner and harvest—"

Edward blanched. "He's a lunatic."

Tuan seemed puzzled. "How did he know where to look for someone like that? An orphan on both sides."

Adin blanched. "I believe Harwiche hired someone to… help that along."

"*No.*" Bran's voice cracked like a whip from the doorway where he stood, his sleep-rumpled figure standing frozen with shock. Everyone fell silent.

CHAPTER EIGHTEEN

Bran swayed on his feet. "My *entire family* was killed so they could sell me to—"

Edward leaped up, his chair skittling backward over the wood floor. He caught Bran's arm before he could fall. "*Bran.*"

Tuan put his paper down and yanked his jacket off the back of the chair. "If it's true that Harwiche has further plans, I need to find out exactly where he is if I can."

Adin agreed wholeheartedly. "He said he was done coming after Bran, but I don't trust him. Then there are the men who sold him to me. They might come after me because Boaz took the money back."

Bran sat. "I'm glad you got your money back, Adin. I don't want those people to have your money, even if that means they kill me."

Tuan laid a hand on Bran's shoulder. "It won't come to that, I promise. Edward, I'm heading out. I'll look into those men and get the paperwork started. Set the alarms, and use the damned panic room if you need to."

"You have a panic room?" Adin asked. "How cool is that? Well. I guess you might need one, in your line of work."

"We needed the security system because of Edward's art collection." Tuan nodded and smiled at Edward. "But I had the panic room added because when I'm working I need to know that Edward is safe. Otherwise, it's hard to focus."

Edward offered Tuan one of his sweetest smiles. "Now we can keep Bran safe as well."

"See to it." Tuan leaned in and kissed Edward, and everyone politely looked elsewhere until they were finished. "I'm going to learn what I can. Boaz, maybe you can stay in touch with Santos in case he hears something?"

"I planned to take Adin to the house Donte uses while he's in this area," said Boaz. "Unless you have a better idea?"

"That's fine. Stay on your toes, Adin."

"I'll try."

"I have some tricks up my sleeve, Tuan," Boaz told him. "And I'm charged with Adin's safety."

Adin glanced at Boaz but his impersonal mask was firmly back in place.

Tuan left first, then Adin hugged Bran and Edward tightly. He and Boaz left as Edward extolled the virtues of his safe room as though he and Bran were going to live in a tree house like the Swiss Family Robinson. It sounded very enticing, Adin imagined, especially to someone so young. Adin doubted the reality would live up to the promise, and he hoped to hell they didn't have to use it.

Adin avoided any comparison between his current stay at Donte's borrowed estate in Marin County with the last time he'd been there. Then, he'd been injured in a bar, attacked by a group of vampires determined to pull on Donte's figurative cape and piss him off. When Boaz had driven him up the private, tree lined drive and the large attractive Tuscan inspired home had come into view, Donte had swept from it like the hero of a Bronte novel and carried him inside.

This time since it was spring, the trees were flowering optimistically, the air was redolent with the scent of newly mown grass, and there was no brooding master to be seen. It was simply a big house that looked as empty as Adin felt.

Boaz didn't speak but helped him carry the things they'd retrieved from the hotel up the stairs to the room he'd shared previously with Donte.

"It's nearly time for lunch, I'm going to see what's in the pantry, but I'll probably have to shop for provisions."

"I didn't sleep well," Adin told him. "If it's all right I'll just lie down for a while."

"I'll leave you to it then." Boaz started to back out of the door.

"Wait."

"Sir?" Boaz waited politely.

"About that. About last night. You were right, and I'm sorry." Adin turned to look out the window, held his good hand behind his back to keep from fidgeting while he made his apologies.

"I was overtired, Dr. Tredeger, and therefore my tongue ran faster than my brain."

"Stop it," Adin ordered. "Just stop pretending you care what I think. I heard you loud and clear."

Boaz frowned thoughtfully and repeated, "I was exhausted last night and I said things in anger that I didn't necessarily mean. I crossed a line and I regret it."

"It's fine." Adin waved him away. "You have a right to your opinion. We're stuck in this situation together. Feel free to share your thoughts with me anytime, even if they aren't…even if it might not be something I want to hear."

The tension seemed to leave Boaz's small frame, but not so much that he wasn't still entirely formal. "I do like you, Dr. Tredeger. That's never been an issue."

Adin's spirits rose a little. "In that case, please—for heaven's sake—no more eggs."

"Yes, sir, Dr. Tredeger." Boaz bowed out of the room. "I'll give that all the consideration it deserves."

Adin shook his head. He heard the sharp *snap* of the door when Boaz shut it and prepared himself for a quiche maybe, or another omelet at supper. He rummaged through his bags for a while, hanging up his clothes, putting others aside for the cleaners. One thing about travelling light, it was easy to unpack and shove the pilot case under the bed, or into the back of a closet. He found a split of champagne from the airline in his carryon and used it to wash down his pain reliever. His sister, the chemist, seemed to sit on the shoulder of his good arm saying *no*, while his arm on the other side said, *yes, yes* as soon as the pain began to diminish.

Within minutes, Adin was so tired he could barely hold his head up. He peeled off his clothes and dropped them at the foot of the bed, then slipped between the welcoming sheets. He was aware of Boaz asking him if he wanted lunch, but he answered that the thing he wanted most was sleep, which wasn't entirely true. What he wanted most was *Donte.*

Donte might be on the move again. That sounded so... ominous. As though Donte were a malevolent spirit or a marauding army. If he were *on the move*, Adin could only pray that at some point he'd look for Boaz, or call him to find out where they were now, and come to him.

Adin's yearning was so powerful he could almost see Donte fidgeting on an airplane, looking at his watch and gauging the position of the sun when he arrived. If he arrived after dawn, it would require that he wait in the airport for evening before he could go anywhere again, unless he went to the trouble of covering from head to toe, which was likely to garner a tremendous amount of unwanted attention in an airport since they'd heightened transportation safety. Donte had to plan his flights carefully and it could sometimes take days to get from place to place if he needed to layover in one city while the sun was out, in order to fly to his destination in darkness.

Adin dreamed that Donte stood beside him on the Golden Gate Bridge, hand in hand, to watch the sun set. The wind blew Donte's dark, wavy hair every which way, and he turned his collar up against the chill. Adin's gloved hands adjusted a scarf around Donte's neck—a rather dashing red scarf in a vibrant silk paisley—like the one he'd talked about with Bran. It did make Donte appear more approachable.

Adin pressed his forehead into Donte's chest and said, "Where are you?"

When Donte whispered, "I'm right *here*," Adin felt a warm, percussive burst of Donte's breath against his temple. It was so real he woke up with a startled cry. When Adin once again found himself alone, his heart hurt. The light outside was gone, and he'd left none lit in his room. It was dark except for the glow from the landscape lighting. Somewhere downstairs he could hear Boaz moving around in the kitchen.

He told himself not to be an idiot. Donte would come when he could, and all the self-pity and star wishes in the world wouldn't bring him one minute sooner. He'd hardened his heart against getting his hopes up, so when he heard that voice again, throbbing through his body as if he heard it on iPod earbuds, *"Caro, I'm right here,"* Adin wanted to believe it.

Something indefinable brushed his naked skin though, like a current of warm air, and finally Adin got up to look out the window, just in case. There were headlights at the end of the drive. Doors opened and closed on what appeared to be a taxi as its occupants moved behind it to transact business. The trunk opened. Then closed. The cab's headlights silhouetted a man wearing an overcoat, and pulling a pilot case, as it drew back out into the street and sped away, leaving the drive in near-total darkness. Adin's heart started to beat so hard against his ribs that he could hear it echoing through his head. He yanked the counterpane off the bed, wrapping it around him like a toga, and took off for the stairs. He took them as fast as he could safely run, dragging the silken fabric with him.

"Shit," he cursed as he stepped on it and had to hop to the front door on one leg, a difficult thing to do when he was well rested and sober but with a soft cast on his arm and slightly wobbly from the medication, it was entirely too much.

He burst outside and ran down the steps, barely concerned that now he was on level ground his makeshift garment flew out behind him and covered him not at all. By the time he ran fifty feet, he could see Donte clearly. He looked tired and grim. When they were about ten feet apart, Adin skidded to a halt on the pathway in front of him.

"Gods, you're a welcome sight, caro." Donte sighed heavily. "Why are you dressed like the Dalai Lama?"

Adin moved the rest of the way forward and reached for the lapel of Donte's coat. He wanted to welcome Donte home but was afraid he'd be unable to keep the emotion from his voice, uncertain whether he would laugh or start sobbing. When at last he tried to speak, it seemed he didn't have to choose one or the other because both tumbled out at once.

Finally he pulled the quilt around him and pressed his face into Donte's chest. "Ah *shit. Donte.*"

"What's all this, caro?" Donte held Adin while he shook with emotion.

For an answer Adin cupped the back of Donte's head and brought him down for a kiss, teasing and tasting, breathing his lover in before Donte parted his lips and his tongue dived inside.

Donte slid his hands from Adin's shoulders downward to span his waist just above the small of his back.

"I've missed you so much. When they wouldn't let me back in, I thought… I couldn't feel you. I thought…"

"Adin." Donte frowned deeply. "I would have spared you that if I could. As it is, there was very nearly one less *Peter* in the world when I heard how he harmed you."

"Whatever." Adin clung to Donte with his good arm. "It doesn't matter. You're here now, and that's all that counts."

Donte pressed a kiss to Adin's forehead. Adin reached out and caught Donte's case handle, intending to pull it up to the house, but Donte stopped him, taking Adin's good hand in his. "I will pull my case," Donte said firmly, "and you will tell me what you and Boaz and your adolescent entity have been up to while I was ill."

Adin leaned his head against Donte's shoulder. He felt whole just then, basking in a resurgence of the powerful connection that bound them. It wrapped around them as they moved up the driveway together.

As they ascended the stairs to the front door, Adin was alarmed to feel a weakness in Donte's limbs, a heavier step, a slight quiver of muscle, as if he didn't have his normal strength. He lifted his gaze and found that Donte was frowning in concentration. Adin pressed his lips together, leaving his questions unasked. It was enough for now to bring Donte inside, to their room and their bed where Adin could hold him and love him—

"I feel your desire, it's very nice."

"Nice?" Adin feigned outrage. "Tissues with lotion in them are *nice*. Girl scouts are *nice*. I plan to rock your world, my lover."

When they got to the door, Boaz stood to one side and took Donte's case from him. His expression was unreadable, but Adin knew how he felt. Adin's relief was giddy and palpable. Boaz didn't acknowledge it but Adin knew he shared it.

"It's good to see you, Boaz." Donte sniffed the air. "Quiche Lorraine. Except for the pun, which he makes every single time you serve it, Adin hates quiche."

"*Quiche me* you fool," Adin quipped, stupidly happy for the first time in days.

"Is that a fact?" There was a twinkle in Boaz's eye that left no doubt he knew that. *The shit.* "Good to have you here, sir."

"Good to be here. I think I'll go up with Adin and get him to tell me whether he's lost his clothes or taken holy orders."

"That sounds like an excellent plan, sir."

"I have a plan," Adin offered. Both Donte and Boaz ignored him.

"Good night, Boaz. I'll expect to you to visit our room with a tray of tea things and something to sustain Adin, since he hasn't eaten."

"Very good, sir." Boaz faded back through the unlit hallway into the kitchen, Adin and Donte started up the stairs. There was enough ambient light from the windows that Adin didn't feel the need to turn on the lights just yet. Something about the quiet, nearly empty house and the darkness, fit his mood perfectly.

"Don't you want to hear my plan?" Adin asked.

"Not particularly, caro." Donte shifted Adin's blanket so he wouldn't trip, and in so doing pulled him snug against a fully aroused vampire. "You'll find I have a plan of my own."

Again, Donte moved slower than normal, his step less certain. Once they reached the landing Adin slipped his arm around Donte to support him as they took the rest of the stairs. "What would that be?"

"I plan to allow you to twine yourself around me—as you always do—whereupon I shall do unspeakable things to you."

"You must have spies; you've sussed out my plan exactly and made it your own."

When they got to the top of the stairs, Adin drew Donte into the bedroom and pushed him back onto the bed. "You need me, don't you? I can feel you trembling."

"I didn't feed after I left France." Donte pulled his tie off, irritated. "The plane was delayed and the airport crowded. It was too brightly lit for me, and difficult to find a quiet space in which to rest, so I sat in a dark bar and drank a bad red wine. I didn't think—"

Adin sat beside him. "*Donte.* You have to remember what you need. Surely you could have found a willing partner? How do you go about that?"

"I just… It doesn't matter. I never thought I'd be weakened this quickly. It's a humbling thing."

"May I?" Adin indicated the reading light next to the bed. "I need to look at you."

"Of course, Caro. What a silly thing to ask."

Adin turned on the light and peered closely at Donte. His first glimpse stunned him. "Donte?" Adin fingered a new and very visible shock of silver in the waves of hair that fell over Donte's eye and said, in awe, "*Look at you.*"

Donte pulled his head back from Adin's grasp. "It's not so big a change, is it?"

Adin searched Donte's face for a clue to why his voice seemed uncertain. "Of course it's not. It's… glorious. You're beautiful. You're like a god. You know that right?" Adin's eyes stung. "I'll never tire of looking at you. I thought I'd never see you again, and my heart just shattered."

"I'm so sorry, caro." Donte drew him into his arms so tenderly that Adin gave in to his tears. Donte stroked his hair like a child's. "This is a case where the cure was worse than the disease, I'm afraid."

"What do you mean?"

Donte's arms tightened. "It required that I be… nearly reborn. Not an outdoor feast, I'm afraid."

Adin chuckled. "A picnic?"

"Yes. Not a picnic, as the saying goes."

Adin drew back. "What aren't you telling me?"

"It required that I be given the blood of a vampire, caro. A transfusion of blood that made me nearly as feral as I was when I was newly made. For a while I lost myself entirely."

Adin shivered again at how close he'd come to losing his lover. "Oh, Donte…"

"I still don't feel quite… I stayed away because…" Donte shook his head.

Adin swallowed hard. "Why?"

Donte seemed to measure his words carefully. "Although I tried to hide how sick I was from you, it became clear when Madame arrived that I wouldn't have lasted much longer. It was the only way. But it might have killed me. I might have been unable to recover whatever thin veneer of civilization keeps me from harming people."

"How could you hide something like that from me?" Adin thumped his chest. "I'm your lover. I'm your *partner*. I had a right to know."

"Of course you did." Donte pulled him in close again. "By the time I realized the problem, it was much too late to deal with it rationally."

"But how could you not tell me you were ill in the first place? You must have felt—"

"I only wanted to protect you and Bran. We made a promise to protect the boy and I wanted to honor that. To be honest, I thought I could find a way to neutralize whatever threat he posed to me long before—"

"You *knew.*" Adin sagged against Donte. "Bran said he thought you realized that he was the cause of your illness, and you didn't tell me because—"

"I was trying to solve a problem, caro. To create a positive outcome for both of us. I never dreamed it could put me in such danger. I'm afraid I'd begun to believe my own hype. It appears I'm not entirely invincible after all."

"You should have told me, Donte. You should have explained the situation and let me make a decision. There is nothing I wouldn't do to keep you safe. Nothing I wouldn't give up to ensure that."

Donte was silent as he contemplated that. "You've never had to make a life or death decision, have you?"

Adin shook his head. "Not really, no."

"Turning Santos… that was a situation in which I had no time to think. He can hate me for it but I carried Auselmo in my heart and I couldn't bear for that living reminder of him…" Donte closed his eyes. "Sometimes with the very best of intentions we commit the worst offenses."

"Donte." Adin gripped the lapels of his suit tighter.

"I thought I could spare you that. I thought I had time."

"Some choices need to be shared."

"I see that now. Forgive me, caro." Donte pressed his face into Adin's neck and nuzzled the skin there. He nipped at it, tonguing the delicate skin.

Adin arched a brow. "You still see me as an impetuous child."

"I don't right now. You smell delicious." Donte groaned, going from sad to seductive with one desperate sentence. His eyes no longer held that teasing, civilized light. His breathing grew erratic. His voice deepened until it was more like a low growl than ever. "*Gods. How I need you. Più amato.* I need everything you have to give me. Probably too much. It might be that this is—"

"I'm here." Adin's breath hitched, catching in his throat. His heart stuttered in fear at the change in his lover. But his cock apparently liked it. *A lot.* "I'm yours. Anything you need Donte, per sempre. I'm not afraid."

"You never seem to understand," Donte whispered sadly. "You should be."

Adin considered this. "You have to know that the monster entices me as much as the man, Donte."

Donte shook his head. "Sciocco."

"Fool I may be, but your fool," Adin told him. "Entirely yours."

CHAPTER NINETEEN

Adin turned off the light, and even as he turned he heard a low growl, a humming from deep within Donte's chest as his arm snaked out to pull Adin close. Their lips met in a bruising kiss, and Adin understood—maybe for the first time—that more had changed in the time they'd been apart, than Donte's hair. At least for the moment the tender lover who undressed him carefully and dotted him with tiny bites and kisses was gone. For whatever reason, Donte was hard and predatory. His grip was desperate, his intent purely to sate himself, to sink his cock and his fangs into flesh.

Adin could feel Donte fight it, sensed that he felt out of control, and maybe a little ashamed of his need.

Adin didn't hesitate, "Whatever you need from me, lover. Take it."

Donte reached for his hips and spun him over, parting Adin's legs with one hand while he unbuckled his trousers with the other. Adin shivered as he felt Donte's nails scrape his skin. He reached for the nightstand and the lube he'd find there and tossed it onto the bed where Donte could reach it. Buttons pinged onto the walls when Donte tore his shirt off, then his trousers hit the floor. Adin felt the weight of Donte's body shift behind him as he peeled the blanket away and ran his cool hand over the curve of Adin's ass.

Adin hissed with the pleasure of it.

Rough hands parted his cheeks, followed by the cool glide of a dollop of lube, and just that suddenly, fingers worked their way inside. Adin grunted at the abrupt intrusion, shifting his hips until he could relax and take what Donte meant to give him. Soon, the burn gave way to pleasure, and Adin pushed back against Donte's hand. He clawed the mattress for purchase with his good hand, balling the sheet between his fingers until his knuckles were white.

"Damn," he panted.

Three fingers pumped deep inside him, nudging his sweet spot with every push. His hips rocked with them and the tip of his cock brushed against the sheet beneath him, every movement he made ratcheted up the tension just that much higher until he knew if he didn't have Donte soon he would start screaming.

"*Please...*" he begged. "Donte. I need..."

"Up on your hands and knees," Donte ordered, and Adin did what he asked without question, keeping his weight off his bad arm, keeping his soft cast close to his chest. Donte nudged between his legs, then pulled Adin back into what had become his favorite position, Donte kneeling with Adin in his lap, his back to Donte's chest, those big delicate hands crossed possessively over Adin's chest to hold him tightly while his cock pistoned in and out of Adin's ass.

Adin lay his head back onto Donte's shoulder and simply let himself be taken. Donte took complete control. Adin lifted his good arm and reached back to cup Donte's head in his hand, stroking his soft hair, even as Donte dropped one of his hands to explore Adin's cock, his balls, and the soft, stretched tender skin behind them. A questing finger rubbed and pushed at Adin's entrance, along with the cock that filled him. Adin cried out, the sound coming from deep inside his throat, shocked to be handled that way.

Donte pulled his hand back, but Adin slapped his own hand down over it, dragging it back and nudging its owner to act on his intentions. Adin had never felt anything like it, he was so full, so overstimulated that precome oozed from his cock in waves. Each fresh surge brought the tingling pleasure of an orgasm without the respite of climax. As cock and finger filled him and brushed his sweet spot, the steady throb of almost unbearable bliss grew deep inside him, building to an impossible crescendo, indicating an explosive release that hovered just out of reach.

At some point Adin became aware of the sounds he was making, strangled cries with each thrust of Donte's hips. Donte's free hand stroked his nipples, pinched and played, scratching and twisting, until the pain and pleasure got mixed up in Adin's head, and all he could think of was Donte. He started to murmur his lover's name, over and over, with each rise and fall and slap of their flesh, until Donte's hand gripped him hard around his neck and he felt the first scrape of the vampire's teeth against his skin.

"*Yes*," Adin cried out. "Do it."

"Who am I?" Donte demanded.

"You're mine," Adin answered. "You're Donte."

"I am Nicolo Pietro di Sciarello. And *you* belong to *me*."

"Yes," Adin sobbed out, arching and stretching and begging for his release. "*Yes*. I belong to you. *Please*, Donte."

Donte shoved him face down on the pillow, and held him there, one hard hand in the center of his back. He continued his punishing thrusts, grinding Adin's hips against the bedding until Adin felt his balls tingle and draw up.

"You wanted me to fuck you because I'm your *monster*."

"*Yes*." Adin gave him everything. Now that his cock was skimming along the bedding, the friction in his ass and on his cock short-circuited his brain. "*Yes*."

"You want me to take you to the brink of oblivion. To devour you."

"Yes! *Yes, yes*," Adin hissed, as the first come spat from his cock. "*Yes. Please, yes*."

Donte struck. Adin felt him drink in deep drafts of blood, satisfying himself, even as Adin's world tilted on the axis of immense pleasure, adrenaline and fear. Donte didn't stop, he didn't let up. At first when Adin felt light-headed, he tried to struggle, and Donte pushed him down as though he were a child, as though he had no strength at all.

Because he didn't.

Soon it didn't matter because Adin could only lie there beneath the monster in Donte Fedeltà, beneath the predator, and cry into the back of his hand. Soon, he knew, soon he would be lifeless, and there was simply nothing, *nothing at all* he could do about it.

Adin didn't feel foolish, as Donte said he should. He didn't feel fear. He didn't feel anger. There was only resignation, and the bitterness of loss.

I love you.

Everything you are.

I could have been more for you. I should have been stronger.

I won't be there to love you when you lose yourself again.

Ah, shit, my lover.

I'm not ready…

When he heard the crash and clatter of china and silver, and the cursing, his head spun and things grew dark, as if he were signing off at the end of the night like a television station. It went from what appeared to be a frightening and fuzzy reality show on a big screen and grew smaller and smaller until even that—the tiny dot of light that remained—winked out.

Adin ran. He had to find…someone. He stumbled over cobblestones in the thickest fog he'd ever seen, barely noticing the ground beneath his feet. He guessed he was in Paris by the texture and age, the sheer familiarity of the dirty stone buildings as the shifting mist briefly revealed them. At first he didn't recognize the place exactly, but after a few moments of squinting, of pressing his nose against shop windows and listening for sounds, he got the vague idea he was once again in the historically protected Marais, where he'd found Bran. The place he'd encountered Bran that first time, the occult shop, had been near rue de Montmorency and the home of Nicolas Flamel. Immediately Adin's heart quickened. Bran. *He had to find Bran, who could share his dreams and access his thoughts and memories. Donte was out there alone and Bran could—conceivably—connect them.*

Hands reached out from the darkness and clutched at him, stabbing him with pins, trying to pull him into the ancient shops along the street; shops that smelled of embalming fluid and decay. The more they held him the harder he fought.

Tremendous noise and flashing lights, along with the sickening lurch and weightlessness of dangling in the air that only a helicopter produced, captured all of Adin's attention for a minute.

"You'll like the resort," Charles told him. "The helicopter is a nice touch don't you think? Shep always takes a private helicopter. He hates driving the mountain roads. Although once we got stuck there when the chopper couldn't fly. Are you all right?"

"Sure," Adin replied automatically. He wondered if Bran was playing with the controls of his consciousness again. He hadn't seen Charles since that disastrous semester at Princeton. "But I don't like helicopters much. They fall out of the sky like rocks. No coasting."

"Ah, you worry too much. You don't want to live forever, Adin."

That was odd. "I don't?" Adin asked. "Why not?"

"What would you do? You're bright enough that you'll be bored to death before you're thirty, and then you'd spend eternity looking for something meaningful that isn't out there, along with every other dumb son of a bitch. You'll never be happy."

Adin heard his father's voice. "I'm happy. Why won't Adin be happy?"

Charles gave a delicate shrug. "Adin isn't like you. He's not complacent. He's never going to be content to live an ordinary life."

Adin's father laughed. "I should hope not. I didn't raise him to be ordinary. And for that matter, my own life has been anything but ordinary."

"Please. You live in the city, you work as a teacher. *You have a wife, two children, and a mortgage. You can hardly get any more normal"*

That's why advertising works so well, *Adin thought. You can spin anything. "My father really has been anything but normal."*

"You'll never be like him though," Charles reminded him gently. "You can't. It's not in your nature."

A voice Adin didn't recognize said, "Adin, if you can hear me, squeeze my fingers. C'mon buddy. I need you to squeeze my fingers."

Adin didn't have the strength. His heart raced and he felt out of breath. His skin was clammy and cold. "Can't. Bran?"

"You don't have to listen to Charles anymore, Adin." Bran's voice. Thank fuck.

"Bran!"

"No, listen to me," Bran said. "I know why you want me here, and I'll deal with Donte later."

"No, now, Bran."

"Later," Bran said firmly. "Right now you need to fight. Squeeze the EMT's fingers, Adin. Do it, or Donte never gets your message."

Charles laughed. "What, that he's in love? Don't make me laugh. Love is for suckers, Adin. Not us. We can take what we want. We have the whole world to play in. Shep and I…"

"You two only care about yourselves," Bran said angrily. "You treated Adin like dirt."

Charles voice changed until it was soft and seductive. "You're a bright little thing, aren't you? A looker too, although your taste in clothes is deplorable. How'd you like to be my new research assistant, what did you say your name was?"

"See what I mean?" Bran asked Adin.

"Adin, be reasonable. Men like us, we're at the top of the food chain."

"No, we're not," Adin said decisively.

"Sure we are, because we're free."

"You're not free. You're just…fickle," Adin's father said. "You're just a conspicuous consumer. And now that I get a good look at you, I'm wondering what my son ever saw in you."

"Bran, are you doing this? It's like the Wizard of Oz. If a dog pulled back the curtain would you be working the controls?" Adin listened for an answer. "Bran?"

Silence. For some reason Adin began to worry. It was as if they'd left him in a room all alone. All the voices had disappeared, all the sounds, the traffic, the helicopter, the EMT's voices were gone as if they'd never existed.

"Bran?" Adin asked, more urgently. "Bran, where are you? Where is everyone?"

"Bran's busy." Santos's voice.

"Perfect." Adin muttered. "Another country heard from."

"Here, take this." Adin felt lips press down on his, dark and seductive. They knew what they were doing and soon a tongue stroked along his lower lip and he parted them, surprised by the pleasure of it. Fluid pushed through to gush past his teeth and over his tongue. Lots of it.

Adin gagged and coughed as a hand came down on his lips and prevented him from expelling the awful, coppery warm liquid.

"Swallow." Adin blinked, and when his vision cleared Donte stood over him.

Adin shook his head.

Donte repeated the word. "Swallow."

Adin had no choice but to do as he was told. When he'd finally gagged all the horrible, salty liquid, down he asked, "What the fuck? Donte?"

Donte's face seemed to dissolve, and instead, Santos's face smiled down at him.

"Happy Easter, Adin," Santos told him, his eyes like dark holes that framed single pinpoints of light. "The oldest and most arcane mystery of all." He smiled in a nearly fatherly way and disappeared. Everyone was gone. Everything was silent.

"Bran?" Adin called out. "Bran?"

When Adin woke, the first thing he saw was Edward. He opened his mouth to say something, but found himself unable to talk past his dry mouth and scratchy throat. He jerked his head minutely and got Edward's attention that way. Edward practically leaped to his feet to bring him soothing hands and ice chips for his dry mouth.

Edward's eyes were red rimmed and swollen. "Adin?" He clasped Adin's good hand gently. Adin tried to acknowledge that in some way but couldn't seem to make his body move.

"Thank God."

Adin looked up dully, reminded of all the times Edward had been there for him. His throat hurt just to look at him. His face crumpled, but no tears would come.

"Now…" Edward soothed. "There's no need for that. You're going to be fine, baby."

A shape detached from the wall on the far side of the room and swept out the door. *Shit.* Donte. He probably blamed himself and was currently going to be harder than ever to deal with. Adin turned panicked eyes toward Edward, willing him to go after Donte and bring him back.

"Let him be." Edward glanced back at the door. He gave Adin an ice chip to suck on. "He should have known better than to come to you in that condition. What the hell did he think was going to happen if he—"

Adin squeezed Edward's hand as hard as he could. "*Go,*" he croaked.

"*Ow.*" Edward pulled his hand back. "Oh, all right all ready. I'll go get him. But if you ask me…" Adin poked him hard and he left.

Tuan came in after Edward left. He gave Adin a relieved smile. "Good to see you awake. I had them airlift you here," Tuan gestured to the private room, "because this facility has a trauma center for victims of paranormal events. They're equipped to deal with all kinds of… Let's just say it's specialized."

Adin blinked at him. He tried clearing his throat, and it was a little easier. "*Thirsty.*"

"Yes, indeed, I'm sure you are." Tuan picked up the cup of ice chips that Edward had been doling out and placed one on Adin's tongue. "Besides trying to track down Donte, Edward will probably inform the doctor that you're awake and I'm sure any restrictions on food and drink will be lifted forthwith."

Adin nodded. "*Water.*"

"Soon, I promise." Tuan's voice was kind. "You won't be the first to be treated for near exsanguination by a lover, and you won't be the last. Humans are like moths to a flame with vampires."

Adin lowered his lashes. Sucking on the ice chips seemed to

help. He swallowed once or twice to test his jaw. "I am, anyway."

"It's nothing to be ashamed of Adin. It's the way things are."

Adin wanted to say he wasn't ashamed at all. At any rate, anything he said would be taken like the excuses a person makes for a drunken spouse or an abuser. It would hardly matter to anyone that Adin was—at last—completely confident with regard to the strange turns his life had taken. During what he had thought were the final moments of his life, even as he'd wept at the thought of losing consciousness for the last time, he was aware he wouldn't give up the time he'd spent with Donte for anything. And he'd nearly lost the chance to tell him...

"Boaz brought Bran. He'll want to see you. He's very unhappy with us that we didn't bring him in last night. He said something about you needing him. But to be honest..." Tuan allowed his normally taciturn face show emotion as he brushed Adin's cheek lightly with his knuckles. "It was touch and go. That was..." Tuan swallowed, "hard to watch."

Adin feared to ask. "I was never alone with Donte, was I? Here?"

Tuan shook his head. "The minute we left the helicopter the medical team took you from us. After you were allowed visitors Edward and I never left you alone. Donte seemed worried about his enemies and I... Maybe I was worried about Donte."

"I need to see him." Adin's cracked and parched throat hurt as fear gripped him. He fussed with the controls for the bed. "Up. *Please.*"

Tuan helped him to raise the back of the hospital bed. Adin's head swam. He pushed against the side rails until Tuan lowered them. When he tried to swing his legs over Tuan wouldn't allow it.

"Stay where you are, Adin. Don't fight me, you're not strong enough to be walking around."

Adin wanted to scream with frustration. The barest push of Tuan's hand was more than enough to press him back down; he was so weak. Tuan sat beside him. Adin's breathing became shallower and his pulse more rapid. He had no strength to fight Tuan's hold on him. He reached out with his heart instead, sending Donte a message, hampered by his physical limitations but carrying the full weight of his determination.

Come back. Stay with me. I need you.

And then he thought of that curious dream, the kiss, the blood, first Santos's face and then Donte's, his hand over Adin's mouth and had a horrible frisson of fear. Had he woken with a coppery taste in his mouth...?

Donte, what have you done?

Gods.

It was only a dream, wasn't it?

CHAPTER TWENTY

Tuan sat with Adin until the door opened and Donte walked in. He had obviously thrown on casual clothes in haste while waiting for the EMTs. He wore a fine-gauge cashmere sweater and a pair of jeans Adin had never seen before beneath one of his many long, dark coats. This one—a vintage wool military topcoat very much like Bran's—swung around his calves when he turned after closing the door behind him. Donte glowered and took up a large amount of space in the small, private hospital room, causing the air to crackle with tension that Adin could feel in his chest.

Adin cleared his throat. Tuan reluctantly excused himself and left.

Donte's hair stood out at odd angles, as though he'd hung onto the outside of the helicopter while they'd flown from place to place, but Adin was too tired to laugh, and too dehydrated to cry. What came out was more like a cough, followed by a helpless gurgle that went silent when Donte pinned him with an angry gaze. Donte wasn't likely to forgive himself. Adin knew he'd have to tread carefully. He held out a hand, but Donte didn't come to him.

"*Donte.*" Adin frowned.

Donte frowned right back and he was better at it. He didn't move. "In case it has escaped your notice, I nearly killed you."

"*Ah, jeez.*" Adin fussed with the sheet covering him. "Yeah. So what's your point?"

Donte ran his hand through his hair and Adin began to understand how it got that way. The usually resplendent Donte didn't seem to care what he looked like. How odd. "You are an idiot."

"Absolutely."

"Sciocco," Donte said explosively.

"Pazzo," Adin countered.

"*Imbecile.*"

"I'm a *clown.*"

"Yes. Even that." Donte inched forward. "You cried."

"Yes." Adin stopped smiling. "I did."

Donte stepped forward once more. "You were afraid."

"I was." Adin never took his eyes off Donte's. "I am."

Donte's façade eroded then, and it was painful for Adin to watch, as if an ancient rocky edifice crumbled and fell away into the sea. "I cannot do this," Donte whispered.

Adin held his arms out. "I know."

Donte was shaking his head no when he moved forward. He leaned over the hospital bed and wrapped his arms around Adin's waist, putting his head across Adin's lap. Adin pushed his fingers—IV tubes trailing after them, attached to the back of his hand—through Donte's dark waves, brushing them back from his face. He found the wisp of silver and smoothed it carefully. Soothing. Caressing Donte's tense face, using his thumb to smooth the tightly clenched jaw. He continued stroking until he felt Donte's body relax slightly, until Adin felt something shudder through it as Donte unwound.

"Shh," Adin said stupidly, because Donte didn't make a single sound. He just held on like a limpet, but didn't breathe, didn't move. Cold and lifeless, except for the ardor with which he clung, and the waves of intense satisfaction that Adin felt through his skin and his muscle to his very bones. The love he felt surrounded them like mist.

My monster.

"Sometimes I hate you, più amato," Donte said then, and Adin knew very well that he meant it.

"Right back atcha, my lover." Adin continued stroking his soft hair.

Donte tightened his grip—if possible—and stayed that way

for another few minutes before he took an audible breath, more for show, and stood. He cupped Adin's face in his hand and peered at him. "You are weak."

"I am indeed. And not just in the usual, I'm human, and you are the apex of—"

Donte tensed. "Not today, *pazzo*, I am not in the mood."

"All right," Adin agreed. "I *am* weak. I can't get out of bed."

Donte pursed his lips and shook his head. "Bran will wish to see you since he appears to have adopted you. He was beside himself with grief. He's probably going to challenge me to a duel."

"And of course you will be a responsible adult and not fan the flames with your usual insouciant charm?"

"You mean I must handle him with soft gloves?"

"I mean exactly that," Adin told Donte.

"I hear you. I can't even be around him, caro. I will not eat him."

Adin said nothing.

Donte shifted uncomfortably. "That is an idiom I find less appealing today."

Adin laughed out loud. He reached out and grabbed the lapel of Donte's coat and pulled him close, pressing his cheek against Donte's, then whispering in his ear, "I could not love you any more than I do. It's not physically possible. Per sempre, amore mio, I'm so, so sorry."

"You have nothing to be sorry for." Donte cleared his throat. "You called me back, and I am here. Perhaps I am the fool."

"Yes."

"Heaven help me." Donte pressed his lips to Adin's, nudging Adin's legs aside to sit beside him on the tiny hospital bed. Adin wound his good hand around Donte's neck, fussing with the IV line to get it out of the way. His broken arm was cumbersome and awkward. He opened for Donte's tongue when they kissed, and pulled him close when he slid down, willing him to forget everything and take what he had to offer.

All his love. All his faith. His body, his heart, his future.

"Ah, lover—" A commotion outside the door caught their attention and they broke apart.

Boaz came into the room followed by Tuan and Edward. "Is Bran here? Have you seen him?"

"No." Donte stood and covered Adin carefully with the lightweight sheet they'd pushed down while they kissed. "I assumed he was with you."

"I left him for a bit to make some phone calls. When I came back, he wasn't in the lobby or the cafeteria. I've checked with the security guards and they don't remember seeing him leave."

Tuan stepped forward. "Where else might he have gone?"

"Nowhere. Why would he? He was adamant that we bring him to see Adin as soon as he was conscious."

"What the hell?" Adin asked, even as he yanked the tape off his arm and pulled out his IV line.

"What do you think you're doing?" Donte demanded.

"We have to look for Bran. Will someone help me find some clothes?" Adin's face was already pale and beaded with sweat. There was no way he'd be able to walk unaided. He gestured to Boaz. "Get me a wheelchair, please."

"Adin—" Boaz began.

"*No.* You were right, Boaz. I didn't give a single thought to what it would mean to bring Bran into our lives. I didn't worry about the consequences and I didn't care about anything else but doing what I wanted."

"I didn't say that, exactly." Boaz opened the cabinets in the room, coming up empty. "I'll need to get you some scrubs. You weren't dressed when we brought you here."

"Oh shit." Adin imagined how it must have seemed, he'd have been lying in bed when the EMTs arrived, he'd probably been covered with sweat and come and bite marks. He closed his eyes for a second. *Great.* "The point is, I brought Bran here, and I'm responsible for him. He trusts me."

Donte nodded. "He loves you. While you were unconscious, you called for him over and over and I'm certain he was aware of it." Donte looked away, his features tightening into a mask that Adin found difficult to interpret. "For the record, I would have liked it had you called to me."

"You can't think—"

"Another time, più amato," Donte answered quickly. "Let's secure the safety of your toxic adoptee, shall we?"

"*Donte.*" Adin caught Donte's arm and growled, "Someday you'll make my head explode."

"I was imagining just that very thing, actually," Donte told him. "But we'll save that for later when we've more time."

"I hope you mean that in the nicest possible way." Adin bumped him weakly with his fist.

"The jury is out, caro. Behave yourself, and I will consider just how I will explode that remarkably empty head of yours later. I can bring both pleasure and *pain.*"

Boaz returned to the room with borrowed scrubs. Donte made short work of working them up Adin's legs, and then lifted his torso in order for Boaz to remove the standard gown and slip the shirt on over his head. Adin grunted when his head came through.

Adin experienced waves of dizziness when Donte picked him up like a baby and carried him out the door. He wondered how much help he could be in his condition but he didn't want to prove Boaz right by allowing others to take care of his responsibility. He clasped his hands around Donte's neck and moaned when he was deposited in a cold wheelchair.

Donte leaned over and whispered in his ear, "Are you certain you can do this, caro? If you cannot, I'll see that Bran is brought to you, safe and sound. I promise on my life."

"Fat lot of good that will do me, since you're *dead*," Adin teased, cautiously letting go and gripping the armrest with his good hand. "Let me catch my breath." Adin didn't want to tell Donte that was far more difficult than he expected.

Donte took the handholds of Adin's wheelchair. "I'll take Adin and look around the hospital. If he's here I will know it."

"We'll all know it." Tuan grimaced. "There'll be a trail of healthy house plants and aging vampires in his wake."

Adin placed his hand on the wheel to stop the chair when Donte would have pushed him. "Maybe I'd better go alone."

Donte snorted. "This is why I love you, you should consider a career as an *attore comico*."

Tuan knelt in front of the wheelchair and adjusted Adin's legs. "I am going to go to administration to see if my credentials will get me a look at the hospital security tapes. I want to see if Bran's left here, or if anyone else I recognize has arrived…"

"We'll find him." Adin's jaw tightened. "And then we'll kill him for giving us a scare."

Adin and Donte began their search of the hospital by trying to consider the places that might interest a boy like Bran. They covered the gift shop, the florist, the vending machines, the dining area, and one or two patio areas where the hospital staff might go for a break or to eat out of doors. They checked the chapel yet still there was no sign of Bran anywhere. Eventually, Donte and Adin made their way to the ER, where they finally found Bran, sitting with his hands folded in his lap. Next to him a teenage girl slept with her legs curled under her and her head on his shoulder.

"I should have known. *Cherchez la femme.*" Donte stopped the wheelchair. "You go on ahead; I'll call Tuan and Boaz and let them know we've found him."

Adin turned and met Donte's eyes. "Thank you. I'm sorry for all the trouble."

Donte shook his head and dropped a kiss on Adin's forehead. He pulled his phone from his coat pocket and left to find a place to make a call.

Adin wheeled over to where Bran sat. "Hi there."

Bran flushed but didn't move. His friend slept on. "Hi."

Adin lowered his voice to avoid waking her. "We were frantic just now when we couldn't find you."

Bran turned and spoke in the girl's ear, she nodded and leaned back. Her brown eyes opened and Adin saw they were puffy and red rimmed from crying.

"Thank you," she told Bran quietly.

Adin watched their gazes lock as something passed between them. Bran looked solemn and sad, and the girl, a sweet-looking thing in jeans and a white blouse with a fitted, feminine jacket caught both his hands and gave them a squeeze. Bran stood then, and she let him go before shoving her dark hair back from her face and taking a deep, shuddering breath. Bran gave her one last smile and left her there, taking a place behind Adin's wheelchair without asking and pushing him toward the elevators, located in a hallway off the central lobby.

Bran pushed the button to call a car and leaned against the wall. "I'm sorry you were worried."

"Of course we were worried. Please don't forget there are people out there who—"

"That was Kelsey. Her brother drowned this morning."

Adin's heart froze. "What?"

"She has a seven-year-old brother, and he drowned in their pool. They brought him in and her parents are with him now. They have him hooked up to machines, but he's already gone. They just don't know it."

Adin felt sick with sorrow for the family. "How do you know it?"

Bran shrugged. "I was there when they brought him in. I was close enough… I just know."

"Does she?"

"She does. But she doesn't understand why. Her intuition tells her he's gone. I can—I did—reinforce that so she wouldn't hold on to hope." Bran's eyes looked older than old.

"Were you able to help her?"

"Maybe," Bran said. "Who knows? How can anyone help with something like that? She seemed to feel better when she was close to me. I helped her find good memories. Sweet dreams."

"I'm sorry."

"Me too." Adin was silent until the doors opened and Bran pushed him into the empty elevator. "They wouldn't let me see you, even though you were asking for me."

The doors closed and they started the ascent to Adin's floor. "I know. I'm sorry. They said that it was touch and go. They wanted to spare you that."

As the elevator started to rise, Adin felt a sick plummeting of his stomach. His heart fluttered oddly and he became short of breath. Bran squatted next to the wheelchair, so they faced one another. "Listen to me, Adin. We don't have much time. You need to ask yourself about your dreams last night. How much was me, and how much was real."

"What?" Adin shook his head. "I don't understand you."

"I think…" Bran bit his bottom lip. "I think someone tried to turn you. If you were depleted enough by Donte's attack, it would have been easy to start the process." Bran reached out and pressed the Emergency Stop button. The alarm rang so unbearably loudly in the elevator car Adin ducked his head and covered his ears. Bran pulled his hands away and continued to speak. "I don't know if it really happened, Adin. *I don't know.* I was in your head and I felt someone else there."

"What do you mean?"

"I mean someone else was manipulating you. Misdirecting you. And either they started the process that will turn you from human to vampire, or they wanted you to think they did. If they made you swallow even a mouthful…"

"I dreamed that someone kissed me, and my mouth filled with…" Adin stopped, suddenly frozen by the possibility that drinking blood represented.

"That's what I mean. If that part of the dream wasn't me manipulating you, if it was real, then it might have started the process. It isn't always easy to tell at first, but it doesn't take much."

Adin drew in a lungful of air although it didn't feel like he got enough. "I dreamed it was Santos who kissed me, but then I saw Donte's face."

Bran put his hand on Adin's shoulder. "You're sweating."

"I'm scared, Bran." Adin's muscles began to tremble. He was dizzy suddenly, as if the floor of the elevator dropped out from beneath him. "I don't feel so…" The walls spun around him as Bran pushed the button that silenced the alarm and put the car in motion again. "Bran?"

"I'm here." Bran's panicked voice reached him from what seemed like a long way away. "I think it's me that's making you sick."

"That can't be it. No one would…" Adin murmured. But he was in deep trouble and he knew it. His heart sped up and his breathing grew erratic. "But I can't…seem to catch…my breath."

The elevator doors opened, and Bran pushed Adin out onto his floor, calling for help. The last thing Adin heard was Bran telling someone to call for Tuan.

Chapter Twenty-one

Before Adin opened his eyes he listened. He heard wind. It lifted his hair and rushed against his eardrums. It batted the rigging and caused the ropes and cleats to slap and knock against the mast. Adin heard sails snap and fill and felt himself lifted up and down. He struggled for balance on the deck of a boat as it rode over waves through the sea. Water lapped against the hull as they bobbed and pitched gently from side to side. Sunshine warmed his face in a direct challenge to the breeze, which kissed him, brisk and chilly. When he finally looked, he wasn't surprised to see he was sitting on the deck of his father's sailboat, the Odd Bean.

Adin's first waking thought was pure elation, a sudden, intense rush of joy at seeing his father at the helm again. His heart swelled when he saw Keene Tredeger's boyish delight. He was in his element on the water, a man who'd grown up reading first Stevenson and Defoe and Melville, then in later years lived on Patrick O'Brian and C.S. Forrester.

The sun was barely breaking the horizon, and his father was holding a mug of coffee that steamed into the air. "Early bird gets the dawn," he said, smiling. "Of course your mother and sister can't be woken at this hour."

"They get the sunset and they see it as a fair trade."

"Little do they know..."

Adin's father was so vividly alive at that early hour Adin wondered if he'd fortified his coffee with Irish whiskey. He looked around on the deck and found his own mug. He lifted it to his lips and sure enough, it was bracing in more ways than one. "You spiked the coffee?"

"Arrrr." His father grinned. "A little grog never hurt anyone."

"Don't let mom hear you say that."

"She'd have to get out of our bunk to stop me, wouldn't she?" He lifted his head and let the wind caress his face.

Adin leaned back and looked up into the sails.

"This is the best thing we've ever done," his father announced. "I've never felt more alive."

"But this is how you died." Adin sipped his coffee. "In this boat. There was a storm and the Odd Bean went down."

Adin's father's face never lost its elated expression, but he was silent for a long time. "I know."

"You and mom both drowned. Your bodies were recovered but we put you back into the sea."

"Thanks for that," his father said. "It's what I wanted."

"Would you do anything differently?" Adin asked. "If you knew?"

"Maybe." Keene shrugged. "I might have waited twenty years before I bought the boat."

Adin nodded. "I thought you'd say something like that."

"What about you?"

"What do you mean?"

"You heard me, what would you do? Differently, I mean. If you had a second chance?"

Adin gasped and reached out blindly, striking his broken arm against the metal frame of the bed. He braced himself for the intense physical pain he knew would follow, but it never came. His arm should have hurt a lot. It should have hurt like *hell*. He opened his eyes and found Tuan sitting in the chair beside his bed. He wore a worried expression on his face, even as he got up and said, "Shh, Adin. Everything's going to be all right."

"What's going on?"

"I don't know if—"

"Was what Bran said true? Am I…?"

Tuan's expression tightened. "Yes."

Adin closed his eyes. "Who?"

"Adin—"

"I asked you who did this to me." Adin ground his teeth together against a wave of nausea.

Tuan lifted his hands, palms up. "We don't know for certain.

We're still trying to get answers…"

"*Tuan.*"

"All right. *Yes.* Based on the information we have so far, and given that none but a handful of people know you're here? We have to assume Donte did it."

Adin shut his eyes, unable to think. How did he feel about that? How was he supposed to feel about that? His entire body felt cold suddenly—as if he'd been bathed in ice—and he began to tremble. Shaking like he was in shock. Maybe he was.

"Tuan?"

"Don't panic, Adin. This is…" He stood and gripped Adin's hand. "This is just the beginning. But you have to know we'll do everything we can. Everything we know how to do to help you through this."

"Can you stop it?" Adin said through clenched teeth.

Tuan shook his head.

"*So cold.*" Adin shivered as he looked around. "Where's Edward?"

"He's with Bran."

"*Fuck.*" Adin held his body rigid, trying to keep it from shaking apart but it was no use. "Bran. Wh-what ab-bout B-bran?"

"Edward will take care of him. You'll be here for a while, Adin. I'm not going to lie to you. This isn't going to be easy, and it's not always successful. There's a chance you won't survive it."

Adin considered this. "W-where is D-d-donte?"

Tuan shook his head sadly. "I'm sorry. I don't know."

The days and nights that followed took on a dizzying, disorienting sameness for Adin. His dreams, which were already vivid and unpredictable since he'd met Bran, took on a nightmare quality as he changed, imbuing him with new senses, dark cravings and a dreadful and utterly insistent set of phobias. The most potent was a terror of the sun that caused such vividly realistic panic attacks—all unnecessary because he'd been locked away early on in a room that had no windows, deep in the basement where they handled cases like his—that he struggled against the restraints until his flesh burned and his screams could be heard throughout the hospital's long corridors. Ultimately, someone would then come to subdue and sedate him leaving him weak and powerless, until the next time it happened.

He had no way to gage the passage of time. It was dark and quiet, sealed off from the outside world to prevent the stimulation of his new and possibly uncontrollable vampire behavior. He could hear nothing from the outside, see nothing, and sense nothing unless someone opened the sliding door and entered his room. Bran's calming presence no longer found its way into his dreams. Consequently, he faced them alone, unprepared for the sinister new longings he felt.

The hospital staff made their way into and out of his room in the faint glow of the poorest light, meeting his needs for the most part, offering palliative care, as if he were a hospice patient, waiting for the inevitable. He wanted, in his lucid moments, to be cured, to be with family or friends, to be free of the room and the dark IV and all its implications. He wanted to be Dr. Adin Tredeger again.

When anyone entered, Adin watched them constantly, breathing in the richness of the blood that rushed through their veins. Even though he needed no sustenance, his eyes tracked their slightest movements. He watched the barely perceptible throbbing of the pulse in their necks, imagining the taste of their flesh.

As men and women worked around him, he discovered new talents. A simple push of his thoughts could cause hearts to race. The monster that was growing inside Adin triumphed to hear it. He could sense the release of sweet adrenaline as breathing quickened as the objects of his experimentation fought the urge to flee.

Rationally, they had to be aware that he was harmless. He was restrained, sedated, and helpless. But a gentle press of thought made fear grip them all over again, it was instinct too old to identify, too palpable—too visceral—to ignore. He could feel the terror that infused them. He could taste it on the air around him. The new thing inside him, cruel and predatory, caused saliva to run in his mouth as his canines ripped through his tender gums pressing aside his incisors, elongating, throbbing and ready to sink into human flesh until everyone left him once again, alone in the dark.

In those quickening heartbeats, there was only the hunt, the desire, the need for a clean kill and—above all—the urge to appease his new, insatiable appetite for blood.

There were moments, too, when he was Adin Tredeger again, aware, appalled, and fully conscious of the thing he could become. When despair and revulsion vied for the top spot on his emotional hit parade, and he cried out for Donte, who never came.

Yet Adin *sensed* him. Donte's presence—while not physical—seemed to color the atmosphere around Adin, hanging there sweetly like the vague scent of a subtle perfume. Every now and again, when Adin woke, he'd find a gift. Something new and different, placed on the table next to his bed or even clutched in his hand. Something simple that gave him pleasure, a faceted crystal orb with a tea light in it that threw rainbows across the sheet covering his nakedness. A perfect conch shell, sleek and smooth on the inside, ridged and tactile on the outside. It smelled like salt and wind and sun to Adin, as though it had been dipped into the ocean then allowed to dry outdoors. Blue glass and an ostrich feather. A golden lump of resin Adin knew to be Frankincense, released its heady aroma into the room. The symbol, sometimes used to signify transition, new spiritual life, wasn't lost on him during what he'd begun to think of as his "Adin moments". The animal within him, the newly awakened beast was content to breathe in its sweet earthy scent. All of Donte's gifts, thoughtfully procured, slyly offered, held the perfect appeal for each facet of the man who was once Adin Tredeger.

Sometimes they made him smile.

Sometimes they made him cry.

"Adin." Tuan's voice.

The predator leaped within him, angry at its captors. Especially Tuan, because Adin wasn't fooled by the patient accountant anymore. He sensed…something feral and predatory under Tuan's skin. "It's about fucking time someone showed their face. Come here and release me before I rip myself apart and come after you."

"I understand your frustration." Tuan moved to the wall and toggled a switch that caused light to flare in the small room. Tuan and Christobel Santos stood inside his room, side by side, solemn and wary. "The process is painful and frightening. We attempt to make it easier to bear with sedation and environmental control, but there's no cure and no guarantee that anything we can do will help."

Adin tried to get control over his roiling thoughts. "I sometimes think I must be imagining everything, but then the hunger comes…"

Santos's dark eyes regarded Adin with pity. "Eventually you will learn to control that, but it will never go away."

"Did you do this?" Adin asked Santos directly.

"I did *not*." Santos stepped forward. Adin watched his face carefully for clues that he might be lying, but found none.

"I need to get out of here."

"It's not safe unless you have someone to mentor you," Tuan told him quietly.

"Donte—"

"No one knows where Donte is." Tuan's face tightened in what Adin assumed was contempt, "He sends you little gifts when he should be—"

Santos spoke. "Since Fedeltà has chosen to abdicate his responsibility, I volunteered."

Adin laughed weakly. "How you must be enjoying this."

"The chance to take Donte's prize? Yes. But unfortunately I find I am unwilling to take pleasure in your suffering. Even at Donte's expense."

"Have you suddenly found scruples?"

Santos picked a minuscule piece of lint off the sleeve of his immaculate suit coat and growled, "Sadly, it seems I have."

"Take heart, they probably won't last." Adin tugged at the restraints that bound him. Impatient. Angry. The monster inside him was ready to feed. "Who do I have to fuck to leave this dump?"

Out of nowhere, Adin heard Edward's voice. "There's someone here to see you."

For a brief and awful moment Adin thought it might be his sister Deana. It was far, far too soon to face his only remaining family member with the sordid truth of his new existence...

"*Adin.*" Bran's voice.

"Hello, Bran. It seems you were right. I'm afraid I didn't dream—"

"It's going to be all right, Adin." Bran tried to console him and it made his heart feel like lead in his chest. *He* should have been taking care of Bran. Not the other way around.

"Bran, I'm so sorry I let you down."

"You never let me down. It's just...I don't know. It's the way of the world..."

"Where are you?" For the first time, Adin was aware of a fixture in the ceiling that resembled half of a Victorian gazing ball. *Camera.* Shit. Had someone been monitoring him this whole time?

"We can see you, and there's an intercom," Edward told him. "We haven't been allowed in until now."

"How long has it been?"

"Nearly four weeks." Edward's voice wavered. "Bran started

school."

Adin closed his eyes. *Four weeks.*

Santos spoke. "If it makes you feel any better, when I was turned it was nearly two years before I could be around anyone. I spent that time in an iron cage like an animal, tearing my flesh from my bones in my rage, only to have it repair itself while I slept. Things have changed since the sixteenth century."

Adin met Santos's dark eyes. "Next you're going to tell me that in order to kill someone you had to walk uphill both ways in the snow."

Santos stepped forward and flicked a finger painfully at Adin's forehead. "You're a pain in the ass, Adin. There will be no end to the satisfaction of the man who will eventually beat that out of you. Thank heavens I have only to teach you how to survive your new existence, and the best way to feed, *without* killing."

Adin noticed he no longer had a cast on his arm when Tuan stepped forward to remove Adin's restraints. Santos stepped around the hospital bed and worked on his other side. Together, they lifted Adin's naked body from the bed and helped him clothe himself. He was not physically weak, far from it. He simply found himself unable to coordinate the movement of his limbs into some semblance of normal activity, as if his mind and his body no longer communicated.

"What the hell?" He balked at sitting in the wheelchair that Tuan provided.

"You'll be relearning balance and coordination, but for now it's best if you take it slow."

Adin scrubbed at his face with the heels of his hands. "Just get me the fuck out of here." He eyed Tuan and Santos until they opened that sliding door and wheeled him out. In the hallway, Boaz waited.

"I'll be packing the things from your room, Dr. Tredeger."

Adin glanced behind him, thinking about the trinkets Donte left for him. It didn't matter how he'd gotten them in there, whether he'd smuggled them in through the nurses or had Boaz lay them out while he slept. It wasn't enough. It had never been enough, really, but Adin had fooled himself into thinking that someday it would be. That someday Donte might love him enough to forgive him his humanity and take him as he was.

That day had not come. In fact, Donte had handed him the betrayal of a lifetime, along with the tremendously thoughtful little gifts he no doubt imagined would make up for his callous disregard for Adin's autonomy. Adin looked back at the tiny gifts, spread out on a rolling table intended for use by patients who could still eat food, and it broke his heart.

"There's nothing in there I want to take with me."

CHAPTER TWENTY-TWO

Tuan pushed Adin's wheelchair toward the elevator with Santos following along behind them like a paid mourner at a funeral cortege. They made their way up from the dimly lit basement like moles. When the doors opened to the lobby, Adin blinked his eyes against the shocking, bright fluorescent lights. He knew Edward and Bran were in the hospital somewhere, but they wouldn't come to him. He would have liked to see them.

Tuan leaned over to speak to him. "I imagine this must seem like too much, but it's the middle of the night and about as quiet as it's going to be. Santos has a limousine waiting to take you someplace where you can get your bearings. Boaz has gone ahead to pull it around."

"Aren't you afraid I'll go on some sort of rampage, and the villagers will have to come with pitchforks and torches to put me down?"

Santos chuckled. "Those sorts of things are usually only required when someone is turned and abandoned."

Tuan nodded his agreement. "Generally speaking, when the initial transition is medically supervised and the newly made vampire has a mentor, the most problematic results can be avoided."

"Thank heavens I have a sponsor." Adin tried not to point out that the subject they discussed with such sangfroid was his worst-case scenario. "Like AA. Will I get a chip? I've been in for a month. Shall I call you whenever I feel like a drink and I don't know if I can say *when*?"

"There's the Adin I know and want to bludgeon..." Santos placed a casual hand on his shoulder. They rolled past the sensor that triggered the automatic sliding doors, exiting into the night.

Once outside, Adin's newly enhanced senses overwhelmed him. The chilly air hit him and he felt every hair follicle tingle as his skin drew up against the cold. The clouds that filled the sky spattered rain intermittently and he heard each drop as it seemed to thunder to the earth. He perceived everything Donte ever shared with him and more. He could see as if it were daylight and his sense of smell was so acute that he was aware of each and every individual odor; from the hospital laundry, to burning fuel from the highway, to the aroma of French fries, carried on the wind from a restaurant he couldn't see. The darkness teemed with living things. Adin felt it quicken with life even as he heard the faint scrabbling noise of insects and the sound of a thousand different heartbeats.

It was too much, though, too new, and he felt inundated by it. He put his hands to his ears while he tried to accustom himself to the vast and varied sensory input, even as Boaz edged the limousine to the curb. He had to pull deep within himself to keep it from swamping him.

Tuan put a hand on Adin's arm to help him rise from the wheelchair. Adin straightened and tested his strength and his balance while Santos pushed the chair away. He felt unbelievably strong, in a way, but uncoordinated, as if he had been placed in a new body and didn't yet know how to make it work.

He stepped back and pivoted around when he felt some sort of imminent danger like an icy slap from behind. His newly honed senses went on red alert. He started to brush Tuan's hands away in order to face the threat except Tuan must have felt it too. He flanked Adin, crouching low, emitting a rumbling growl that made the hair on Adin's arms stand up. A ripple of air brushed Adin's skin in the charged atmosphere, telling him Santos had moved to his other side.

Adin's skin tingled and it took a while before he realized he had given up breathing. He waited for what seemed like an eternity, watching the shadowy alley beyond the well-lit emergency room entrance. He couldn't see anything but felt something coming, an imminent menace, from the darkness there.

What finally materialized and stepped into the light didn't make sense. It was Donte as Adin had never seen him before, wearing a sleek black turtleneck and soft-looking leather pants that fit like skin. He wore nothing flowing or fashionable as he normally did, he was garbed for function, for ease of movement, and armed with a wicked-looking katana.

Donte was dressed for war.

"*Donte.*" Adin heard his voice and couldn't believe the power of it. That one word blew out of him like thunder. Adin's nascent inner monster was determined to protect itself.

Donte stopped where he was. "This is between Santos and me."

Adin turned to Santos with a frown.

Santos froze. "I beg your pardon."

"You heard me," Donte growled. "For the record, you may arm yourself or you may die where you stand."

In the blink of an eye, Tuan pulled a telescoping steel baton from his pocket and flicked his wrist to open it. "What is this about Fedeltà?"

Donte didn't take his eyes from Santos. "I should have killed you when you took Adin the first time, Christiano. I should have let you die five centuries ago. I allowed sentimentality to cloud my thinking and it ends tonight."

Santos stepped forward, still relaxed. He held his hand out for Tuan's baton. He took it and hefted it, whipping it back and forth experimentally. "Have you nothing with a blade?"

Tuan shook his head.

Santos turned to Donte. "While I can appreciate that you might wish to kill me, what can I have done to you that you feel it must be here and now?"

Donte didn't answer Santos's question. He merely lifted his sword in preparation to attack and said, "Tuan, take Adin and go."

"I don't think so." Adin's angry words ricocheted off the damp pavement. "Explain yourself, Donte."

"Adin is right. I'm not going anywhere." Tuan rolled his shoulders. "And I'm sure you know that I don't need a sword to fight."

"Do you defend Santos?" Donte asked Tuan incredulously.

"What if I do? This makes no sense, Fedeltà."

Adin caught a movement out of the corner of his eye. Boaz opened the driver's side door of the limousine and got out. He came around the car to stand on the curb between them off to the side.

Santos stopped posturing with the baton and spoke. "Adin will be under my protection."

Wind whistled and the steel of Donte's sword sang when he leaped forward. "Like hell he will."

"Stop!" Adin stepped between Donte and Santos, giving the latter a firm shove back toward where Tuan stood, waiting. Donte barely had time to pull back his strike. "Santos will see to my needs until I am less angry with you, Donte. You should thank him."

"Are you out of your mind?" Donte moved into the light so that Adin could see his face. His dark eyes were angry and hurt. "You are angry with *me*?"

"Wait." Tuan caught Adin's arm when he would have turned away. "Donte, are you saying you didn't turn Adin?"

Donte gripped his sword tighter. "I did not. You must know I did not."

"How would I?" Tuan asked.

"You never left his side while I was there." Donte shook his head as if the question were ridiculous. "I had no right. He told me he didn't want—"

"You think *I* turned him?" Santos asked, genuinely shocked. "Why would he accept my protection if I turned him?"

Santos didn't move, even as Donte advanced, even as the tip of Donte's blade pressed against his throat. "If you lie…"

"I swear on my father's soul—the soul of a man we both loved—that I did not," Santos said evenly. "Can you say the same?"

Donte lowered his sword. "I can. On that same soul I swear. I did not."

"What the fuck?" Adin sagged. Both Donte and Santos reached for him then, although it was Tuan who finally thought to bring Adin the wheelchair. When Adin was seated he massaged his forehead absently. "I don't understand."

"This is troublesome," Santos remarked, shooting Donte a look loaded with meaning that Adin didn't comprehend.

Adin looked up at his lover's face. He stood tall and appeared more coldly unemotional than Adin had ever seen him. It was impossible to guess what he was thinking. It was enough to swallow the pain of his betrayal. If they'd all been wrong...

At that moment Edward emerged from the hospital with Bran in tow. When he took in the scene at the curb where Donte and Santos stood, still armed, he froze.

"What's going on here?" Edward asked carefully.

"It seems," Tuan frowned, "we have a mystery on our hands. Both Donte and Santos insist they had nothing to do with turning Adin."

"Well...*shit*." Edward folded his arms and glared at both men. "He didn't get it from a toilet seat. Who the hell else *could* have done it?"

Donte turned to Edward and sheathed his sword. "Who knew he was here?"

"Just us." Edward gestured toward the group of men who surrounded Adin and ticked them off on his fingers. "You. Tuan, Me, Bran, Boaz, Santos, and Adin himself..."

"Surely you don't think I turned myself," Adin growled. "Would there be any reason, any advantage for one of the medical personnel to turn me?" He looked up at Edward and saw Bran standing stock still under the overhead lighting, staring at

Boaz with an expression of shock on his face. "Bran. What is it?"

Boaz gazed back at Bran without expression.

"*Boaz*. Why?" Bran asked.

Boaz said nothing but suddenly every eye was on him.

Edward was the first to speak. "Boaz? Did you do this?"

Boaz sighed. "Do you mean did I put an end to Adin's rubbish and move everyone forward to the inevitable outcome of the situation in order to protect Donte Fedeltà to whom I am sworn? *Yes*. I did."

"How?" Tuan asked.

Boaz held his hands out palm up. "I'm not without resources, and this is a hospital full of vampires and vampire blood. How do you think?"

Adin gripped the arms of the wheelchair. "You tried to make me think it was Santos."

"Or Donte. Frankly, I was surprised to see that it mattered one way or the other. But it certainly wouldn't do for Donte to kill Santos. I never expected that."

"What did you expect?" Donte asked. "That I would welcome the violation of my lover in such a fashion?"

"Well. Frankly, yes." Boaz eyed Donte. "Because he weakened you. And we couldn't have that."

"*We* couldn't…" Donte seemed to have no words. Tuan's hand dropped onto Adin's shoulder when he would have risen from the wheelchair.

Santo turned to Boaz sadly. "This was a grave impertinence, Boaz, even for an imp. But it's Donte's to deal with. You are no longer welcome in my home. Don't make it necessary for me to refuse you aid in the future, and steer well clear of my family."

"I will," Boaz said calmly.

Adin wanted to slip his hand into Donte's, his face was so pained it was hard to look at him.

"Boaz," Donte said finally. "Every breath you take from this moment on is the direct result of the love I bear your parents. I never want to see you again."

"Fair enough," Boaz agreed. "Because we both know that every breath Dr. Adin Tredeger has taken since he met you has cost you the respect of your peers, your time, your safety, and every resource you have. We both know that the love of this human *pet* of yours would have been your undoing, and we both know that it was my loyalty to you, the love I bear you, and the responsibility my family undertook centuries ago to keep you safe that made me the only person—the only entity on the planet— who cared for you enough to do what was right in the face of what was comfortable and convenient."

"Get out of my sight before I change my mind and tear you apart," Donte spat.

"I'm going." Boaz sauntered back around to the driver's side door of the limousine and opened it. Before he got in he peered over the roof. "I'm sorry to say you'll have to get another ride, Dr. Tredeger. I'm responsible for this vehicle and I have to return it before I go home."

Adin shook his head, unable to speak past the lump in his throat.

Boaz hates me. Maybe he's always hated me. How did I miss that?

The car's engine started and Boaz drove sedately off, taillights winking in the shallow puddles left by the intermittent rain. The six of them, Donte, Santos and Adin, Edward, Tuan, and Bran watched it go. Adin realized that of all of them the only human—the most *normal*—was Edward. Somewhere, the gods were probably having a good laugh.

CHAPTER TWENTY-THREE

Donte reached out to Adin and lifted him into his strong arms. Adin followed his instinct and pressed his face to the junction of Donte's neck, where the silky turtleneck he wore hid the tendons and flesh Adin was aware of in a new and more profound, more sensual way.

"You smell good." Adin closed his eyes. "Take me home, Donte. Please. Take me somewhere safe."

"Caro," Donte murmured against his skin. "If I could barter my life to return yours to you—"

"Don't, Donte." Adin sagged against him.

"I'm so sorry. I never wanted for this to happen. No matter what you may believe. I could never have wished for this…"

"I know that. I know… I should have had more faith in you. I'm sorry."

"Shh…caro. I'll ask Tuan to bring my car." Donte dug his keys out of a tight pocket and handed them off. It fell to the rest of them to wait until Tuan came back. No one spoke. There was little left for any of them to say. Adin noticed Bran hugged himself tightly against the cold and wished he could have thrown an arm around the boy. As it was, Edward filled in, drawing Bran close, patting his back, and giving him a reassuring smile.

It made Adin happy to see that, but he felt his own loss keenly. He genuinely liked Bran, and now he didn't know what would happen.

Once Tuan brought the car around Edward and Donte helped Adin into the passenger seat. Edward took over the positioning of his seat belt, locking him in and then patting him as if he were a child. He brushed his lips across Adin's forehead and murmured things in his ear that Adin didn't understand because of all the other noises that crowded in on him.

Everything burned into his consciousness at once until it

became his fondest wish to be isolated, somewhere outside of the city. Away from the lights and the cacophony and the sensory overload for a while, if not forever, because even in the middle of the night, even in the dark, things were simply too much for him and he experienced the terrifying desire to claw his way free and run like a trapped animal.

Donte keyed the ignition and seemed to read his mind. "I know how overwhelming everything is for you right now. I believe we should head for your home in Washington. I can make arrangements for another car and driver so we can travel comfortably."

"All right." As they pulled away from the curb, Adin turned to the side and waved to Edward and Bran. Bran looked like he was trying not to cry. Edward turned to him and said something, then chased the car a few feet until Adin rolled down the window and Donte applied the brakes.

"Bran will e-mail you first thing so you can keep in touch. You can video chat live and…"

Adin leaned out of the car to motion Bran over. "It will be all right, Bran. I promise you. We'll find a way to talk often while we're trying to figure all this out."

Bran's face was so hopeful that Adin wanted to capture it and hold onto it. He wanted to imprint it on his heart so he would never allow himself to let Bran down again. He asked for Donte's phone and used it to take Bran's picture.

"I'm going to miss you," Bran told him.

"I'm not going far. Promise me you'll call me if you need to talk about anything. Anytime you want."

Bran hesitated.

"Promise me."

Adin got a smile and a nod from Bran as Edward put his arm around the boy. Adin waved once again and watched them as he and Donte edged out into the night.

When they could barely see the hospital in the distance, Adin remembered something and sighed with regret.

"What?" Donte asked, taking his hand.

"I left your gifts behind. I thought…"

Donte's expression tightened. "I know what you thought."

"Now I wish I'd brought them."

"I'm sure Tuan can be persuaded to gather them up for you."

Adin nodded.

"And I have forever to find new things to gift you with," he added. "If you'll still let me."

Adin squeezed Donte's hand hard and growled, "Who's the *pazzo* now... Even if you had done this to me—"

"Don't say anything you don't mean, Adin." Donte glanced at him, then back at the road.

"But I do mean it. I barely understand what's happening to me. But even when I was furious with you, I loved you. I longed for you. I would have forgiven you eventually, if you'd done it. I know I would have… It might have taken time, but I would have."

Donte's voice grew hoarse. "I don't deserve absolution. Even though I didn't turn you, it was because of me that—"

"Maybe, but my forgiveness is mine to give along with my love and my future. It's all yours, Donte. Everything."

Donte was so silent Adin worried for a minute. "You said something like that before, when we met. *'My life is mine to give.'*"

Adin remembered. "For the record, I had already begun to change my mind about being turned."

"What did you just say?" Donte's voice was tense.

Adin shook his head. "A lot of what I believed about love changed when I had to leave you in France."

"I don't understand."

"I thought then…what would I do for one more hour? What would I do if that was the last time…?" Adin's throat closed.

"I didn't know." Donte pulled over into the deserted parking lot of a restaurant.

"I realized I'd have moved heaven and earth, let Peter break my other arm, every bone in my body, even turn me, if it meant I could be with you again."

"Caro. I had no idea. You left for America with Bran and I believed you understood that I would come when I could. When I spoke with Boaz I told him that I would be there as soon as it was safe for me to travel."

Adin smiled bitterly. "I never got that message."

"What?"

"Boaz told all of us you never called."

Donte's face registered the pain of that betrayal. "I had no idea how deep his resentment went."

"I'm sorry to come between you. He loved you in his own way."

"He can't have loved me if he harmed the person I cherish most. That's not love."

"He said you were a prince among men."

Donte flashed his white smile. "I'm not even a count anymore."

Adin felt the beginnings of a fathomless hunger bloom throughout his body. It made beads of cold sweat break out on his upper lip until he whispered aloud, "Donte…"

"Hungry?" Donte eyed Adin's face, watching him with curiosity as the changes began. It seemed that Adin had his own blood song to sing. He felt it surge through his veins until it rang in his ears, driving him toward something he didn't know how to find.

"Yes." Adin hissed as his canines elongated. He shivered against the sensation of teeth tearing past his gums. He noticed the way his body hair rose on his skin and the desperate, wrenching emptiness that clawed at his belly.

It hurt.

"Can you help me?"

"I can, caro. But not the way you think. If you take a small amount from me, then it will stay your cravings until we can find something for the both of us. Shall I help you that way?"

Adin simply didn't know. He'd never fed. He'd never had to. His needs were taken care of intravenously in the hospital and his cravings had been muted by medication. He still couldn't make himself believe he'd ever use his teeth to tear someone's flesh. "Yes. But…"

"This first time I'll open my own vein, here, on my arm, see?" Donte lifted the sleeve of his turtleneck, bringing his arm up and using his other hand to point out the place he planned to puncture. "When you get close to the skin you will feel it, press your lips just there…"

Adin did as he was told. He was shocked to feel blood beneath the surface of Donte's skin like a hidden spring. He could smell it and it made his mouth water. "I want it…" was all he could get out. The truth was just the idea of tasting what he smelled made his eyes close in ecstasy.

"Ah, caro." Donte bit his own wrist and Adin fell on it, lapping up the rich, red droplets until the wound closed.

Adin whimpered when he could find no more blood and Donte repeated the process twice more until Adin sighed happily.

"That's right, caro. You don't need much just yet." Donte nuzzled him for a kiss and Adin knew they both tasted blood on his lips. Donte smiled indulgently at him, stroking a light finger over his cheek. "You…"

"What?" Adin asked. He was slightly ashamed at the greed with which he'd taken Donte's blood, but discovered that beyond the need, beyond the thrill of having Donte's flavor, his essence coursing through his veins, he felt nurtured in some indefinable way that made his love for Donte burn brighter in his chest than it ever had before.

"I would turn myself inside out for you," Donte told him. "I find I very much enjoy feeding you this way for a change."

Adin was so relaxed he felt boneless. "Me too."

"But soon you'll need others. It's not a terrible thing if you learn to give pleasure while you take sustenance."

Adin frowned. "I don't want to give anyone pleasure but you."

Donte laughed gently. "Do you want to know a secret?"

"Not if it means I have to—"

"Hush, caro." Donte resumed his seat behind the wheel and started the engine again. "You will not win this argument. Your body will demand blood. But there are ways of finding it without sharing intimacy with anyone. I save all my pleasure for when I'm with you. But I can give others pleasure for the gift of their blood, and remain completely unmoved."

Adin leaned back in his seat, tired, replete for the moment, and happier than he'd been in a long time.

"Bet you thought you could do that with me," he teased.

"I admit, the thought occurred to me in the airplane when we first met."

"I am irresistible." Adin lifted the lever that caused the seat to sink backwards.

"Of course you are."

"I'm still vampire catnip."

"Indeed." Donte reached into the back seat and pulled his coat forward for Adin. "Here, pull this up over you, so you don't get cold."

"How often do you get cold?"

Donte stopped in the act of tucking Adin in. His hand still hovered over Adin's chest. Adin caught it and kissed the knuckles, giving them a tiny nip in the process.

"This is going to take some getting used to, isn't it my lover?"

Donte smiled indulgently and continued to drive. The wipers

picked up speed as the rain came down harder. "We have plenty of time, più amato."

Want a little more of Adin and Donte? Take a peek at

MATINS

Coming in 2011 from ManLoveRomance Press

Adin sat in the window seat of his Bainbridge Island home and gazed out at the crisp winter morning. Gray clouds hid the sun, and since it had recently rained the naked trees stood in stark silhouette against the sky. Adin was surprised to find that his thoughts—for once—didn't mirror the weather.

Life… for lack of a better word had become very pleasant over the weeks they'd spent in Washington. After a number of minor changes, new double-paned windows with lightblocking shades inside that could be drawn on the days that the sun shone, some clever manipulation of the perceptions of the neighbors on Donte's part, and what Adin had privately begun to think of as his crash-course in *Vampire 101, The Care and Feeding of Baby Vampires*, he'd managed to find a sort of equilibrium.

Long, late evening walks led to more intimate conversations than he'd ever dreamed he'd have with Donte, who seemed to believe he was on some sort of probation—which was patently ridiculous. As Adin watched him crawl backward from behind the sofa in their living room, tacking cable to the baseboards, it once again occurred to him that he'd never, ever been loved like this.

He knew how lucky he was and—alive or undead—reveled in it.

"I feel you watching me, Adin," Donte said without looking up.

"Your ass is doing marvelous things. I should have you lay carpet, just for giggles."

"Carpet is a filthy thing. Humans have no idea what goes on unseen by the naked eye in *carpet*."

"Thanks for that image." Adin shuddered. "I'm glad we have wood floors then."

"I agree. I like them; they show age and craftsmanship. They're organic. It feels nice to walk on wooden floors. I've always liked them. And stone."

"Are you ever going to tell me what you're doing?"

"It's a secret." Donte tapped his Bluetooth headset and said, "Almost there."

"Who are you talking to?"

"None of your business." Donte smirked at him. Aside he said, "No, that was for Adin, he's curious what I'm doing. What can I say? *Babies*. Always into everything."

"Donte, I can and will strike you if you don't stop calling me a *baby*."

"I should probably go, someone's getting fussy. Must be getting tired." Donte shot Adin a look guaranteed to start a fight, at the very least. "It's hard to tell these days if he just needs a nap or—"

In the blink of an eye Adin shot to his feet and hurled himself into Donte. He slammed into Donte's body and wrapped both arms around his neck, pushing him down to the couch. On impact it moved several feet across the wooden floor and smashed into a final resting place against the wall where Donte had been working.

"One of these days, you're going to scratch that floor." Donte positively grinned, and okay, on Donte it was rather chilling but it heated Adin's blood like nothing else ever could.

"Are you still on the phone?"

"No."

"Good, because I don't want whoever it was to hear you screaming my name." He tore Donte's tailored shirt right off, the sound of buttons hitting the floor loud in the still afternoon air, but not as loud as Donte's gasp of excitement. Still he held Adin back from doing the same thing to his trousers.

"Adin. Buttons do not sew themselves back on to a shirt when you do that…"

"I thought we planned to keep your tailor and all his progeny in business for generations to come."

Donte was uncharacteristically quiet.

"What?"

"Boaz took care of things like mending."

"I see." Adin pulled back a little, bracing himself on his elbow and thumbing light circles on Donte's chest. "You miss him."

"I cannot miss what never existed. I don't believe I ever really knew him."

Adin kissed Donte's dark nipple until it hardened, then rubbed his lips over the bud. "Possibly, none of us did. I didn't realize how deeply he resented me. He never gave me even a hint until the very end."

"I don't know how I missed it." Before Adin could give him a pinch, Donte caught his hand and gave it a gentle nip. "I'd rather he didn't spoil our afternoon, though. I'm sorry I mentioned it."

"Ah. All right. Where was I?"

"You were going to make me scream?" Donte took two of Adin's fingers in his mouth and sucked. "Wasn't that what you had planned?"

"Yes, I remember now. I have this movie called *The Grudge* and—"

Donte pushed Adin up to his knees and jerked the buttons of his jeans open. "I have always liked buttons so much better than zippers. Good for you wearing the easy-to-open variety of blue jeans."

"Oh, so it's all right for you to tear open some clothes…"

"But these—" Donte gave an experimental tug on one of Adin's buttons "—are so very sturdy."

"What about yours?" He reached for the fly of Donte's trousers. "Alas, a zipper."

Adin carefully unzipped Donte and they writhed around on the couch, freeing each other of their clothes until they were naked, skin to skin, cock to cock, and some world-class friction had stopped their silly banter.

"*Yes.*"

Adin gripped Donte's ass before reaching down his thighs and drawing his legs up. Donte felt behind his head for a bottle of lube that Adin had tucked into the space between the cushion and the arm of the sofa. In fact, Adin had tucked lube in just about every crevice of his house, at one point even placing a bottle between some of the pots on the back porch because if his hunger for blood was new and fierce, his hunger for Donte had grown exponentially beyond that, giving him superhuman vigor and really vivid porn-star fantasies. His concession to Donte's fastidious personality was to leave quilts on the leather furniture. He picked Donte up with one arm using his brand new and frightening strength, to slide one under his ass.

Quilts, apparently stood up to washing better than leather couches. Who knew?

"Donte," he growled and went in for a deep, satisfying kiss. He slicked his fingers and probed Donte's entrance gently, earning a sweet sigh when he found his way past the tight muscles. Once he got started, he couldn't help adding another finger, pushing them in and out of Donte's tight heat, stroking over the bundle of nerves that made him shiver and eventually, would send him flying apart.

Donte's eyes darkened, his black pupils blooming in the dark irises as he grew more aroused. Adin was aware of Donte's need. He felt tension under his fingertips from the way Donte's muscles bunched beneath his fingers, heard the small grunts he made as he strained for more contact, he smelled Donte's arousal, and underneath all the physical cues, he heard the song of Donte's blood as it called him.

His canines elongated so he rubbed them gently against the skin of Donte's neck.

"Do it." Donte arched against him. "You once told me it meant something to you to nourish me. I believed I'd never have the pleasure of returning the favor, and now I find that I want it more than anything."

Adin pressed his cock against Donte's tight entrance. He lifted Donte's hips and began a long, agonizingly slow push into

Donte's ass even as he struck deeply with his sharp teeth, piercing the skin below Donte's jaw cleanly and lapped at the blood that welled there.

Donte let out a shuddering breath. "*Ah. Adin. Più amato.*"

Adin smiled against his skin as he pulled his cock back and thrust again, over and over, biting and sucking, until their blood sang louder and louder—a cacophony of sweet harmony and intense need. Their bodies surged and fell together like waves, only to draw back again and again, meeting and crashing, drawing apart, obliterating any remaining restraint between them as they fucked and delivered stinging love bites all over each other's skin, until Donte was indeed screaming Adin's name.

At some point they fell off the couch, and continued to roll frantically, with Donte on top for a bit, riding him and clutching his shoulders in a viselike grip.

Adin watched as Donte went over the edge, his head thrown back, sweat dripping from his damp hair. He froze to a shaking stillness and held on to Adin's hips as if he'd never let go. Donte was beautiful. Adin had no words, no adequate thoughts, even, for a sight like that.

Donte came in convulsive waves, his ass clenching Adin's cock while Adin rode out his own release, his hips stuttering, out of control. Donte crushed Adin to him and pierced the flesh of his neck to feed.

They came to rest somewhere in the middle of the living room, half under a cocktail table. Donte lapped at the deepest wound in Adin's neck while it closed.

After holding one another for a long time in the breathless, utter silence of the undead, Donte peeled his body off Adin's. "No need to order the pizza boy tonight."

"That's good, it feels wasteful throwing out the pizza." Adin crawled on all fours to find his clothes.

"You look like a beautiful cat when you do that, caro."

Adin found his T-shirt and put it on. "Are you ever going to tell me why you moved all the furniture and spent the day tacking cable to my beautiful walls and baseboards? I hope you know how to spackle."

"Whatever *that* is, I'm sure I can learn it, given time." Donte dragged on his trousers. "Get dressed and I'll show you right now."

Once Adin complied and was basically dressed, Donte donned his now buttonless shirt then tapped his Bluetooth earpiece.

"Redial," he commanded with all the aplomb of an erstwhile Italian count wearing sex-shredded clothes. He waited for a minute and then said, "Donte here, I think I'm done."

Adin snorted. "Done. I'll say. You've definitely been done."

Donte shushed him with a hand to his lips and listened. "All right. Let's try it out."

He picked up the television remote, and when the set turned on, Adin saw Bran and Edward. Both grinned at him in what he assumed was real time. Edward leaned toward the camera. "Hi, Adin."

Bran waved frantically. "Got it, Donte. It's brilliant. You're on the big screen. I can see your... have you been getting busy? Oh, *ew*! That's completely gross."

Edward's eyebrow shot up. "Seriously. I'm sure you realize you are going to be using this with an impressionable young man. I hope you have a modicum of—"

Adin waved him off. "No one buys that, coming from you, Edward, so just give us a break."

Donte left the room for a minute.

"It's so good to see you Bran. How are you doing?"

"I started school, Adin. I go to your old high school. It's all right, and everything, but I miss shopping and hanging about with you."

"Me too." Adin had to stop himself from putting his hand on the screen over Bran's. He really missed him. He wished he could spend time with him, take him on errands. He missed the long talks they'd had when Bran could still fumble around inside his memories. "You won't see inside my head anymore though."

Bran's face fell. "I know. And I liked it there, too. You've done some pretty odd things, but your family was nice."

Edward glanced up at this. "Have you seen Deana yet?"

"No. We've just talked on the phone." When Edward started to say something, Adin held his hand up. "Don't look at me like that. I don't even know where to start."

"You'd better start soon. She deserves the truth, and she needs to hear it from you."

"It will melt her brain. She's a scientist."

Tuan stepped out from somewhere behind Edward and off camera. "Then maybe she already knows more than you think. Have you ever considered that?"

Adin frowned. He hadn't considered that at all, actually. "No."

"Have you heard from Santos?" Tuan asked.

Donte returned to the room carrying a small table, on which he began to set up a chess set.

"No we haven't," Adin admitted. "Donte?"

"No, and good riddance. Santos believed he should mentor Adin. That insufferable—"

"I expect he'll keep his distance now that Boaz isn't keeping us in touch anymore."

"Boaz," Donte growled. "Has anyone seen him?"

"No," Tuan answered. "No one is really looking for him either. It's not illegal to do what he did, precisely, although there are ways to address it in court. It could be considered a civil crime. The case would be heard by a tribunal of supernatural judges, privately."

"It's not a matter for the courts." Donte gazed at Adin. "I doubt I handled it wisely, but for the sake of Boaz's parents, I let him live. I hope I don't come to regret that."

Adin glanced over at his lover and the thought came to him, unbidden, that Boaz had never, ever done anything—until the moment he turned Adin—that was not the direct result of Donte's orders. He hated himself, but a tiny, painful part of his heart worried that even now, Boaz was simply following orders and staying away until Adin cooled down. He looked at the screen and found Bran watching him closely. *Speculatively*. Adin had the absurd idea that Bran was thinking along the same lines. The boy looked back at Donte and his eyes narrowed.

"Donte—" he began, but Adin interrupted him.

"Look what we have here, Bran? My chess set?" He met Bran's gaze and held it. "What do you say to a game? I warn you, my new vampire instincts are far more lethal than my human ones were. I might not let you win this time."

"As if," Bran sneered, derailed for the moment. "That will be the day, when you have to *let* me win. I kicked your arse in France and I'll be happy to do it again. Even long distance. No fair coaching, Donte."

"You're on." Adin and Bran argued over how to choose who played white and who black, then began their game. They were evenly matched and it took all Adin's concentration to play.

He was so deep into the game that he was surprised to hear a knock on the door about a half hour later, but he assumed that Donte had ordered the pizza boy after all. They both liked the young man, and the feeling was mutual. The agreement was consensual. They fed on him, tipped him well, and he always left relaxed and happy, with a grin on his face, as Adin had learned to give pleasure with his bite—enough to get a man or woman off—in the same way Donte did.

Apparently the world was full of people who enjoyed the pleasure the undead could give. Often they wanted more. Adin and Donte declined sexual relations with those humans but traded gratification for food. Adin smiled as Donte returned from the door, expecting their usual young man to be following him in. He was therefore surprised to see Donte's good mood had seriously deteriorated and that the person who strode in behind him wasn't someone unfamiliar, just completely unexpected.

"*Sean?*" Adin rose from the chess table, startled.

Bran muttered, "Uh-oh. I've seen you before."

Sean entered Adin's tiny living room. He stood next to Donte as if he'd been placed there simply for comparison. He was fair, and had the bluest eyes—the most memorable eyes Adin had ever seen—except for Donte's brown ones. Red hair tumbled to his shoulders in thick waves. He wore a worn leather jacket and jeans and held a motorcycle helmet under his arm. He was as small as Adin remembered, barely his own height, but thinner, and wore a T-shirt studded with metal shamrocks at the neck that read, "FecK you. I'M IriSH."

"What on earth are *you* doing here?" Adin asked.

"Santos sent me. He said you were out of a majordomo now that your Boaz has done a runner, so I thought to myself, I'm exactly what you need." He followed this up with a cheeky grin that was scant millimeters short of a leer. "I'm out of a job, temporarily, and you're out of a butler. Kismet."

Donte folded his arms. "Over my dead body."

Sean shot him a sly look and said, "Thank you, I don't mind if I do."

Adin raised his eyebrows. It could be awfully fun to watch Donte explode. And he would, eventually. Santos had to know that. He'd planned it that way, *the prick*. Adin and Donte still had some things to work out between them. Surely it wouldn't do for Adin to have even a single shred of suspicion that Donte had taken part in turning him.

"While you might be very good, Boaz was an imp, not a vampire, and he was extremely useful for things that required attention during the daylight hours."

Sean cocked his head to the side a little. "I find there's little I can't do once I set my mind to it."

"I see."

There was nothing in the world that could make Adin want

another man after he'd had Donte, not the way they were now, in very human love, immortal, and vaguely animal at the same time. They were monsters for one another, so hungry they devoured each other yet still felt starved…

No. Sean was attractive and there had been a time when Donte had left Adin, or so he thought, and he'd considered…But after everything that had happened? No. Now, there was no way.

Still. Dark and angry was Adin's favorite look on Donte, focused and lethal instead of brooding. He liked that. An off-balance Donte was never, ever boring, and they had a long, long time together ahead of them.

Adin smiled sweetly at Sean and asked him, "How are you at mending clothes?"

Z. A. MAXFIELD is a fifth generation native of Los Angeles, although she now lives in Orange County, CA She started writing in 2007 on a dare from her children and never looked back. Pathologically disorganized, and perennially optimistic, she writes as much as she can, reads as much as she dares, and enjoys her time with family and friends. If anyone asks her how a wife and mother of four manages to find time for a writing career, she'll answer, "It's amazing what you can do if you completely give up housework." Check out her website at: http://www.zamaxfield.com.

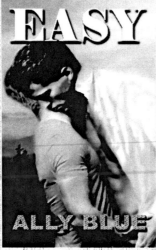